Castle Gordon

SUE JASKULA

Publisher contact information: jaskula.sue@gmail.com
Artist credit: Diana Carlile - http://designingdiana.blogspot.com/
Formatting and Interior Design by Woven Red Author Services, www.WovenRed.ca

Permission granted by Angus and Melissa MacAuley, for reference to the name and history of Port Albert Inn, Port Albert, Ontario - © 2010, 2018, Inn at the Port. https://www.innattheport.com/

Castle Gordon/Sue Jaskula—1st edition
ISBN e-book: 978-1-7781490-1-6
ISBN Paperback: 978-1-7781490-0-9

To the people of Kincardine, Ontario, Canada,
who have maintained the allure of Scottish heritage
and created a town that feels like home.

Acknowledgements

Special thanks to Harry Gregg and Glenn Hedley who enthusiastically provided candid, first-hand information via phone calls, Facebook messages and video chats. You not only answered my specific research questions about life in Kincardine in the 1940s, but you gave me a true sense of the struggles and the joys of the townsfolk.

I also extend a warm thank you to Angus and Melissa MacAuley, for allowing me to fictitiously integrate the name and history of Port Albert Inn into my story. From the first time I visited the community of Port Albert, vivid stories came to mind which begged me to explore. You may not have seen the last of me!

Another huge thank you to my new friend, Rowan MacKemsley, historical fiction author, for reading my first draft and providing her candid thoughts and kind words.

Finally, this book could not have come together so nicely without the efforts of my fabulous cover artist Diana Carlile and my knowledgeable formatter Joan Frantschuk at Woven Red Author Services. Thank you both for your patience and words of wisdom.

Chapter One

Kincardine, Fall 1945

Cold wind seeped through Anna's hooded cloak; her hands and feet gone numb as she raced through the trees in the dark shadows of night. The rough waves beating the rocky shore provided the only aid to hold her course. "Stay hidden, stay in line with the lake. If you stop running, he will find you," Anna whispered, urging herself forward despite her panic.

Without a sliver of moonlight to act as a guide, she stumbled awkwardly, instantly halting her escape when her knee smashed against a rock as she pitched forward. The hard ground cut through her gloves as her hands broke the fall. Pain sliced up her leg when she pulled up to rest against the offensive boulder. "Damn it. Now look what you've done." Stuffing her stinging hands into the pockets of her coat, she hugged it tightly around her, tipped her head back, and prayed for a miracle.

Minutes later, a hand touched her shoulder through the grey shadows. Anna's gasp was loud in the still of the night.

She jolted upward with a wince of pain and the hand retreated.

Sitting motionless, barely breathing, she wondered if the touch had been real or imagined. "Is someone there?" She swept a hand in front of her in the darkness, hoping to connect with someone sympathetic to her plight, but terrified Ian had followed her, and she now sat injured and alone at his mercy.

A thumbnail flicked a matchstick; the flame temporarily blinding, caused her to turn her face away. In the light, her profile was visible to her intruder. Porcelain skin with delicate features, and tendrils of flaming golden hair peeked out from under her hooded coat. One leg lay straight in front of her; she wore a small shoe that now touched his boot. "Yer a bonny wee lass out alone at night. What ails ye?"

Scottish accent, thank God. Anna sighed with relief when the flame doused.

"How long have ye been out here?" He lit another match and crouched to her level, bringing the flame low. He extended his free hand. Anna shook her head and closed her eyes to the stranger. "Take my hand." He clasped her gloved fingers in his warmth.

Weakened by pain, cold and diminishing adrenaline, she stood with his help, but immediately faltered when she attempted a step. The trees spun before her, and she slumped against her rescuer.

"Well, damn," he mumbled. Unaware of her injured leg, he lifted her under her knees, and sensed his way along the path in the dark.

Anna came to with a start and shook her head quickly at the foreign surroundings. Several pillows propped her up against the solid wood headboard of a double bed; her legs stretched out in front of her. She caught her breath with her first glimpse of the man who now administered gauze bandaging to her bare knee. "Who are you? And where are we?"

"Ye can speak then. I might ask ye the same." He smiled but concentrated on wrapping her injury.

She winced when he secured the tape holding the bandage in place. "That should do it. I apologize for taking the liberty of removing yer pant leg. I had no other way to assess the damage."

She raised her focus from her injured knee to his face when he glanced up in the dim light. His blue eyes held hers from under fair brows that matched the strawberry blond in his hint of beard. Darker red than his beard, his hair was almost mahogany, shorter on the sides with a long sweep on top. One errant piece now fell over his forehead. His touch had been soft but the span of his shoulders and chest showed strength with muscles that strained the fit of his white t-shirt.

"Can we have a go again wi' introductions?" His head tilted in question and his smile widened now that he looked directly at her. "And maybe a wee bit of detail as to why ye'd be out alone alongside the lake in the middle of the night and in this weather."

She looked down at her hands and examined the small wounds from her fall. She recognized his kindness by his soothing tone and gentle ministrations to her injuries. His expression showed compassion and she immediately felt safe, but also uncertain how much to reveal to this decadent stranger.

"Since I carried ye half a mile, blood dripping from yer knee down my arm, how about starting wi' yer name? I'm Joseph Hendrie." He extended his hand.

She shook it, then flinched when the cuts cracked open. "Anna Gordon."

"A fellow Scot ye'd be?"

Ignoring the request to divulge family connections, she gazed around the small cabin. A warm fire glowed, at the end of the room opposite where they sat on his bed. The kitchen area was to their left. A quiet hum came from a small surprisingly modern refrigerator that stood alongside a countertop with one drawer and two cupboards underneath. She recognized a Coleman burner pocket stove sitting in the middle of the counter, indicating his time in service. Standing on four legs, the sink was to the side of the counter. It had an attached drainboard on either side and cloth-wrapped pipes underneath which led through the outside wall. Two shelves had been nailed to the wall above the sink and held neatly stacked dishes and a small collection of non-perishables. A glowing single bulb hung from the ceiling, above a bare wooden table with two chairs. One door was slightly ajar to their right which Anna hoped led to an indoor washroom. Another shelf receded into the wall beside that door and held two towels and neatly folded jeans and button-down shirts. The door to outside was on the other side of the washroom and had a long wooden thumb latch wedged in place with a small deadbolt lock above it. "Where are we? Is this your cabin?"

He too ignored the request for details and reached for Anna's hands. Warmth seeping through her from his touch, she instinctively pulled her hands back to her lap.

"I'm only assessing yer injuries. I wilnae hurt ye."

She slowly put her hands out in front of her, palms up, and cringed but kept them still as he wiped the scratches with a warm cloth.

"Ye went down hard. Ye must have been going at a fair speed when ye tripped." It was a statement, not a question but Anna felt the need to explain.

"It was so dark. I think my foot caught on a tree root and my knee hit a rock on the way down. I cannot thank you enough."

When he glanced up, his forehead creased. She met his gaze once again and tried to gauge his reaction to her carelessness.

He reached for the bottle behind him, and sprinkled powder on her palms as he had on her knee.

"Is that sulpha powder?"

He answered her question with one of his own. "Shall I bandage yer hands as well?"

"No, no, I'll be fine." She pulled them back to her lap.

"I'm nae sure why ye'd be running away at this hour of the night, but I cannae keep ye here love; 'tis nae appropriate."

"I must get to the library. I am friends with Elsie Blair, the librarian. She will give me a place to stay until I can … well, until I can sort some things out."

"The library downtown? Ye have yerself turned about, heading north from town, toward Tiverton. Ye'd be a couple of miles off yer destination."

"Damn it." Her shoulders slumped and she shook her head slowly.

His brow rose at her strong reaction. "What are ye hiding from?"

"Who, not what. I really can't say, that is… could you give me a ride back to town?"

"I dinnae have a car here and yer in no shape to be running around in the cold. Who is after ye? Ye didnae answer the question."

"How do you live in this primitive cabin, out of sight of anyone else, with barely a provision in sight, but you have the medical supplies and knowhow to bandage my knee as you did?"

"I have plenty of food and I stay here away from the main street because I prefer my privacy. I have an emergency kit for just this kind of scrape." He waved his hand in the direction of her knee before he stood and walked toward his kitchen. His rushed answer was clear without further words. He did not want to talk about it.

"What do you do all day?" Anna asked.

"I go to work and ye ask a lot of questions for someone who does nae like to answer mine. I have whiskey or tea."

He held the small kitchen cupboard open and turned to face Anna.

"Oh, um, no thank you. I am fine really; I need to get out of here."

"'Tis snowing and yer nae going anywhere on that knee. 'Tis barely holding wi' the bandages I wrapped around it. Ye should really have stitches."

"I appreciate your help, but I need to get back to town." She attempted to pull her legs to the side of the bed but winced at the pain.

"Ye must be new in these parts."

She smirked. "I ah ...you're not the first to ask."

"As I thought. Storms come up off the lake, even in the fall, when ye least expect and get ye turned around, or worse yet, frozen in the woods where no one will find ye until spring."

Anna shivered at the thought, then flipped her hand dismissing his warning. "That makes no sense. I walked on the beach just yesterday with only a fall coat. I can't stay here. I don't know you and Ian will—"

"I wilnae hurt ye and no one will ken yer here, so yer reputation is safe. My mate used my truck tonight; he is meant to pick me up early in the morning. I will take him to the job and come back to get ye." He took two small glasses from his shelf and poured a generous shot of whiskey into each.

"Have a wee dram, it will warm ye."

Anna took a sip and tipped her head back feeling the golden liquid burn down her throat. "It does take the edge off. This is fine whiskey; it tastes like home. Where would you get— Never mind, you're right, I do ask a lot of questions, my apologies. And I am not worried about you hurting me. I feel safer here than where I'm staying." Anna tried to curl her legs up to give him room to sit on the bottom of the double bed but again cringed when she bent her knee. "I am so sorry. This is your bed, and I am taking up all the room."

"Yer fine, keep yer leg out straight so the wound does nae crack open again."

She set her glass on the bedside table, then used both hands to lift her leg so it stretched to the far side, allowing him room to sit on the bottom corner of the bed. "Please sit down."

Their eyes met when she smiled up at him. His gaze locked a moment too long before Anna blushed and turned away.

He cleared his throat and turned to pull out a chair at the small table. "I will be fine over here. Do ye want to tell me who has done ye such a disservice?"

"It's kin. I have some loyalty to keep the problem to myself." She frowned.

"What kind of kin scare their own enough to have them running through the frigid darkness of night?"

"My husband's brother, that's who." The words were out before she had a chance to think it through.

His head jolted back. "Married are ye then? Yer husband best be protecting ye more closely and having some strong words wi' his own brother."

She took a deep breath to compose herself. "It's not that simple and I don't want to burden you with a long story. You have been so kind."

"Yer in luck. I happen to have trouble sleeping." He smiled and tipped his head in anticipation.

She smiled back at his kindness. "I may as well tell someone. My husband … that is, Graham's plane was gunned down just weeks before the surrender."

"My condolences." His grin disappeared and he nodded curtly.

"Thank you. We had sold everything we owned when we both enlisted in the Royal Air Force shortly after we married in 1940. We intended to come to Canada after the war and make a home here near Graham's only family."

"The offensive brother?"

She smirked and nodded before she continued. "Yes, his brother, sister-in-law and two children live here in Kincardine. I arrived just over a fortnight ago and have been arguing with Ian ever since." She turned from him and stared off through the window as she relived the last two weeks.

Chapter Two

"Might I remind you that I am a grown woman and a widow, not a child. I do not need a chaperone." Hands on her hips, Anna glared at her brother-in-law. While her tone remained calm, her expression voiced her irritation loud and clear.

Ian also remained still. His hands folded over each other rested on his massive oak desk while his placating smile further raised her ire. "Sit down, Anna."

"I will not be told what to do. Did you not listen to a word I said?"

"I am not demanding; I am requesting. Please sit down." He gestured toward the wing-back chair behind her; one of two that faced his desk.

She glanced in the direction indicated, lowered her fists from her hips but remained standing and turned back to the faceoff with her brother-in-law. His home office was meant to impress, although since she had been in Kincardine, Anna had never seen anyone else enter the room. Dust free, leather-bound books perfectly aligned shelves that extended the full length of one wall, many first editions of famous authors, the majority of them she knew to be unread. Opposite the books, heavy curtains hung over whisper thin sheers covering another full office wall with floor to ceiling windows. The dark forest green of the drapes blended perfectly with the rich gem hues of the boldly patterned oriental rug which spanned the room corner to corner.

"Fine, stand if you wish. All I am saying is my brother clearly arranged the transfer to guarantee his money was safe against the possibility you did not return from the front lines. His note says as much."

"This is ridiculous. If he had time to write to you while he lay dying, why did he not send me a letter?" Anna asked.

"At the risk of stating the obvious, your whereabouts were unknown and likely because he entrusted me with your care should he meet his demise."

"Men do not need to take control of every situation for things to be done correctly. I am quite capable of taking care of myself; I will not stand for this." She pressed her lips in a tight line.

"You married him." Ian chuckled at his retort while Anna continued to frown.

"Don't be a jackass, Ian. Graham and I loved each other, and he admired my independence. I meant you needn't control the situation, not him. Transferring funds via your bank for security makes sense, but I will take it from here." She sat in the chair offered; her mood softened with memories of her late husband's thoughtfulness. "I would like to see the note again and tell me exactly when you received it." Anna tipped her head and squinted at him suspiciously.

"How many times must I review this with you? I discussed it with my lawyer, and he agrees, Graham's instructions are clear. I am to ensure your safety and manage a trust for you, dispensing funds as I see fit."

"Graham would never have named you as trustee without discussing it with me."

"You might have considered such discussions, or better yet written up Wills, before you both volunteered your services. Perhaps you rushed into marriage, without learning much about each other."

"You are being presumptuous. We knew each other better than most pre-war couples. We had weeks together before we ran to the priest, and then weeks again before we shipped out. Not to mention the years we have corresponded and spent together on leave numerous times."

"Weeks, well then, just the same, we shall assume he had some notion somewhere along the line that I may be needed to oversee his funds." Ian flipped both hands in the air, his wide-eyed sneer indicating he had fully explained the situation.

"We will not assume any such thing. We had plans to come to Canada, start a business and live on a nice farm property. When I enlisted in the Air Force, we arranged for everything to be sold other than the few things we stored. As Graham's wife, and without children, it is now my money and I intend to use it as we planned. He would have wanted it that way."

Ian took a deep breath in and let it out in a huff. "His request states otherwise. My lawyer confirmed that since the note is handwritten and dated, it stands as a Last Will and Testament." He tossed the single page down on the desk in front of her.

Anna shook her head as she read it through for the third time.

My Dear Brother Ian,

I have been struck down and fear this note will reach you after my demise. As you know my darling Anna has enlisted in the Women's Auxiliary Air Force. The RAF sent word to her through internal channels, but without a home address, I believe word of my fate may also get to her after I am gone. We considered coming to Canada if the war ever ends. You and Marcy and your children are our only remaining family. Please provide shelter for my Anna until she can meet and settle with someone new. I will arrange transfer of funds to this end.

```
I, Graham Davidson Campbell, grant the
Bank of England, Threadneedle Street,
London, England direction to transfer all
funds from the account in the names of
Graham Davidson Campbell and Anna Castle
Gordon to my brother, Ian George
Campbell, via immediate wire transfer to
the Bank of Canada, Queen Street,
Kincardine, Ontario, Canada to be held in
trust and disbursed at his behest.

Dated:           Signed:
```

April 30, 1945   Graham Davidson Campbell

She ran her thumb over his name; her brow furrowed when she glanced up at Ian. "Why is his note to you hand-written but the bank request is typewritten? And why does the handwriting simply end off? It appears it should have a second page. There is no closing greeting."

His gaze remained downcast at his desk. He shook his head slightly and did not reply.

"Ian." She raised her voice.

He faced her and again took a deep breath, letting it out slowly before he answered. "How am I to know what was happening when he penned the directive. Perhaps one paragraph was all he could write in his deconditioned state, and he had a clerk type the bank transfer so it would be more formal."

"Do you have any idea how difficult that would be in an army hospital?" Anna's lip curled in disgust at his ignorance.

He threw up his hands and shrugged.

She sat back and crossed her arms in front of her. "Almost impossible. The war zone was not like your bank office with little assistants dashing about tending to your administrative needs. Military aides rarely had access to telegraph machines for emergencies, let alone typewriters; and they certainly did not have the wherewithal to word a bank order such as this."

He stood and walked around his desk. "I will not argue how the note came to be; the point is entirely mute. He asked me to house you and disburse his money at my behest." He snatched the paper off her lap and stabbed it with his finger. "Right here, it says right here at my behest'."

"By my interpretation, he sent funds to reimburse you for accommodating me temporarily, not for you to keep me prisoner forever. It says, 'to this end' which means to provide accommodation until I see fit to move on." She stood and walked to the window, calming slightly when she pulled the curtains aside to watch colourful leaves blow off the large maple tree, with the warm fall wind. "We believed our love could survive anything, even a world war. The war changed everything." She leaned her head against the cool window.

"Of course, it did. I am just saying—"

His irritating voice interrupted her warm memories and she spun from the window. "No, I'm not done."

He threw up his hands, rolled his eyes, and dropped back in his oversized desk chair.

"Graham gave the ultimate sacrifice in the name of a peaceful world. You were not there; you have no idea. I worked ten, twelve sometimes twenty-hour days often near the front lines, within range of enemy fire and some of my war sisters lost their lives; something you would know nothing about."

He slumped his shoulders; then faced her like he might defend himself, but she continued as she walked toward him. "While we dedicated ourselves to the war effort, you sat safely behind a desk managing rich people's money. Do you have any idea what your brother contributed to the Royal Air Force, how respected he was by his peers?"

He shrugged one shoulder but remained silent.

"Then Graham's plane got struck down mere weeks before the surrender. And now you expect me to forget our married life and our future plans, forget the terrors of war ever existed and sit quietly in this dull house with your delusional wife and read a book while you spend all our money?"

"My wife is delusional because she is sick. I ask you not to speak ill of her. And I am holding his money in trust, not spending it."

"My money, Ian. It is my money," she stated calmly, once again stepping forward to face him.

"Anna, please. You took ill on the voyage over; I am merely affording you the opportunity to rest. We can reach an amicable solution in time I am certain."

"I am rested to the point of boredom. After only a fortnight, I have spent so much time reading, that Elsie, the librarian has had me round for tea. And I am healthier than you and you know it. You wired that I would have the ability to live an independent life and I intend to do so. I want the full account transferred to my name now."

"My wire stated you would have access to funds. It made no reference to getting them all at once. Clearly, Graham chose to keep the Campbell wealth in the family."

"I am not uneducated, Ian. This is 1945, women are entitled to their husband's estate, all of it I should add, in the absence of children. The account was in both our names; and the majority was Gordon family wealth, my inheritance from my family that I brought into the marriage." She poked at her chest as she explained.

"You don't even have a marriage certificate in your possession." He raised both hands and pointed at himself in a grandiose gesture. "I, on the other hand, have Graham's signed transfer giving me full authority over the funds. Unless you have the means to fight it in court, you shall have to trust me—"

She again jammed her fists on her hips, stood in front of his desk and stared down at him. "My marriage certificate is in the trunk of my belongings being shipped as we speak. I will fight you and I will win. You do not intimidate me, Ian. I am prepared to work for a living, set up the business Graham and I planned, and buy my own property with my own money."

"As I was saying, if you would stop interrupting. Once you are feeling your old self, if you wish to take on a job, I am all for you earning money to buy yourself whatever you like. And of course, I will set aside a generous monthly allowance for you. In fact, I have already set up an account in your name. You can come to the bank this week and endorse a signature card. I will introduce you around and show you how things work." He swept his hand across his desk.

"I am quite knowledgeable in completing bank transactions. I worked in my family's business for years before enlisting. Again, I remind you, I am an adult who does not require guidance."

He forced a smile. "But, as your husband clearly stated in his dying wishes, you shall stay here with Marcy and me. We will make a comfortable home for you, and I will control how your inheritance is spent." Ian put the note back into his desk and slammed the drawer for emphasis.

"I do not believe they were his dying wishes. This cannot be happening." Anna sat back in the chair and dropped her head to her hand.

He mistook the gesture as weakness and his voice took a soothing tone. "Do not burden yourself, my dear. It is only proper that a man should oversee your finances and I am the best qualified to do it. You have admitted you are barren, so you are not likely to marry—"

"Who told you that?" she spat back at him, jumping from her seat once again.

"Stop the interruptions, Anna; you must learn to tame that fiery temper of yours." He chuckled at his observation annoying her more.

Hands splayed on her brother-in-law's desk, Anna leaned closer and glared at him. "I asked you a question."

"Marcy told me, but that aside, I presumed since you and Graham had no children, there must be a problem."

"And of course, you would assume the problem was with me? I did not say anything about being barren. Graham and I were separated by war more than four out of the five years we were married and our conjugal visits during those years were few and far between."

"He was stationed in Britain the same as many soldiers who managed to procreate. You had blackouts after sunset for heaven's sake. I am sure you had plenty of opportunity—"

"Black out curtains and painted windows prevented light from escaping during bombing raids. They did not force people to lay about coupling. Your knowledge of war proceedings and frankly, procreation only adds to my assessment of your ignorance. Do not dare assume anything about—"

He flicked his fingers dismissing the conversation. "Nonetheless, we are off-track Anna and there is no need for this bickering. Your childbearing issues are certainly none of my concern. The point I tried to make is women your age, are less likely to get married and make a family home; and certainly, buying a home of your own as a single woman is unheard of." He came from behind his desk and stopped in front of her. Hands on her shoulders, he turned her toward him. "We are your kin; we are happy to have you here and the children have taken quite fondly to you. Graham was fine fellow, and he had the good common sense to entrust your care to me."

Anna's late husband and his brother shared features of dark blond hair and hazel eyes, but the similarity ended there. While he stood a few inches taller than Anna, Ian Campbell's disproportionally short limbs and well-fed stoutness, contrasted Graham's tall, fit frame.

Appearances aside, Graham's meticulous manners put Ian's insolence to shame; not only irritating Anna but causing her to question their shared ancestry. She shrunk from his inappropriately intimate touch and took a step back. "Save the feigned sincerity; you scarcely knew your brother. You were children together in England and then you emigrated when you were barely an adult. And having a job in a bank does not mean you are the best suited to control my account. You knew nothing of your parents' farm and even less of my parents' jewellery business. Simply because women in these parts have not lived independently up until now, does not mean I will not be the first."

He smirked and shook his head quickly. "So be it. We are talking in circles here. I will not belabor the point today. If you feel the desire to work, then by all means make an effort to ingratiate yourself to the town folk and do you as you please. I need to get back to the bank." He strode toward his office door.

"There are no jobs now, the good paying positions went back to the men at the end of the war."

He turned abruptly. "Heavens, you need not tax yourself at hard labour. You could work with your friend, Elsie at the library or at the Bruce Telephone System on the switchboard, or perhaps the ladies' clothier in town might be an option; at least it would be if you would dress appropriately instead of roaming about in men's trousers." His hand swept the length of her.

"They are ladies' pants. It is what we wore under our coveralls. Do you suppose I should have sweat over aircraft engines in a cocktail dress and high healed Mary Jane's?"

He huffed and ignored her question as she expected. "Marcy's brother is a brilliant craftsman; he works as a lead hand at a local furniture company. Surely, you have heard of the fine furnishings created in Bruce County."

"Your point?"

"They produced parts for bombers during the war, employed hundreds of people, even women like yourself."

"I know how women worked in the war effort, Ian. I just told you—"

He held up a finger and took a step toward her. "My point is the young sons of the owner have returned from the war and taken over management of the business. They have only recently resumed making furniture."

"Once again, I ask, what is your point?" Anna glared at him.

"Well, only that the brothers have a well-established business around these parts and Marcy's brother, Everett has been with them since before the war and he is single for one thing."

"Forget it."

He pressed his hand downward. "Listen to me. I was going to say, he also does finish carpentry on the side, rebuilding porches and replacing windows and the like. He mentioned he needs someone to do the book work for his side business, take orders and so forth. Since you have business experience, he would likely consider setting you up in his home office; perhaps you could also help him around the house. He is quite well off, who knows what could come of it. I am certain Marcy would put in a word for you."

"Just what I need, another man telling me what to do." She dropped her head to the side.

"Well, you are a little feminist?"

"Once again, I remind you, this is 1945, not the 1800's. Women have rights."

Chapter Three

Yet another new book in hand, Anna approached Marcy's room the following morning, but stopped short when she heard Ian mention her name. She ducked into the linen closet in the upstairs hallway and held the door slightly ajar so she could see between the hinges.

"Now what?" Ian asked Marcy as he paced across the floor at the foot of her bed.

"I like the idea of introducing her to Everett." Marcy's weak voice was almost imperceptible.

"I am sure you would like to see him married off."

"He deserves it as much as any other, especially after all you put him through." She propped up on her elbows and glared at him.

He stopped pacing and leaned on the footboard. "All I put him through? You mean all he put me through."

She frowned and shook her head abruptly. "That aside, he has lived alone much too long."

"Due in part to his abhorrence of children, and, well…" He flipped his hand and turned to the window. "Given she is barren, it seems like an excellent match."

Anna covered her mouth to stifle a gasp.

Ian turned back and met Marcy's sneer. "What? You are the one who brought it up." He glared back at her.

"I said they had not had children, not that she could not. No woman wants to be spoken of in those terms and my brother does not abhor children. He simply does not blend naturally within the confines of societal expectations, as you well know."

"Call it what you will. Perhaps Anna could change that. She seems outgoing enough in an unseemly, liberated way." He shrugged.

"I doubt my brother could be swayed from his habitual routine after all this time. I was thinking more of myself. I would be delighted to have her for a sister-in-law; to have another female in the family to visit and chat with. Lord knows, she will not be well accepted by many women in town."

He stepped closer and leaned on the bottom rail of the bed. "Whatever do you mean? How do you know what the women think of newcomers? You never go out."

"I have been to church and women at the tea have complained that some war brides have been, well, stealing their men in the last few months."

"That's ridiculous." Ian began to pace once again.

"I thought so too to at first. But I suppose it make sense. Plenty of men stayed overseas or didn't come back at all and now these foreign women show up or come back on the arm of our soldiers, and frankly they are competition for the single women in town."

"Well, there are no women vying for your brother's attention." Ian chuckled, drawing his wife's frown once again. He stopped and faced her with a smirk. "You know I'm right."

"Perhaps I could invite Everett to tea and introduce them." She dropped her elbows and fell back to the pile of pillows behind her.

"You just get well and leave the introductions to me." He stepped to the side of the bed and patted her hand.

"I am not going to get well Ian, and you know it. My muscles weaken with each day that passes and my mind..." She blinked repeatedly when tears pooled. "Maybe you should marry Anna when I am gone."

He tipped his head and paused before he replied. "That's preposterous."

"You hesitated; see you think it's a clever idea."

"We will not discuss such morbid issues. I am off to the bank. Finish your tea now so you can rest."

He turned from her bed and left her crying to herself.

～

Anna pinned herself against the linen shelves while Ian passed, then waited several minutes in hiding before she snuck out, retreated down the hall quietly and began her entrance once again only to find Marcy already sound asleep. She sat in the stiff chair and glanced down to the single bed where her sister-in-law lay motionless with pillows propped behind her head and under her knees. Marcy wore her dark hair in a tight French braid which emphasized sprouting greys and pulled her plump facial features into a stern look even while she slept. Unlike the lavish decor of the rest of the house, Marcy's day room was drab. Excepting a hideous purple paisley print bedspread, the room was devoid of colour, window coverings and personal items. Despite the meticulous cleanliness, a sickly musty smell lingered reminiscent of the dying. Anna shook off the reminder of the bleak rooms at the army hospital where she often sat to provide company for the injured soldiers. Idly reading her book in this dull room, staring at her lifeless sister-in-law did little to erase Anna's sad memories and even less to boost her low spirits.

She stood and slammed her book shut, startling Marcy abruptly awake. Her arms flailed in front of her as her gaze darted the room. "What is it; what's wrong?"

"This room is dismal, not to mention stifling; that is what's wrong." Anna strode to the window, flipped the lock on the side and threw open the sash, gulping in the fresh air.

"Oh, no. Ian would not like that. We are not to open windows so late in the fall season. I will catch my death of cold."

"Well, Ian is not here, and we both need some air. This room smells like mould. It has just gone November and it is a balmy fifty degrees out today. No wonder you feel unwell, cooped up here in your bed all day, barely moving a muscle." She stood with her arms across her chest, facing her motionless sister-in-law.

"I used to go out, but Ian—"

Anna pressed her hand forcefully in front of her. "Ian, Ian, what about Marcy? Why do you let him control you? What do you like to do? Why do you not go on any outings with the children or with your acquaintances in town?"

"I go to church." Marcy cringed.

"Okay that's a start. But attending weekly worship with familiar faces is different from socializing with friends."

"My favourite outings were to the lake. I used to take Clara and Thomas but …" Marcy words lingered off as she stared at the blank wall remembering better days.

"But what? Do the children not like the beach?" Anna's firm voice brought her back.

"Oh yes, very much so. The thing is, I …"

Anna huffed in frustration as Marcy wandered off again. "You what? Look at me and focus on your words; finish what you started to say."

"I hear voices in the shells," Marcy whispered.

Anna perched on the windowsill, momentarily unsure how to respond. "Everyone can hear the sound of waves in a shell when you bring it to your ear. My mother taught me that trick years ago. What you hear is simply the amplification of the air that makes its way into the shell cavity. It bounces around against the inner surfaces and resonates a lovely ocean-like sound. In any event, I can't imagine there are shells large enough on the shores of the great lakes for such a thing."

Marcy slowly shook her head but did not reply.

"Okay, what do you mean, voices?" Anna threw up her hands.

"The shells come from freshwater mussels and they look like a longer shaped clam shell." Marcy cupped her hand over her ear. "They call to me: 'come to the sea, come and be free'. I told Ian that I had been tempted to follow the voice out into the water one day and he immediately assigned Nellie to care for the children. He will not let me alone with them and he forbids me to go near the lake." Tears streamed down her cheeks, and she turned her head away.

Anna moved to sit on the side of the bed, taking Marcy's hand in her own. "He is your husband not your keeper. And it is a lake, not a sea, so there you go. The voices don't make sense. There is no reason not to go to the beach. Perhaps you were dreaming or overtired. Why do you not tell him how it upsets you to stay in here?"

She turned abruptly back to Anna. "Oh, heavens no. He does not stand for a woman who speaks up to him."

"I've noticed." Anna smirked, which Marcy ignored.

"I make every effort to keep peace between us, and I daresay, he is a good man for putting up with my idled brain and weakened muscles."

"Your brain is perfectly fine. Being locked in a stuffy, drab room away from your children is making you melancholy. Have you had a doctor examine you? I am certain your muscles would be stronger with daily exercise. Perhaps you have issues with hormones or, or…I don't know an imbalance of the blood or lack of nutrients." Anna circled her hand in the air.

Marcy's tears pooled again. "I don't know what that is. Ian said the doctors will tie me down and stick tools through my eye sockets to take out the nerves in the front of my brain. He insists the tea is just the thing to help, and it does soothe. It helps me rest, but I daresay, you are right, I am losing my mind up here day after day and I miss the lake, despite the calling."

Anna reached for Marcy's teacup and sniffed the remaining contents. "Dear God, they would not do a lobotomy on a perfectly healthy woman. What is in this tea and what do you mean it settles you? He likely has you drugged. No wonder you hear voices."

"No, he would not do that. Ian says—"

Anna held up a forceful hand once again. "Stop, just stop with the Ian this and Ian that. Tell me what Marcy wants."

Her head lolled to the side, before she turned slowly back to Anna. "I want to go back to the beach. The shoreline is so beautiful, and the children love it there. They sit and watch the boats and then the big ships quite often come and go through the harbour. Oh, and they used to visit the lighthouse keeper, Daniel Eastman, he always had a story for them. Then sometimes, we would stop for ice cream at O'Brien's on the way back through town. But that is much too far for me to walk now." Again, she gazed off, lost in thought.

"Then ignore your husband and let's go to the beach."

Marcy shook her head quickly and shrunk back into the pillows. "I have never heard a woman speak so much like a man. You should go to the shore by yourself. Ian will not like what you are saying. He takes care of me, and he knows what is best. Things run much more smoothly if I go along with what he says."

"Get up, we are going together." Anna jumped up, pulled the covers aside and grabbed Marcy's ankles, drawing her to a sitting position.

"What are you doing? I have Nellie for helping me out of bed." She swatted at Anna's hands.

"Nellie is busy raising your children while you waste away in here. We are going to the beach today," Anna demanded.

"Oh no, oh no. We can't do that. Ian will… well… really? Do you think we could just for a few minutes?" Marcy's eyes brightened and a smile grew on one side of her mouth.

"Can you stand?"

"Of course. I shall take my walking stick."

"Then let's go." Anna held out her arm.

Marcy timidly reached her hand through it. "You must not tell Ian." She grinned and leaned against her sister-in-law.

"It will be our little secret. Let's find you a day dress and a coat and go get some fresh air." Anna held herself tall and smiled with accomplishment for the first time in several days.

~

Two hours later, Anna and Marcy returned, elbows linked, giggling as they entered the front door.

"Marcella, get in here this instant," Ian bellowed from his office just right of the front door.

Marcy cowered and visibly weakened so that Anna had to hold her lest she faint to the ground. "There, now; I have you," Anna said.

Marcy turned and clutched both Anna's forearms with a surprisingly tight grip. "I have angered him. We shouldn't have gone. What will I do? What will I say?" She spewed questions in a panicked rush.

"I will come with you, and we will tell him we have been for a walk. That is all there is to it." Anna stepped back from

Marcy's death grip and smiled despite her own trepidation at facing the wrath of Ian Campbell.

"Good day, Ian." Anna beamed confidence as she entered the office first at Marcy's insistence.

Ian bolted from his chair at their entrance and glared at Anna who stood firm as Marcy crumpled into the closest chair, resting her head against the wing of the high-back.

"What the devil? Why have you taken her from her sick bed? You have no idea the depth of her weakened condition. She cannot be trapsing about town with the likes of you. Look at her, she can barely stand."

"What the devil, yourself. We were not trapsing and we did not get anywhere close to town; we went for a stroll to the lake in the warm sun. It's three blocks away. What asinine doctor has told you that fresh air and sunshine are bad for any ailment?" Anna's calm, pleasant voice challenged Ian's tirade.

"You shall speak appropriately in my presence young lady." His face reddened and he balled his fists at his sides.

"Your hollering and accusations are the cause of her collapse into the chair, and I will speak however I please to whomever I please. And save the young lady, reference. We are barely a few years apart. Must I remind you again that I do not need a guardian?" She tilted her head and smiled sweetly, despite her irritation.

"Several years older and if you expect me to treat you like an adult, you should start acting like one." He turned and pushed a button on what appeared to be telephone with no dial.

Anna stared with wide-eyed astonishment when she realized what he had done. "Please tell me you do not have a servant call system."

With a huff, he landed hard in his desk chair, but did not provide an explanation.

None was needed as Nellie entered the office a moment later. She was a petite woman, younger than Anna. Her curly blond hair was drawn into a ponytail with a bright red ribbon that contrasted her dull grey belted dress. "You rang, Sir?" She turned, startled when she noticed Marcy slumped in the chair. "Oh heavens, Mrs. Marcy; are you ill?"

"Miss McGavin, please help my wife back to her day room. It seems she has taken on too much activity. And ask cook to make her the calming tea."

"Wait." Anna extended her hand to Nellie's arm, deterring the nanny's assistance.

Nellie frowned, her gaze darting between Ian and Anna, unsure whose directive to obey.

"Unhand her this instant," Ian demanded. He came from behind his desk and stopped abruptly just inches from Anna when she held up her free hand toward him.

"Both of you calm down. Marcy and I went for a stroll in the warm fall sun. I did not push her through army calisthenics. She had full energy and a cheerful outlook the whole time we were out. As long as I am your guest, I intend to encourage her strength and re-entry into society with daily outings and positive conversation. Ian, I believe your oppressive treatment of your wife has damaged her ability to think for herself. Your insistence that she kennel herself in that bleak room upstairs away from the beach and from all aspects of day-to-day life, not to mention her own children, is negligent. Heaven forbid, it is basic cruelty; and I challenge you to find me a doctor who says otherwise. Also, I would like to know what is in this tranquilizing tea you administer repeatedly throughout the day. Have you considered the herbal ingredients may be contributing to her confusion or interpretation of sound, instead of soothing her nerves? Many plants can have ill effects you know." Anna dropped her hands to her sides but held herself tall despite Ian's intimidating stance just inches away.

"I will not allow you to speak to me this way." His jaw clenched so tightly that the veins in his neck pulsed visibly, and his words were barely audible.

Instead of pulling back from his angry retort, Anna, inched her face even closer to Ian, causing him to recoil in shock. "You may be able to reduce your wife to simpering obedience, but you will never command me. I will speak my peace to you or to anyone else who crosses me. This woman is being held prisoner away from her own children and any mental illness she has shown is a result of your treatment."

"Get out of my sight." He maintained eye contact as he abruptly pointed toward the door.

"If you recall, you are the one who insisted I stay. If you are prepared to transfer the entirety of my account, I will gladly take permanent accommodation elsewhere and mark my place in town entirely independently."

He took a long deep breath through his nose, clapped his arm back against his side, turned, and walked to the window. His hands remained fisted by his sides, and he did not speak; the effort to compose himself appearing a challenge.

Anna turned to Marcy, winked, and patted her shoulder. Wide-eyed, Marcy flinched at Anna's touch. Nellie's astonishment was equally apparent judging by her matched expression. Clearly neither of these women nor many others stood up to Ian Campbell in the past. Anna faced him again and spoke to his back. "As I expected, my money means more to you than your wife's well-being."

He did not turn back to the women, nor reply to Anna.

Anna extended her hand once again to rest on the shoulder of the now wilted Marcy. "We will be fine, Nellie. I can accompany Marcy back to her room and sit with her."

Marcy hesitated, glanced to her husband's back, then turned to Nellie with a shrug. She finally accepted Anna's hand and hauled herself to feet.

"See, you are just fine." Anna smiled at the women. She drew Marcy's hand through her own arm to be sure they made a strong exit, lest her assessment of Marcy's good health be proven wrong. Anna stopped them at the door, and she alone faced Ian who had returned to his desk. "We will consider dining with you if you are able to compose your manners and treat us with civility. Otherwise, we will take dinner in the kitchen with the children." Anna raised her brow in question.

"Everett's here," he replied curtly, his focus downcast, avoiding Anna's glare.

"What?" Marcy jolted back with renewed strength, yanked her arm from her accomplice and spun to face her husband. "My brother? Now? On a Tuesday? Why did you not say something sooner? Dear God, now he has been privy to our dirty laundry."

Ian stood behind his desk once again and faced his wife. He ignored her concerned outburst and answered her slew of questions calmly. "I invited him to dinner as we discussed earlier today. That is why I am home early. Little did I expect to return from my office to find you out galivanting the town." He circled his hand in the air to convey his distaste once again.

"Tell him we will be thirty minutes. I must change." Marcy reached to flatten her windblown hair as she scanned the room, avoiding all eyes on her.

"Of course, dearest. You are undoubtedly flustered at this turn of events. But you need not have to rush into dinner attire if you had—"

"Nonsense," Anna interrupted another admonishing rant. "We are perfectly presentable just as we are. Nellie, please bring the children for dinner with their uncle."

"Oh no, not the children—" Ian started.

Ignoring his protest, Anna took Marcy's hand, pulled her forward and marched from the room, leaving a gape-mouthed Ian standing alone behind his desk.

"Everett, how are you?" Marcy asked. "I am sorry we kept you waiting. Had I known you were coming, we would not have stayed so long at the beach."

He jumped from his seat as they entered the formal living room. Dressed in his Sunday best, hat in his hand, he appeared to Anna to be in his mid thirties. His suit hung loosely on his thin frame, and he fidgeted nervously as he stood under their scrutiny across the room. His dazed expression conveyed his surprise at Marcy's confident entrance on Anna's arm. "What? How?"

"Oh, close your flap. I went for a walk with Anna. I don't need you to slice into us too."

"I, no, of course not. I am delighted you have had an outing. I simply did not expect, that is, Ian…" He ceased his stammering when he stepped forward and accepted a brief hug from his sister.

Ian entered the room, composed and smiling like the heated exchange in his office never transpired. "Thank you for joining us on such short notice. As you can see, we have the pleasure of both these lovely ladies for dinner today." He reached to shake his brother-in-law's hand as he made introductions. "Everett please allow me to introduce my late brother's wife, Anna Gordon. Anna, this is Marcy's brother Everett Rossi."

"Pleasure to meet you." Anna forced a smile and nodded.

At the front of the house, adjacent to Ian's office, the living room displayed matched full-length windows with the same heavy set of drapes. The late day sun shone in a stream through the opening in the sheers causing Everett to squint at the women as Anna took a seat beside Marcy. The dark upholstered chesterfield suite allowed comfortable seating for four in the centre of the room. The wall opposite the windows housed a large hearth with a massive fireplace mantle, boasting garish antique collectibles but devoid of personal items.

"The pleasure is all mine." Everett beamed at Anna and formally bowed almost in half before returning to his seat opposite the women.

With a loving smile for his wife, Ian turned from the tea cart beside the fireplace mantle. "Shall I get you ladies some tea, or a spot of sherry perhaps? I have a lovely bottle one of my customers brought from Walkerton."

"What, no serving staff?" Anna whispered behind her hand to Marcy who struggled to stifle a giggle.

"Anna!" Ian barked. "Do you have something to say?"

Before she could reply, their attention was drawn to the living room door when Nellie entered with one child on each hand. They were night and day in appearance. Clara stood tall and slim with soft features in a darker complexion, deep brown hair, and brown eyes, while fair haired, hazel-eyed Thomas, even at his young age, mirrored his father's image.

"Oh. Children." Everett's scowl showed his distaste.

Marcy shrugged one shoulder in reply but remained silent.

Anna's brow knit at the exchange between the two. "Yes, your sister's children who have names. How long has it been since you have seen your niece and nephew, Mr. Rossi?"

"Oh please, call me Everett." He smiled awkwardly.

"Everett, of course. Are you not able to address the children by their given names? Am I correct in guessing you have not spent much time with them?" She smirked, knowing she was pushing Ian to his limit but the satisfaction of irritating such an obnoxious man was too enticing to stop.

Everett shook his head almost imperceptibly and glanced up to Ian, pleading for guidance.

"Anna, that is enough. You will not challenge my brother-in-law nor any guest in my home in such a disrespectful way."

Anna ignored his scolding, smiled, and motioned the children forward. "Clara, Thomas, come and say hello to your Uncle Everett."

"Children do as you're told when an adult speaks to you," Ian demanded, when they cowered behind their nanny. They hesitantly released Nellie's hands and stepped forward.

Anna dove to the floor, ignoring a gasp from Ian as she did. Encouraging them forward with outstretched arms, she knelt between the children and their uncle. They ran to her embrace with confident smiles. "I have an idea. Since he is new to me too, how about if we greet him together?"

They silently nodded their agreement. Anna stayed on the floor and crawled forward on her knees toward Everett before sitting back on her heels and pulling Thomas onto her lap. The three presented themselves in front of Marcy's brother as if he were royalty. "Everett, this is your niece Clara, and she is ten." Anna smiled at the child and tipped her head toward their uncle.

Everett extended his hand which Clara shook awkwardly before darting back to the safety of Anna's arms.

"I am Thomas, and I am six." The small boy pounced from Anna's lap landing mere inches in front of his uncle, causing him to recoil, blinking in surprise. He once again extended his hand awkwardly, but Thomas bolted forward and encircled his uncle in a hug. Everett held his arms frozen in the air as if touching the child might cause harm.

"That is enough," Ian barked, his voice piercing the awkward silence of the room.

Thomas stepped back and smiled the beaming grin of every innocent child, before skipping back to Anna. She pulled her arm from behind Clara's back and extended it toward their guest. "And I am Anna Gordon, you may call me Anna."

Everett shook her hand lightly and nodded silently.

"Miss McGavin, please take the children to the kitchen for dinner, and tell cook we will be ready in half an hour."

"Yes, Sir." Her right toe tapped the floor behind her, as she bent her left knee in a slight dip, bowing her head to Ian before she extended her hands for the children.

Anna's head jolted back. "Did you curtsy?"

Nellie stared silently as Anna continued to clutch the children to her sides, once again intercepting the nanny's duties.

"Why are the children not dining with us? Their uncle is here for a family visit." Anna directed her glare to Ian.

Ian bowed his head slightly. "He is not here to visit the children."

A scowl and a firm tip of their father's chin had the children rushing back to their nanny.

Anna returned to her place on the couch. "I don't understand." She tilted her head innocently challenging Ian once more.

"Children, go sit on the couch with your mother," Ian commanded. They smiled as they scrambled up between their mother and Anna, a tight squeeze which left Nellie standing awkwardly behind the sofa, unsure what to do next.

"Everett, pour the ladies a glass of sherry and a scotch for each of us would you. Anna, out in the hall, now." Ian pointed toward the living room door.

Anna turned to the children before leaving, stuck out her tongue and crossed her eyes, causing fits of giggles as she left. Even Marcy smiled, enjoying the rare sight of the children's laughter.

Ian pulled the door closed behind them as they stepped out into the hall, then clutched Anna's upper arm holding her in place just inches from his face. "You know damn well that Marcy's brother is here to meet you."

She glanced down at his grasp, then back to his face. "I know nothing of the sort. You left Marcy and me completely unaware he was invited for family dinner."

"You are a flippant, ill-mannered little wench, and I have no idea what my brother ever saw in you. I would not tolerate you in my bed for a minute."

His insults were interspersed with spit which had Anna shrinking back with a disgusted snarl. "Well, that is a relief." She shook her arm out of his tightening grip and wiped her face with the back of her hand. "I am tired of playing games with you, Ian. Clearly my husband knew nothing of your insulting character, or he never would have transferred a penny into your name for safe keeping nor suggested I stay in your home for even a day. You are insufferable and the reason I treat you with disrespect is because that is exactly the way you treat everyone else in your path. Respect is earned and you certainly have none of mine."

He grabbed both her arms and squeezed them tightly when she tried to wiggle away. When he pulled her forward and crushed his mouth down on hers, she held her lips firm and did not return his advance. He stepped back, released her arms, and wiped his fingers across his lips. "As I expected, stone cold bitch. I will wear you down and you will obey me, or you will never see one cent of my brother's money."

Anna reached back and swung her arm toward him, striking his face with all her force. The slap was loud in the silence of the hallway. "If you ever lay a hand on me again, I will call the police. I will tell your wife and everyone in this town that you are a rapist, and I will have Marcy, and your children removed from this house."

"And I will tell everyone you are a liar and a fortune-hunting widow who married my brother for our family money and then seduced me to steal my fortunes as well. I have an upstanding reputation in this town as a gentleman and a professional while you are an unknown, foreign woman who will be lucky to find acceptance, let alone trust. You are at my mercy, and I intend to show you who is boss of this house. Now get back in there and charm Marcy's brother and leave my children and their nanny to my charge or so help me, you will deal with my punishment." He squinted and leaned toward her.

"Go to hell," she snapped back, before she stormed through the living room door and slammed it behind her.

He entered seconds later and nodded to Anna when she forced a smile and sat down in the empty chair beside Marcy's brother.

"I am so glad you have returned, Miss Gordon. Marcy was telling me about your war experience as a mechanic with the Women's Axillary Air Force. How very impressive. I am afraid I did not have the opportunity to enlist, not for lack of trying."

"Imagine that. And it is Mrs. Gordon, but as I mentioned, you may call me Anna."

"Children, you will go with Nellie now and have your dinner in the kitchen with cook." Ian grinned like the reputable upstanding citizen he claimed to be.

Clara and Thomas pouted at Anna. Despite her anger she shrugged, and then held her arms out. They ran to her, and she pulled them tightly into a hug then held them back at arm's length. "Adult dinners are boring anyway. You will have more fun with Nellie. Ask Lorna for a biscuit for dessert; she baked oatmeal with hazelnuts and chocolate chunks earlier today."

They nodded but their disappointment showed.

"How about I take you for a picnic tomorrow at the beach. Your mama will come too. Maybe we could even venture as far as the lighthouse so I can meet your friend Mr. Eastman."

Clara jumped and clapped her hands. "Oh, may we, Mama?"

Ian snarled. "There are vagrants lurking in the woods by the pier, waiting to prey—"

"We will not be picnicking in the shipyard, nor will we bother the shoremen. The children are perfectly safe with their mother and me." Anna squinted at Ian, daring him to argue.

Marcy glanced to Ian briefly, then nodded to the children.

"Yay, thank you Auntie Anna," Clara said.

Their excitement diminished when their father cleared his throat behind them, his intention obvious by the stare that followed.

"Say goodnight to Uncle Everett before you go," Anna whispered when they hugged her a second time.

They turned in unison, holding each other's hand tightly as they stepped toward Everett. "Goodnight, Uncle Evet," Clara said.

Thomas tilted his head and stared at his uncle but stayed silent until his sister punched his arm. "What'd you do that for?" Thomas turned to her.

"Come children." Nellie stepped forward with her hands outstretched, hoping to avoid another awkward moment with the child-hating uncle or the overbearing father.

"Goodbye children," Everett said as they retreated through the door.

"Rossi is your last name? So, you would be Italian then? They were quite involved in the war." Anna stated before retrieving the small sherry glass from the table beside her.

"I am Canadian born and raised, Ma'am. My father was an Italian immigrant from north Italy. He settled in Toronto just after the turn of the century. As I said, I was declined when I tried to enlist. They said I had a heart murmur on examination." He smiled and blinked several times.

"Is that right?" Anna forced a smile in return.

"I am afraid so. And with Marcy so young when our parents passed, naturally I followed them here to Kincardine. Then with her declining health after the children were born, well, it only seemed right that I stay close by and help."

Anna's brow knit. "And yet you're a stranger to the children?"

"Well, I'm more inclined to help—"

"Yes, Marcy would be lost without her brother," Ian finished for him.

Everett jerked his head up to Ian at the interruption causing Anna to mirror the confused reaction. "I have heard some family history from Marcy. I understand your parents were UK and Italian, just like Marcy and Ian. It's odd that you and Marcy have such dark features while Clara is dark, and Thomas is so fair."

Everett blushed to the tip of his ears, then his gaze darted first to Ian, then all about the room. Anna turned her furrowed brow to Marcy who had just dropped her head in her hand. "I'm sorry, did I say the wrong thing?"

Ian had continued to stand since entering the room, occasionally leaning one arm across the fireplace mantle, as if his height somehow helped him hold authority. His curled lip showed his displeasure at Anna's line of questioning. "Ancestry is of no interest to anyone but one's own kin. No need to create gossip over who did what with whom."

Her confusion mounted. "But we are family and I have no mind to gossip about any of you and to whom would I speak? No one knows me. It never crossed my mind to question who did what. Am I missing something?"

Ian ignored the question, stretched down to stoke the fire with the brass poker, then switched his stance to the other side of the mantle, changing his line of focus from Anna to Everett. "Everett has done well indeed since coming to Kincardine. His carpentry business is profitable, and he holds a reputable position here in town as well."

"I make furniture, Ma'am." Everett's gaze jumped to Anna briefly who shook her head quickly at the abrupt change of subject.

"Do not sell yourself short, my man. You are a lead hand and an excellent craftsman." Ian raised his glass toward his brother-in-law, before taking a long drink that drained half the contents.

"Wealthy carpenter, furniture maker, you sound like an eligible bachelor. Why have you not married?" Anna tilted her head innocently.

"Anna, for God's sake," Ian berated.

Everett's face turned crimson once again, but he smiled shyly at Anna. "Quite okay, Ma'am. It is a reasonable question."

"Please Everett, call me Anna."

"Thank you, Anna. The thing is, I have never been particularly comfortable with children. To be honest, they terrify me."

"But you have a delightful niece and nephew now and marriage is not always—" Anna began.

"What she means is—" Ian cut in.

She glanced over her shoulder to Ian. "I am quite capable of elucidating my own words without your clarification. Please stop interrupting our conversation." She turned back to Everett with an encouraging smile, but Ian cut her short once again.

"I believe our dinner will be ready, shall we?" Ian stepped toward Marcy and offered his arm to help her up from the couch.

Before Everett, could follow suit, Anna strode to the door and through to the dining room, seating herself before anyone else caught up. As with all the other rooms in the house, the dining room was a formal affair. The long dark oak table had been set for four at one end, with two on each side. The place settings had no less than five plates, seven pieces of silverware and four crystal stemware each. Several tapers in sterling silver candelabras were lit and the large buffet was strewn with plates covered in large silver domes. Anna half expected a suited butler to appear to serve their food. She received yet another scolding glare from Ian when she jumped up as Lorna entered, wiping her hands on her apron. "Let me help you serve, Lorna."

"Cook is well-paid to carry out such tasks. Return to your seat this instant," Ian barked.

Anna scowled at him and shook her head. "Cook is her job, not her name and Lorna is exceptionally good at said job so what say we let her do that and manage the service ourselves. We are all capable of spooning food onto our own plates. This is ridiculous. You are a banker, not royalty." Anna placed the bowls laden with steaming vegetables into the centre of the four place settings while Lorna did the same with the meat and gravy.

"Thank you, Lorna." Anna smiled at the cook as she retrieved the serving spoons from the top buffet drawer.

The cook leaned her hefty weight, nudging Anna in appreciation, then winked at her before she retreated quietly into the kitchen.

During the several courses of dinner, three of the four adults altered mostly between awkward silences and angry retorts. Everett seemed to play it safe by agreeing with Ian in most discussions rather than express his own opinion, while Marcy remained stoically silent in the presence of the two men.

"All I said was I plan to continue my parents' jewellery business and buy my own cottage." Ignoring the chocolate dessert in front of her, Anna twirled her wine stem between her fingers, staring at the dark contents as it swirled in the glass.

"You are ludicrous to think you will secure a loan without a man to sign for you." Ian raised his voice although they all sat just inches apart.

Anna stood, narrowly missing knocking her chair to the ground behind her. "Watch me." She glared at Ian who had the decency to keep his mouth shut for the first time all evening. "I have had enough of your contempt for one night."

Everett stood as Anna clearly intended to leave. "Nice to make your acquaintance Ma'am. I hope we will meet again someday soon."

She nodded without reply to Everett. Turning at the door, she addressed Marcy who sat stunned and completely still. "I will collect you before noon to picnic with the children. Please be ready."

Her nod was barely perceptible.

Chapter Four

Anna lay awake staring at the canopy of the ancient four poster bed. She bolted up and pulled the covers to her neck at the rattle of the bedroom door handle. The children had come to her one night during a storm when their father had thrown them out of his room; but tonight was clear and cold and they had long since gone to bed. That could mean only one intruder.

"Who's there?" she called out.

He entered the room with a brandy snifter in his hand and staggered slightly as he closed the door behind him.

"Get out or I'll scream." Anna sat up straight and pulled the heavy quilt to her neck.

Ian fell into the chair adjacent her bed and inched it forward in jerky movements, the thick amber liquid sloshing unnoticed to the top rim of his glass. Once close enough, he stretched his legs to rest on the bottom rail of the bed, entwined his fingers around the stem and rested the glass on his protruding belly. "Anna, Anna, Anna. I find you quite attractive you know. That feisty temper of yours challenges me, you are quite a woman. And beautiful too, petite, and slender with such a clear complexion and long golden hair just like the Scots in the old country. Quite a temptress, you are."

"You are vulgar and drunk. How do you get such a variety of alcohol in this dry town?"

"I have people who are gracious enough to deliver what I need. Not too many luxuries in life that cannot be purchased if you have the means."

"Bootleggers you mean?"

He ignored the question and raised his liquor taking a long draw that almost emptied the glass, then licked his lips when he finished.

"Leave my room and go to bed with your wife," Anna said forcefully, fighting the onset of nausea.

"She is not well you know. I do not expect her to live long."

"She is perfectly healthy. You are driving her mental state into ruin and causing physical symptoms as a result."

He flopped his hand downward dismissing her accusation. "I was thinking since you are barren and we already have children who seem to have quite a fondness for you, that once Marcy is gone, we should marry. You and I, you know. Then you need not fret about Graham's money. I would oversee our finances, just as I have managed Marcy's. It is really quite a brilliant scheme that would work in everyone's favor, do you not agree?" His head lolled to his shoulder.

Anna kept her voice calm despite her anger. "Your wife is healthy and even if she were not, you are the last person on earth I would consider marrying. I will get my money back and I will make my own way in this town if it kills me trying."

"Well let us wait and see how that works out." His drunken eyes squinted in his puffy face, and his sneer sent chills up Anna's spine.

He stood and staggered slightly before he came to the side of her bed. She leapt out on the side opposite him, pulling a pillow up to protect her modesty. "Remove yourself from my room right now before I scream the house down." She backed away from the bed but had only inches before she was pinned to the far wall.

"No one will hear you in this guest wing. The children and Marcy are tucked in quietly on the other side of the house." He tossed his brandy snifter to the ground, the remaining contents splashing over the rug before the glass rolled across it. He then dove across the bed with precision dexterity given his inebriated state, grabbed a piece of her nightgown and yanked her toward him.

She tried to fight him off with the pillow, the only weapon available to her. He drew himself up on his knees in the middle of the bed, still clutching her nightgown in his fist, grabbed the offensive pillow with his free hand and tossed it the way of the brandy glass.

Anna squirmed and fought with her fists, screaming all the while. "Help me, someone help me."

"Damn you, woman. I will have you and you will learn to mind me." He spoke through clenched teeth. Lunging at her a final time, he grabbed her by the neck, pulled her down to the bed and cruelly backhanded her across the face, causing stars to spin before her eyes.

Barely conscious, she heard more than felt him rip away her night gown from the top down. The cool air of the room on her bare breasts, jolted her to awareness. Ian knelt between her legs, fumbling with the zipper on his pants. Anna was bare above and below the remnants of her nightgown now circling her waist. She briefly squeezed her eyes shut to fight the building nausea at his combined body odor and heavy brandy infused breath just inches from her face. Graham's words came to her mind as if he had spoken aloud. "If any one of those air force boys makes a move on you, now you will know what to do my love."

With Graham's strength running through her, Anna pulled her arm up to gain momentum then plowed her elbow forcefully into Ian's chest. The blow distracted him long enough for her to twist away to one side, raise her leg as she brought it past him and kick it full force into the centre of his face. One hand holding his bloodied nose, he fell onto the floor, allowing Anna time to jump from the bed and bolt from the room.

Running through the house, clutching her shredded nightgown to her neck, Anna screamed continuously until she finally reached the master suite just as Marcy stuck her head out the door. "What's going on out here?"

Anna pushed past her, slammed the door behind them and turned the lock.

Marcy gasped when she turned on the light and saw blood streaming down Anna's cut face. "What happened to you?"

"Your husband, that's what. He attacked me in my own bed and tried to violate me. I am calling the police to have him arrested."

"Marcy open this door immediately," Ian yelled.

Anna leapt forward and yanked Marcy's arm when she started toward the locked door. "What do you think you are doing? Did you not hear me? He tried to rape me. Look at me; my nightgown is in shreds. He came in drunk, said you were dying, and he would marry me in your place. Then he hauled me to the bed, beat me and tried to violate me before I got away from him."

Marcy's reaction was inappropriately devoid of emotion as Anna screamed in her face while Ian continued to pound on the door.

"What is the matter with you? Snap out of it. I need your help."

Marcy shook her head slowly. "This is my fault. I suggested it, just after you arrived. You told me you were not sure if you could have children and when I told Ian that, well, it came up in conversation that if I died, it would be logical for you to step into my place."

"I would not marry that vile, abusive man ever. And you are not dying. And that is not the point." Anna shook her head abruptly, stunned at Marcy's reaction.

"Marcella, if you do not open the door this minute, I will break it down," Ian screamed.

"He will, he has done it before. You don't know the half of his temper. I have to open it." Marcy's statement was matter of fact.

"Wait." Anna scanned the room and settled on a glass vase that stood on the low dresser by the window. She tossed the flowers to the ground and held the jug over her head ready for attack as Marcy unlocked the door.

Ian shoved through the opening, slamming the door against the tall dresser behind it. "What the hell are you doing?" He glared at Anna. "Put that down."

"Step out of my way. If you come near me, I will call the police and have you arrested."

"You tried to seduce me. I refused you and you pushed me down the stairs. I have a bloodied nose to show for it. What the devil shall I be arrested for?"

Anna slowly lowered the vase. Her mouth hung open, shocked by his explanation. "Go stand beside your wife and let me pass," she demanded, anger having taken over her fear.

He held up both hands in surrender and walked to Marcy's side. "Ready for bed my dear?" He placed a hand softly on her back.

Marcy shook her head slowly and climbed into her bed, turning away from Anna as she left the room and closed the door behind her.

Chapter Five

Anna shook off the recollection of the last few days and turned back to Joseph. "I'm sorry I got lost in thought. So much has happened since I arrived, I fear I am still trying to process it."

He smiled and lifted his glass to her. "I'm happy to hear ye out or help if I can. Did yer husband nae leave things set for ye?"

"Apparently, before his death, or as he lay dying, Graham penned a note issuing a transfer of all our funds to his brother's bank pending my arrival in Canada to stay with them."

"Well thought out on his part. So ye've got the means to get a cottage of yer own?"

"There is the problem. My brother-in-law insists Graham's directive implies my money be held in trust to be disbursed at Ian's behest. I mean he has offered an allowance but, the money is mine and I have big plans."

"Have ye seen the note?"

"I have and while the initial page looks like it is written in Graham's hand, it ends off halfway down the page and it's not signed. Then there is a typewritten direction for the Bank of England to transfer funds into Ian's name here in Kincardine at the bank where he works."

"Typewritten? There's yer forgery right there. No one had access to a typewriter as they lay dying in an army hospital. Perhaps a telegraph in an urgent situation."

"Precisely what I said, but Ian thinks Graham dictated it to a clerk or an aide and they somehow had the transfer request typed up and sent to the bank."

"Sounds farfetched to me." Joseph smirked.

Anna nodded. "Me too, but how do I prove it? And that presents problem number two, his lawyer insists the document represents Graham's Last Will and Testament providing the funds to Ian." She flicked her hand in front of her as she explained.

"Ye should fight him in court and gain control of yer funds. Women can sue. The estate is rightfully yers."

"Right, and ask him to disburse money so I can pay a lawyer to sue him? That will never happen. The man is deranged, and he has his bankers' and lawyers' old boys' clubs to back him. What have I got?"

"The law for one thing."

"Yes, laws protect women's rights to some degree; the problem comes with the enforcing. And how does a recluse Scot living in a cabin in Kincardine know so much about current affairs and women's rights?" She smiled despite her curiosity.

His smile in return held more mystery than answers.

Her brow knit, waiting for an answer that didn't come. "I am guessing you were in the military?" she asked.

His grin disappeared. "I was a battlefield medic alongside the first Canadian Infantry. Yer husband?"

She nodded. "He was in the Royal Air Force, and I enlisted in the Women's Auxiliary Air Force. I worked as a mechanic, mostly."

He nodded back with appreciation. "With that experience, I imagine ye'd manage on yer own quite nicely. What business did ye and Mr. Gordon plan to take on here in the new country?"

"Well, my mother's family name was Castle, she was from Newcastle on Tyne, in England."

"I ken it." He nodded.

"My da was a Gordon, originally from Aberdeen, Scotland. They were jewellers in London, where I was born and raised. My full name is Anna Castle Gordon and I intend to continue in the business of fine jewels like my parents. I want to call my shop, Castle Gordon to honour them both."

"A clever name and a fine honour to their memory, indeed."

Her eyes cast down briefly when she blushed at the small compliment, flustered that this man brought such warm feelings when they had only just met. She cleared her throat and faced him with a confident smile. "I did not have time to change my name when we got married. My husband was a Campbell, not Gordon, and his family were hard working farmers, so he intended—"

Joseph flinched. "Campbell? Ye were married to Graham Campbell?"

She straightened, ignoring the pain the sudden movement caused. "You knew Graham?"

"Well, I … I'm nae sure. I met several Campbells over the years," he stammered.

"What did he look like? Did he wear the Royal Air Force uniform?"

Joseph smiled then copied her movement, focusing on his hands briefly before he answered. "Unfortunately, every soldier looked the same as the next to me. Like I said, I worked as a battlefield medic. I'm afraid most of the uniforms I saw were covered in mud or blood or torn away so I could work. They all wore khakis to my memory."

"You're a doctor then?"

"'Twas nae my job to doctor them. We stabilized the ones we hoped could make it and prepared them for evacuation to field hospitals or medical centres." Joseph stood, raked his fingers through his hair and walked toward the door. "I need some air. Ye should get some rest." He closed the door firmly behind him and left her alone in the quiet cabin.

By Anna's watch half an hour had passed when the door creaked open. "Mr. Hendrie?"

He stepped into the dim light of the room. "Please call me Joseph, or Joe is fine."

"I'm sorry if I brought up bad memories."

"Na harm done. Finish the story if ye'v a mind to."

"Oh, I'm certain I have intruded enough on your kindness."

"Nonsense; anything to distract from war stories. No need to rehash those. Tell me about the note. Do ye think this Ian forged it? And what caused ye to run out in the middle of the night? Ye wilnae get yer money if ye leave it all behind."

"Forgery crossed my mind, but that is not the worst of it. Ian Campbell keeps his wife closed off from her children and feeds her a strange tea of his own concoction. I am not convinced he is beyond poisoning her. He suggested we marry once Marcy has passed as if that's something he could control."

His forehead creased. "Ye mean control his wife's death or force ye to take her place?"

"Either!"

Joseph chuckled and Anna couldn't help smiling back. "This all sounds ludicrous now that I am telling it instead of living it."

"So, ye have suspicions, but ye have money in the bank and hardly sound lacking in resourcefulness. I think the court action is the way to go so at least he can't abscond wi' all the funds."

"As I said, him trying to steal my money is just the beginning of the nightmare." She pinched her lips in a straight line.

"What else has this tyrant of a man done?" He chuckled again.

Anna clutched her hands and shook her head, tears pooling.

"What has he done?" He came to sit on the bottom corner of the bed and reached to take her hand in his.

"The reason I ran, that is, the reason I cannot go back. Well, I, that is he…" she bit her bottom lip as her words lingered off.

"Did he attack ye?"

She nodded slowly then wiped a finger under each eye. "He tried to have his way with me, and I managed to fight him off. I ran to their bedroom and confronted his wife. She hardly seemed at all surprised. He caught up with me and told his wife I tried to seduce him; that I pushed him down the stairs."

Joseph gently ran his finger below the cut on her face. "Did he do this?"

She nodded.

"Bastard." He stood, took the whisky glass from the bedside, and replaced it with a glass of water from the sink. "Ye wilnae get the answers ye search tonight m'eudail. Get some rest, we will sort ye out in the morning."

"I have taken your only bed and it's late; you need sleep."

"I'm fine on the floor."

"But I cannot—"

He held up a finger, stopping what she had been about to say. "Many a night I slept on worse than a bedroll on the floor. I will be fine."

~

"Where am I?" Anna woke with a start, the glowing embers of the fireplace, the only light in the cabin.

"Yer safe; 'tis me, Joe. I have gone to work and come back wi' my truck. I will take ye back to town if yer able to walk."

"It's still dark out." Anna stretched her arms above her head and yawned.

Joseph pulled the cord on the small bedside lamp, filling the room with a soft glow. He glanced down to the bed as her blanket fell away. With the light of the lamp, her slim curves showed through the blouse she wore. He was also aware her bottom half was scantily clad in just her underthings. He cleared his throat then turned away before he spoke. "I've mended yer trousers this morning, so ye have something to wear back. I have no doubt my jeans would be of no use to ye, given yer wee size."

"You sew?"

"I learned a fine stitch as a medic. Works on trousers just as well as it did on wounds. Will ye be needing help up? Otherwise, I will wait outside."

"Oh no, I am fine. I need two minutes in the privy, and then I'll be right out." She reached for her pants that were laid out at the end of the bed and ran her fingers across the fine stitching. "Thank you for doing this. I'm embarrassed, your stitching is finer than mine."

Her thanks drew his attention back; his gaze dropping from the pants in her hand to her bare legs now dangling over the side of the bed. Her skin was porcelain pale, her smooth shapely legs marred only by the sight of her bandaged injury. "Forgive me, I didnae mean to look." He turned away again and pointed to the door on the right. "Loo is through that door. There is soap and a towel at the sink if ye would like to wash up."

"No harm done; I think you had a good look at my legs last night when you were bandaging me." She pulled the pants on, then stood to fasten them, stumbling as pain sliced up her leg. "Damn it."

He bolted toward her and grabbed her arm before she fell back. Gaining her balance, she glanced down to his hold, then up to his incredible blue eyes. Once again, their gaze locked, before she shook off the moment and turned away. "I'll be fine, really, you have done so much already."

~

"I cannae leave ye out in the cold, hiding behind a locked building."

"Yes, please you can. I know how to get in. It's barely dawn, no one will see me in the darkness. Elsie showed me how to maneuver the cellar entrance. She knows about … well, she has become a friend when some others in town have not been quite as welcoming."

He shook his head slowly. "I'm still nae sure how I feel leaving ye to yer own devices wi' an injury."

"Elsie comes in at eight and she will accommodate me until I can sort things out. That's why I was trying to get here last night. You said yourself an air force girl is likely to be resourceful and you are right. Well, provided I start off heading in the right direction." She smiled and tipped her head to her shoulder.

Joseph chuckled but stayed silent.

"Wipe the worry from your face. I am no young innocent. After years of war, I am well trained at managing on my own."

"I have no doubt yer capable and ye can manage. But I feel the need to tell ye—"

Anna placed her finger on his lips, drawing a wide-eyed expression from Joseph in return. "You have done more than enough for me. I would be sitting frozen on the lakeside path or limping in the wrong direction for miles if you had not rescued me. You have been very kind, and I thank you."

He took her hand and ran his thumb over her palm. "No need to thank me. I have enjoyed yer company, Anna. I hope to see ye around town then."

"I would like that." She smiled shyly, before stepping carefully down from the truck.

Joseph shook his head as he watched her retreat into the darkness. *Eejit, ye should have told her.*

Chapter Six

Anna pulled the cord to the single lamp beside the oversized reading chair and attempted to fight the chill of the large brick building by pulling her legs up under her. She winced at the painful reminder of her botched escape and returned her feet to the floor, hoping Elsie would not be long and the furnace would soon be warming the area. The silence of the room, the sight and smell of so many books surrounded her like an embrace for her senses. As her discomfort diminished, she allowed the details of her rescue to occupy her thoughts. She couldn't wait to confide in her friend about the horrors of the night before and then find out all she knew about the handsome and mysterious Joseph Hendrie. She smiled recalling his gentle hands and piercing blue eyes. The mass of his shoulders brought images of his arms around her. She impulsively pulled the edges of her coat to wrap herself in a tight hug and grinned at the feelings the mental image stirred.

"Who are you and what are you doing hiding amongst the reading stacks? How did you get in here?" The demanding male voice interrupted Anna's warm memories.

Lost in her thoughts, she had not heard him creep up. She gasped in reply to the angry questions thrown at her from just a few feet away. He quickly tapped a row of button switches, flooding the room with bright light.

She had no intention of outing her friend in answer to the demands of the chief librarian. By Elsie's description which led Anna to believe her friend may be smitten, she expected a demure, soft-spoken man. Instead, before her stood an intimidating large-framed man with dark hair and dark eyes to match, clearly unhappy to find a patron invading his revered space. Anna ignored her nerves and stood to face him, initially flinching at the pain the sudden movement caused. "Thank goodness someone has arrived. I fear I got locked in the building last night and have had to spend the night curled up in this reading chair. Short of exploring through the basement for an escape, I found no way out without a key to secure the building behind me. I did not want to leave the door unlocked to vandalism by vagrants."

"That is preposterous. I check the building myself every evening before closing." He puffed himself up, with his pride of management.

"I was in the, that is to say, I had to use the facilities just before closing time and I, um…"

"Never mind, there appears to be no harm done. If you leave now, we shall keep the matter between us." He flicked his hand several times dismissing her.

Anna recognized his embarrassment at a possible breach on his own part and knew a hasty departure would be the best plan of action but without Elsie's help, she had nowhere else to go. "Is Elsie in today?"

"Why would you ask? Did Miss Blair allow you stay here last night?" He raised his chin and stood stock straight with a scowl on his face.

Anna shook her head quickly. "Oh, no, on the contrary; she runs a tight ship here, always by the rules. She is an acquaintance is all. I am new in town, and she has been very kind at recommending books. I wanted to—"

He glared at her warily before interrupting. "Either way, she is not in today. She has every second Wednesday off." He turned to walk away.

Anna hesitated and he quickly spun back.

"Did you need something else Miss? What did you say your name was?"

She ignored the request. "No, nothing else. I will be off, my apologies for the intrusion."

He nodded curtly and turned back toward the main desk without reply.

Once again out in the cold of the early morning, Anna had no choice but to return to the Campbell household.

~

After the privacy and comfort of Joseph's cozy cabin, Anna cringed when she stepped into the familiar foyer and was immediately assaulted by the mass and formality of the Campbell's home. The light from Ian's office diminished her hope of escaping conversation with him. As she hung her coat in the front hall closet, he stepped from his office and jerked his head back at the sight of her. "Where the devil have you been at this early hour?"

Ian was the last person she wanted to see on re-entering the house. Her anger surfaced, and she almost retreated to the cold, her injury and discomfort aside. "Stay away from me or you will wish you had."

He waved a backhand, dismissing her threat and smiled as if nothing had transpired between them. "Out for an early stroll, were you? You must be chilled. Would you care to join me for tea? Cook made some delicious scones for breakfast."

She squinted, appalled at his expectation that they remain civil. "I will not join you, now or ever without other people in the room. I will also keep my bedroom door barred at all times and if you attempt to enter, I will have a weapon ready, and will not hesitate to use it. You will not be so lucky as to walk away with only a black eye as you are sporting now."

He chuckled, raising her agitation higher than she thought possible. "Oh, Anna darling, I am not used to the kick of the brandy I got into last night. I meant no disrespect. I will be forthright; in my slightly inebriated state, the thought crossed my mind that you might be lonely and enjoy the company." He turned his hands up in front of himself with a shrug.

"Disrespect, you think that attack was merely a lack of respect? You are a rapist and if I had not had the where-withal to protect myself, you would have completely violated me. I will never be lonely enough to welcome you into my bed and I will never enjoy your vulgar company on any civ-ilized level. I will however have a lock installed on my bed-room door immediately and will remain in this house only until I find a way to obtain the funds to leave. Until then, you will keep your distance."

He again shrugged one shoulder and smirked at her.

"Do you hear me?" She glared at him; her lip curled in disgust at his nonchalance.

"How could I not, I am sure half the town has heard you. If you are done your tirade, there is a note for you on the entryway table and breakfast in the dining room." He tipped his chin toward the tray on the table behind her before he turned and slammed his office door behind him.

Pain shot up her arms drawing her attention to the blood oozing through her gloves; the cuts on her hands having broken open from the force of her clenched fists. Through tears she reached to the small envelope bearing only her first and last name on the front.

Marcy stared down at Anna as she ascended the stairs. "I can explain his behaviour."

Anna checked over her shoulder to be sure Ian remained closed behind his office door. She nodded to Marcy who followed her into her bedroom and closed the door.

Anna removed her gloves gingerly and placed them on her bedside table, then turned to Marcy.

"What happened to you? You can barely walk and look at your hands!" Marcy's mouth hung open.

"After your husband tried to rape me and you did nothing to defend me, I escaped the house. Rather, I tried to escape, injured myself further in the process and now I have been forced to return until I can secure alternate accommodations." She patted her scraped hands with a clean handkerchief, then glared silently at her sister-in-law.

"What's the note?" Marcy tipped her head to the envelope Anna had tossed on the bed.

"I haven't opened it." Anna winced as she bent her knee to sit on the side of the bed. She ripped the seal, drew the single sheet out, then rubbed her fingers across her forehead before she read aloud the few words scribbled on the page. *"Go home. You're not welcome here."*

"Can this week get any worse? Who would send such a thing?" Anna extended the note to her sister-in-law.

Marcy glanced at the page then tossed it and the envelope into the waste bin. "Give it no mind. Some women here are the jealous type; they want the bachelors for their own. In my opinion, if they haven't snagged a man by now…" She waved her hand through the air then stepped closer and lowered herself quietly beside Anna, drawing a puzzled expression.

"Why are you so, so"—Anna shook her head quickly. — "limber or should I say, awake and engaged in conversation? Don't you usually lay in your daybed at this time of the morning?"

"I have considered your advice and decided to decline Ian's tea, make more effort to walk regularly and interact with the children and my acquaintances."

Anna's brow rose. "That is a big switch in a short time. Would your actions have anything to do with punishing your husband for attacking me?"

She ignored the accusation, stood again, and began to pace the room. "I need to explain something to you."

Despite her exhaustion and pain, Anna perked up, curious by Marcy's renewed disposition. "I'm listening."

Marcy pulled the stool from the vanity and sat facing Anna. She cast her gaze to her hands in her lap and stayed quiet for a moment.

"What's on your mind, Marcy?"

She lifted her head and took a deep breath before she began. "When Everett and I were younger, I fell in love with a man by the name of Domenic Curto. He emigrated from Italy with his family and came to work for my papa alongside Everett. Domenic had long dark hair, strong arms and soft lips; the most handsome man I ever met." She stopped speaking to swallow her emotion. "Domenic and I planned to marry. We had promised ourselves to each other, and well, not just with words, but—"

Anna forced a brief smile. "I understand. How did Ian come into the picture?"

"Ian was a bank teller in Toronto at the time, in his young twenties. I had just turned eighteen. He and Everett had met and got on quite well, but initially Ian and I never gave each other much notice. Papa did business at the same bank where Ian worked. When Domenic asked for my hand in marriage, my father refused. Everett and I were born into wealth that my papa had worked long hours to establish. He told me he didn't want me to marry a new immigrant and at the time the Rossis and the Curtos weren't well known to each other. Papa had barely refused us, when next thing I knew, Ian began courting me."

"Ian would be aware of your father's wealth, having managed his finances." Anna smirked.

It was a statement, but Marcy nodded in reply. "You are not the first to imply Ian married me for my father's money. Other people gossiped about it too."

"Okay, so why didn't you tell your papa that you loved Domenic and that you as well as others suspected Ian was only after your family's money? And where was your mother in all of this or Everett for that matter? I would expect him to stand up for you if Domenic were known to him."

"Unfortunately, Papa ignored my pleading even more than the local gossip. Everett was no help; he thought the sun rose and set on Ian." Again, she glanced down at her hands for several seconds before she looked up and continued. "My mama had passed years before. She was lovely and soft spoken, and she could control Papa's temper. She would have talked him into the love match. But I had no chance to talk reason to Papa after Mama died so..." She shrugged one shoulder.

"What happened when Ian came calling?" Anna leaned forward, resting her arms on her knees, and pressing the handkerchief between her palms.

Marcy stood and once again began to pace. She stopped at the tall window and pulled the curtain aside, staring outside as she reminisced. "He was pleasant, polite, and said all the right things to my papa and my brother especially. He told them his parents lived north of Toronto and owned acres of premium farmland, that they were wealthy and had sent him to business school where he graduated top of his class." She spun back from the window and rolled her eyes. "All lies I later found out. Anyway, he proceeded to court me like an English gentleman, never more than a peck on the cheek; and he exuded his charms throughout family events and at church. People congratulated Papa on what a fine match we were. I eventually told Ian that I still loved Domenic and that we had lain together."

"And?"

"He didn't care. I mean it angered him and he called me some horrid names. And, well, he certainly was not as attentive after that, but—"

"I don't understand. If you were on to his act and he knew you didn't love him, then how did you end up married?" Anna's forehead creased.

Marcy flicked her hand. "It all happened so fast, and I had no defence against three men. I begged Papa to let me marry Domenic, but he insisted I marry Ian. He married me off quickly, along with a sizeable wedding gift to give us a good start, he said, which I never laid eyes on. Then we relocated to Kincardine and Everett followed along."

Anna shook her head quickly. "I find that hard to believe. You don't suppose Ian forced the marriage for the money; perhaps told your papa that you had been intimate with Domenic?"

Marcy nodded. "I am certain he said something along those lines to my father. Ian acted like he was doing our whole family a huge service by marrying a soiled woman."

"That's likely why they both made haste to change the subject before dinner last night. No one would want to discuss whether your children look Italian or British decent."

She nodded again. "Ian refused to touch me for several months after we were married to assure himself that he would not be raising another man's child. The truth is, I was a still a virgin, but without my mother alive to explain things, I had no idea that what Domenic and I had done would not conceive a child. I was terrified for weeks after the wedding until my menses came. After that, I was happy Ian stayed away. He never made me feel the way Domenic did."

"It doesn't sound like your brother was much help. In fact, it almost sounds like he was part of Ian's scheme." Anna's brow furrowed deeper, and she shook her head. "An accomplished businessman like your father surely must have had some questions about Ian's character even if his own son did back the plan."

Marcy turned her hands up in front of her. "Ian was incredibly convincing, and Everett always took his side over mine. What's done is done, no point second guessing the why."

Anna's brow knit at Marcy's dismissive comment. "Well, thank you for sharing that and I am sorry you had to go through with an arranged marriage and leave your love behind, but what has this family history to do with why Ian attacked me or why he is so arrogant to everyone? He got a rich wife, a promotion in a new town, an ally in his brother-in-law and a lovely family. He should be happy he got away with deceiving your father and making himself look good in the process."

"Despite Ian and Everett's relationship back in Toronto, once we all got to Kincardine, Ian made life difficult for both Everett and me. Ian pushed Everett away despite his loyalty. The details don't matter, but there was money involved other than the dowry and I believe their arguments about it caused distrust."

"What money?"

"It likely had to do with Papa's inheritance. Everett and Ian oversaw the details and left me out of all discussions." She flipped her hand again. "Aside from all of that, I am trying to say I'm sorry you had no idea you were walking into such a hostile home, or that Ian can be somewhat calculating when it comes to other people's money. It takes everything in me to get through each day and avoid Ian's anger and Everett's dejection, even years later. I know you think Ian is the culprit in my mental health, but some days, I welcome his calming brew simply to remove myself from my own world."

Anna shook her head. "Ian is the culprit of your sadness, Marcy. Starting at day one from the sound of it. If only Graham had known the half of it. He said Ian sent letters home describing the beautiful countryside and his prosperous life in Canada as a successful banker. He portrayed a picture-perfect life with his beautiful wife and his devoted brother-in-law. That's why we wanted to settle here."

"Well, nothing is ever perfect. And I am only telling you all this to warn you. I learned long ago that Ian is a moody, unpredictable man and it is best to heed him or get out of his way. In fact, perhaps you would be better off, as the note said by returning to your homeland." She tipped her head toward the discarded warning.

Anna squinted suspiciously at Marcy's comment. "I will do no such thing. Graham and I had plans and I intend to carry them out. Kincardine is a beautiful town to start fresh and neither Ian's foul moods, nor you, nor the unwelcome committee can scare me off."

Marcy nodded curtly. "I will let you rest then."

She retreated and quietly closed the door behind her, again drawing a puzzled expression from Anna as much at the renewed strength of the woman as her words of warning.

Chapter Seven

Now almost noon, Anna lay curled in a fetal position on her bed, staring unseeing at the dust particles floating through the sunbeam from the break in her bedroom curtains. Desperately tired, aching from her fall and exhausted with emotion, she wanted nothing more than sleep. The peacefulness of slumber evaded her as her thoughts wandered to Marcy's confusing family account and the mysterious note and then to Joseph Hendrie. His kindness touched her heart while his physical presence touched on emotions she had never experienced.

Anna had been attracted to Graham, and certainly their physical connection had been exciting. He had been her first love and she had marveled at the varied positions and techniques he taught her over the years, to give them both pleasure. But despite Anna's reassurances to Ian to the contrary, her visits with Graham over the last year had become few and far between. Although she enjoyed his company, his touch had become unfamiliar, and she had longed for the end of the war in the hope they could reignite the passion they once had.

Anna's draw to Joseph went beyond that kind of basic attraction. His presence had immediately stirred a deeper need, something she felt was subconsciously more intimate. She recalled the warmth that seeped through her when he drew her hands forward to examine the cuts, then his pained expression when they discussed the mine fields, followed by her immediate response to go to him and nurture his post war suffering away with a gentle touch. His hungry gaze at her bare legs when she climbed out of bed, matched her own instinctive need. She had forced down the impulse to invite him back under the sheets to satisfy them both.

Anna rolled on her back, her hand wandering between her legs to press against herself attempting to abate her lustful thoughts. She bolted up at the knock on her door; sitting frozen until the door handle jiggled and pushed against the dresser, she had used to bar the door. "Auntie Anna, it's picnic day. Auntie Anna, what is stuck behind the door?"

"Just a minute Clara," she called back. The dresser that seemed feather weight after her angered conversations with Ian and Marcy, now challenged every aching muscle she could muster to move it back. Barely budging it far enough to open the door part way, she squeezed through the opening to meet the excited children in the hallway.

"Good morning my sweets." She reached to them and ran a hand down each of their faces in turn.

"I am sorry, Mrs. Gordon, I could not keep them away any longer." Nellie tilted her head and cringed.

"Don't apologize Nellie; and please call me Anna. There is no need for formality with me."

"Can we picnic, can we, can we," Thomas begged. He pulled on her pant leg, causing her to flinch from the pain of the wound beneath.

"Mrs.... Anna are you feeling well today? You look like you just woke up." Nellie tilted her head, her brow creased with concern.

Anna pulled her fingers through the back of her hair in a futile attempt to straighten it. She smiled at the nanny, then down to the children. "Yes, I am fine. I slipped getting out of the tub last night and banged my knee and cut my cheek against the corner of the bathroom sink." She touched the cut on her face and grimaced at the reminder of her night.

"Oh, children, we should not bother your aunt today. She has had a bad fall."

Disappointment was an understatement judging by the tears that pooled in Clara's eyes. Thomas merely slumped his shoulders then sat down, cross legged on the floor. "I knew it. I told you we wouldn't get to go."

"It's okay Auntie Anna, we can go another time," Clara said quietly as she wiped her face on her sleeve.

"Nonsense, I promised you a picnic and a picnic we shall have. We have but one problem."

The two children jumped up, renewed hope on their faces. "What is it? I can carry the basket if you are hurt," Clara piped up.

"You are sweet, thank you for offering to help. But that is not the issue. Have you looked out the window yet this morning?"

They both shook their heads. "No, we have been in lessons with Miss McGavin since breakfast," Clara said.

"Well, a storm blew in last night, a rather cold biting wind with snow. So, I do not think we will get to the beach today."

"Awwwwwe."

Anna held up a finger. "But wait, I am not done."

"Thomas, let her finish," the nanny scolded.

Anna winked at Nellie, then continued. "I am fine here; you may leave the children with me."

She shook her head quickly. "But I could not think of it, Mr.—"

Anna held up a forceful hand. "I refuse to hear another word of Ian Campbell. I insist, take the rest of the day to yourself."

Nellie dragged both hands down her cheeks, her expression nothing short of incredulous. "I, I cannot thank you enough," she stammered. "I have not had a day off for weeks."

"My pleasure, go find yourself a book, put your feet up and relax."

"Thank you, thank you so much; I shall do just that."

Anna shoed her hand at the younger woman and chuckled at her exuberant appreciation. "You are very welcome, Nellie."

Taking one child's hand carefully into each of her own, Anna smiled down at them, and they beamed back at their aunt. "We are going to the kitchen to make ourselves a special lunch with soft bread and sweet jam and cheese and biscuits. Then we will take the basket and a blanket, and all your dolls and teddy bears and we will make a grand picnic in the side parlor."

Clara looked up; her eyes wide in fear. "Oh, we are not allowed—"

"Uh ah, I am in charge, and I say for today we shall be allowed to dance about the parlor. Now, let's go get your mama so she can join in the fun."

～

Alone once more, her door securely guarded by the weight of the dresser, Anna's thoughts soon returned to Joseph and the instant connection she experienced with the decadent stranger. Spending time with him had brought on a comforting nostalgic feeling like she had visited home. She punched her pillows as self doubt crept in. "Who am I kidding? So, he shared his military loss, so have thousands. No doubt he is kind to everyone and has not given me a second thought all day. Show up around town with a guy like that and people will want you here even less. Smarten up Anna," she grumbled to herself and attempted to put him from her mind. Her best intentions were not meant to be.

The following morning, after a fitful sleep filled with passionate dreams, Anna was again startled awake by a knock at her door.

"What the devil are you moving about in there?" Ian asked.

Anna opened the door several inches and stuck her face out to her intruder. "Stop with your 'what the devil'. It is horribly irritating, especially at this ungodly hour."

"It is half past eight, the whole world is up and active. Why are you moving furniture?"

"The whole world would not be active if they were awake until four a.m., and I am not rearranging furniture. I use the dresser to block anyone who may decide to invade my privacy, thereby allowing me time to secure a lethal weapon." She forced an insincere grin. "Did you knock for a reason?"

He smirked and ignored her explanation. "A crate has been delivered to you, full of your clothes and some personal belongings."

"You opened it?" she screamed, then forced the door back, squeezed through the opening and shoved past him, despite her state of undress.

"I merely cut the bindings and pried the lid for you," he called to her back as she descended the stairs.

Shaking with fury, she stopped halfway down the staircase and turned to glare at him.

He held his hands up and stared back with wide-eyed innocence.

"I cannot even… rrrrgh. Get out of my sight," she ground out through clenched teeth.

Minutes later, tears sprung as she filed through her personal belongings, remembering better times when she and Graham had shared their own flat before the war. It seemed like a lifetime ago when they were happy and young; when she was naïve to the horrors of the world, and inexperienced at death and destruction. Glancing up, suspicion mounted, when she again saw Ian watching over her movements.

"Did you need something? Or are you afraid I might find something from Graham to prove you lied about him transferring our funds to your name?"

His brow raised and his mouth dropped open at the accusation before he recovered himself. "Of course not. I merely—"

"I will not need an audience. Go away Ian."

He huffed his displeasure at being dismissed but retreated to his office leaving Anna alone to savour unpacking the few remains of all her possessions.

Clara joined her not long after Ian had retreated. She took a place on the floor beside her aunt. "Are you okay Auntie Anna, why are you crying? And why are you still wearing your nightgown and robe?"

"I am fine. Sometimes adults cry when they are reminded of happy things from the past or just when they want for easier days."

"Are these your things? Can I look too?"

Anna shifted over and pulled the girl closer to her side, allowing her to lean over the edge of the trunk. "Of course, you can. In fact, I would appreciate your help if you were not too busy."

Clara perked up and nodded, excited to be involved in a project with her aunt.

"I need to take all these things upstairs," Anna said.

"I could ask Da to carry your trunk."

"No," Anna snapped causing the child to flinch. "Sorry, I mean, he is busy, and I prefer not to bother him. I think we can manage if we take only a few things at a time and then I can put them away upstairs as I go."

After their third trip up the stairs with arms laden, Anna stopped and sat on the side of her bed, clutching a small blue box to her chest.

"Look at these," she said.

Clara jumped up to the bed and peered into the small jewellery box Anna now held open on her lap. "Ouuu, pretty."

Anna poured the contents into her hand. "These are called precious gems. I had the stones set into these beautiful pieces when I worked at my parents' jewellery shop." She extended her open hand to show Clara three rings and several raw stones.

She pointed to the ring with three sparkling clear stones in a row. "Is that a diamond? Mama said I should marry someone who can buy me diamonds."

Anna smirked at the sentiment. "That would be nice I suppose, although marrying someone who returns your love is much more important than how many gifts he is able to buy you."

"But—"

Anna patted the girl's knee. "We should save that conversation for another day. But yes, this one is a diamond ring, and these green stones are emeralds, and the red are called rubies. There were others, even more rare and certainly more expensive but they were sold with all my things back in England."

"What could be more expensive than these? I like the green ones." The child touched the jewels gently, her eyes wide with fascination.

"To jewellers and collectors, the value is not always about the price. When you find something like this to love, you learn to appreciate the beauty because of its quality and rarity more than the cost. I had an alexandrite, or I should say my da did. I set it into a stunning oval design with a split-shank pavé band. It was the most beautiful ring I have ever seen." Anna fingered the few rings she had in her hand, frowning at the loss of her treasured collection and more so, the loss of her previous life.

"What colour is alexite?"

Anna chuckled. "The stone is called alexandrite and it contains a mineral that changes colours depending on the light. In daylight, it appears green, lighter than this emerald, but in the dark of night, it is ruby red like this one. Alexandrites were mined mostly in Russia or Brazil but the one we had was from India."

"Whoooaa."

Anna forced a smile despite her nostalgic mourning. "Yes, we had some beautiful gems back in England. But these are all I have left."

"What will you do with them?" Clara asked.

"I am not sure yet." She told the child truthfully. A sudden desire came over Anna to discuss her plans and share her treasures with Joseph, knowing somehow that he would appreciate the importance to her, especially the items related to her departed family. Although Marcy had seemed intentionally more attentive since Anna's return after the fateful night, neither she nor Ian had ever shown any interest in Anna's past nor her families' lives in Scotland and England.

Anna patted Clara's hand and then tucked the jewellery box into the drawer of the bedside table. "Let's you and I keep these jewels a secret from the others. Can you do that for your Auntie Anna?"

With a huge smile, Clara nodded emphatically, excited at being entrusted with an adult secret.

"Shall we go find your brother and see what mischief he has gotten up to. Poor Nellie must be wondering where you are as well."

Chapter Eight

Anna sipped her morning tea, alternately daydreaming out the window and reading the news. She stifled a gasp when Ian's entrance to the room startled her as it had every time since she had returned three days prior. Keeping her focus on the paper, she met him with silence.

"Good morning, Anna."

She nodded but otherwise ignored his innocent formalities.

"There is a man coming by this morning to fix the bottom few steps to the basement before cook takes a tumble again. Be a dear would you and let him in."

Anna snarled at him and the casual way he addressed her. "I thought Everett was the master carpenter of the family."

"Oh, he is much too busy for mundane jobs like this. I imagine this handyman that Pastor Simon recommended is a bit of a simpleton, so do not engage with him, just let him in and about his business. Perhaps stand by with a book to be sure he doesn't nick the silver." He chuckled.

She responded to his self-amusement with a frown. "Are you joking? Can you not be civil to anyone? I will also be asking him to install a bolted lock on my bedroom door."

He waved his hand dismissing the insult as he turned to leave.

"Wait," Anna called after him.

He turned with a charming smile. "Yes, my dear."

"Do not call me that and save the fake sincerity for your bank customers."

He huffed and rolled his eyes. "Did you want something?"

"I shall wait for your repair man and direct him if you will make an appointment for me with your bank manager."

"To what end? I can manage your finances quite efficiently on my own."

"I wish to discuss a business loan with your manager."

"Why? He will not accommodate a single woman, foreign no less, who—"

Her vicious glare had him rethinking his words to avoid the likelihood of another argument. "Of course, I would be happy to arrange an introduction to Mr. Lonsdale."

An hour later, she answered the knock at the front door. Her surprise mirrored his and they both stood momentarily speechless.

"Mr. Hendrie, how did you find me here?"

"I came to fix a step Mrs. Gordon." He stepped in when she pulled the door open in invitation.

Facing her, his brow knit in confusion. "This is the Campbell ye ran from?"

"I, um, yes."

He shook his head. "And ye'd be back and appearing quite unscathed."

Fingers splayed; she pressed her hand downward. "Please, let me explain."

He held up his hand. "Ye dinnae owe me an explanation."

"But I need to tell you what happened. Will you come and sit in the living room?" she pleaded.

He stared at her for several seconds. She was more beautiful in the light of day, comfortable in her own home versus running scared in the dark of night. Her golden hair lay in curls down her back; her eyes, now fixed on his were clear and as dark blue as the Pacific Ocean off the Isle of Skye.

"Could ye lead me to the step that needs fixing?"

She took his aloof behaviour to mean he questioned her original story. She was crushed he would turn on her, after what she clearly mistook as a mutual connection. Her disappointment surfaced as accusations. "Why are you working as a handyman? I thought you worked for a company in town. Your mates? The truck?" She stood firm; her head tilted looking for answers.

"Seems there is a lot we dinnae ken about each other." He ignored her inquiry, but she remained facing him, one hand on her hip, the other still holding the front door.

"The step?"

Her shoulders slumped as frustration mounted at the inability to defend herself to this man she had felt so comfortable with. "Right; I also need a lock installed on my door if you happen to have one in your tool kit," she requested.

"I can come up wi' something."

"I will show you to my room first."

She leaned against the wall across from her bedroom door and watched him work, unable to draw herself away.

"Ye need nae stay. I can manage a door lock on my own."

"As could I if I had the tools. I have been barring the door with my dresser. This will be much easier."

His brow knit in anger. "Ye need to find a way out of this place. Yer nae safe here."

"I am working on it."

He hesitated when he faced her, and she wondered with renewed hope if he may have another suggestion to help her out of her predicament. He shook his head and turned away. "Could ye show me to the kitchen step needs fixing?"

Now down the basement of the house, she leaned against a cellar post, arms crossed, a few feet from where he worked.

"Since ye seem to want to linger, could ye hand me that screwdriver; nae that one, the red Robbie."

"The what?"

"'Tis a Canadian invention, the Robertson screwdriver, the square head there wi' the red handle." He stretched an arm back, holding the screw up to show her. "See the square in the head of the screw."

"Oh my, I never saw one of those."

He took the offered screwdriver from her hand and turned back to the stair tread. "Nae likely. There are three sizes of drivers, each wi' corresponding screw heads; green is the smallest, then red and black is the largest. Easier to tighten wi'out as much pressure; ye can use one hand and it saves injuries of the flat head screwdriver slipping."

"How efficient." She smiled, and crouched down to rifle through his toolbox, drawing memories of busier days in the air force not so long ago, but feeling like a century.

"The square-head screws were used in car manufacturing, but after near bankruptcy due to shady European licensees, Robertson refused to license his invention to Ford in the U.S. Wi'out a guaranteed supply, Ford turned to Phillips-head screws, so Robertson lost his market in the American industry. Then Ford dropped his orders wi' Robertson for the Canadian car plants as well. But Robertson's are still the favourite here in Canada, especially wi' furniture makers and boat builders and so forth."

"Interesting, we used mostly Phillips screws in my camp. I am sorry, I don't mean to intrude on your work. There is not much to do here. As I said, if anyone had tools, I would have installed the lock and fixed the steps myself."

"Aye, I imagine ye could have done well enough."

"And I, well, it's nice to have company, even if only to discuss screwdrivers." She hesitated to say what she was thinking. Silently, she stood and leaned back to watch him work once again.

He glanced up at her and smirked. "Ye look terrified. I wilnae bite ye, but ye may chew a hole in that lip if ye keep gnawing on it like that. What is on yer mind, Anna?"

"The other night, was, that is, I was… Oh dear, I am stumbling for words today and it was so easy to talk to you before."

"I always find words flow better in the dark of night, than the starkness of day, dinnae ye find?" He turned once more to gaze at her over his shoulder. His piercing blue eyes held hers and her cheeks flushed at the memory of her wanton thoughts and passionate dreams. He grinned and turned back to his work.

"I never thought about it before," she whispered. "But I suppose you are right."

"How are things?" He kept his focus on his task when he asked.

Thrilled with the opportunity, she crouched to his level to explain her circumstances. "Nerve wracking, I suppose is the best term. After you left me, I snuck into the library, but unfortunately, the chief librarian found me instead of my friend, Elsie. I couldn't betray her confidence, so I said I got locked in the night before. I had no choice but to retreat to the cold, and unfortunately without Elsie to accommodate me, I had nowhere to go but back here."

"I'm sorry to hear that. Anything I can do to help?"

She almost cried with relief at his offer. "Thank you, but no. And thank you for allowing me to explain."

He nodded but didn't reply.

"I avoid Ian and have kept my door jammed with the dresser until today. Installing a lock will calm me, at night at least. I have been spending time at the library, when Elsie is there that is; and I do things with the children and Marcy.

That would be his wife I told you of. She has taken my advice to avoid his questionable tea and she seems better for the outings."

"And the funds?"

She stood and spoke with confidence. "I am still planning to buy a small cottage like I told you and run my business from home to start. I have calculated if I save every monthly allowance, I will have enough for a down payment in just a year."

"Ye plan to stay here an entire year?" His eyebrows raised.

"No, I cannot wait that long; that is a worst-case scenario. I asked Ian, well, I demanded only this morning that he arrange an appointment for me to meet with the bank manager to discuss a loan. I also received delivery of my trunk of belongings. When we liquidated our assets, we set aside a small box with a few of my jewellery pieces. I worried it might not arrive, but the gems were there wrapped as we left them. They will be collateral for the loan as well as providing a profitable start to the business."

He stood and turned to her. She hadn't realized he was so tall until she stood just inches from him, he still in his boots, her in only day slippers. She glanced up and he grinned down at her. The way his smile coursed heat through her caused her to blush once more at his proximity.

"That sounds promising," he said.

Taking a step back did nothing to erase Anna's urge to reach up and pull him toward her as she had done in her dreams. She cleared her throat. "I hope so. It looks like you are all done here."

He nodded, then motioned her ahead of him up the stairs.

He reached for the screen door then turned back, hesitant. She held the inside door and they stood awkwardly fixed on each other for an instant. "Is there something else?" she asked.

"There is a dance every Saturday at the pavilion, a few blocks from here. This week is called the Fall Fling, even though we have already had snow. People come from all around, might be a good way for ye to meet the locals. Fancy a night out?"

As much as she craved time with him, the idea of a night out together in public caught her off guard, especially after the notes telling her to leave town. "Oh, I'm not sure. Some people in town do not seem so happy to have me here."

"I will come around about seven. If ye've a mind to go, I would be honoured to escort ye."

Suddenly shy, Anna's gaze cast down. She cringed when she glanced back to him. "I am worried what people will say. Maybe I could meet you there if I decide to go."

"Fair enough." He smiled again and nodded to her. "Dinnae overthink it, m'eudail. 'Tis only a small band; a few guys playing jazz and Betty's famous punch."

She smiled thinking back to the wartime performances when she danced the Lindy Hop with the soldiers. "Thank you, Joseph. Perhaps I will see you there."

"I would like that." He winked at her before he turned to leave.

She closed the door quietly and rested her head against it. She did not want to read too much into his kindness but confiding in him seemed to come so naturally and his mere presence calmed her not to mention the ardent feelings he stirred. "What am I doing?"

"I will tell ye what yer doing, lassie."

Anna gasped then spun around. Lorna leaned against the kitchen door frame, shaking her head slowly.

"What? Were you eavesdropping?"

She grinned at Anna. "He is a catch, and he would be sweet on ye. A woman been around as long as me, has an eye for such a thing. I will also say, a man the likes of Joey Hendrie asks ye to a dance, ye go to the dance."

"Oh, Lorna, you are such a romantic."

"An' yer a fool if ye dinnae go to the social on Saturday." She huffed, rubbed her hands on her apron and turned back to the kitchen.

Anna smiled at the cook's advice, then squealed, ran up the stairs and bolted into Marcy's room, startling her awake.

"Marcy, come with me to buy a new dress."

Chapter Nine

Ian sat alone at one end of the sofa reading the paper while Marcy played a game with the children at the card table in the corner of the room. All four glanced up when Anna walked into the living room, the full skirt of her dress swishing side to side as she entered. The small cap sleeves just covered her shoulders and the slight V-neck led to four large white buttons down the front of the tightly fitted boddice to the flare of the skirt just below her waist.

"I think you picked well, the colourful flowers suit you much better than the plain lavender dress," Marcy said.

"Thank you, I like this one too." She placed her coat and purse on the chair while she pulled on elbow length, white gloves. "I will be off. Thank you again for the use of the car."

Ian dropped the corner of his newspaper. His gaze roamed the length of her before he snapped the paper back in place and spoke from behind it. "I have gone to the trouble of arranging a meeting on Monday morning. You should be home organizing your notes and your business plan, not out galivanting on a Saturday night."

"I appreciate your effort, but I could have arranged an appointment myself and I am quite prepared. I do not need a whole weekend indoors to have a discussion with a banker."

"You have no idea what you are getting into," he shot back.

"I am not sure if you are referring to the bank meeting or the local social, but either way, I would again ask you to mind your own business and stay out of mine."

"You look pretty Auntie Anna." Clara broke the awkward silence in the room a moment later. Her smile beamed with adoration. "I can't wait until I am old enough to go to a dance."

"Well thank you Clara." Anna smiled at the children and spun around to swirl her skirt into a full circle.

"You do look lovely," Marcy agreed, although her melancholy expression paled in comparison to her children's excitement.

Anna wondered the last time Marcy would have danced without judgment or felt the excitement of butterflies over a man. She guessed it had been in the arms of her Domenic. She smiled briefly at her sister-in-law, attempting to keep pity from her expression, as she bent to kiss each child's cheek. "Good night, I will see you tomorrow for church."

Anna retrieved her coat and purse and left the room without looking back to see the lone tear falling down Marcy's cheek.

~

With butterflies churning enough to make her stomach nauseous, Anna entered the beach pavilion alone. A wood stove stood in each corner, embers glowing through the small front panels. Coupled with the crowd of people, the fires kept the room impressively warm against the cold wind outside. A platform stood at the end of the hall farthest the entrance. Instruments were set on the stage, but the band had yet to start.

"Do you have a ticket, Miss." The girl's voice startled her.

"Oh, I, um, I will I need to purchase one, please." Anna undid the clasp of her handbag then flinched when a firm hand gripped her shoulder, drawing her back from the ticket girl.

"She's wi' me." Joseph stepped up to the table and retrieved a ticket from his pocket.

"You were confident enough I would attend that you bought a ticket in advance?" Anna smiled up at him.

He opened his mouth to answer, closed it again and smiled back at her.

She tilted her head, eyebrows raised.

"Okay, aye. I hoped ye'd come." He took her by the shoulders, turned her to face the ticket table and pulled her coat off her shoulders. "Let me take this for ye."

The ticket girl winked at Anna and gave her a knowing smile.

"Ye look bonny in yer fancy dress."

Her apprehension over their mutual connection vanished. She smiled back in answer to his mischievous grin and took his offered arm after he handed off her cloak and gloves.

He wore tan cotton pants, the crease pressed to a point in front and dark brown dress shoes that clicked on the floor when he walked. His red tie complimented the tartan front of his dark V-neck vest. Somewhat of a rebel without a suit jacket like most other men, his white shirt sleeves were rolled up his forearms allowing her hand to rest on his bare arm. "You have cleaned up nicely yourself. That's a smart tartan."

"Hendrie is an associated folk name of Clan MacNaughton so we wear the red, green, navy and black, MacNaughton tartan." He pressed his hand down the front of his vest.

"And you wear it well."

He winked at her compliment and motioned them forward. "Shall we?"

Excitement consumed her to be out socially engaging with healthy young people, but more because she felt confident on Joseph's arm as she entered the room of strangers.

The band soon had Anna tapping her dancing shoes. "Come on, let's dance. Do you remember doing the Lindy Hop at any of the dances for the soldiers?" Her face beamed with excitement at the memories as she extended her hand to him.

"I'm nae much of a dancer."

"Come on," she begged at his reluctance.

"I think you lied," she yelled to him over the music, after he spun her out and back against his chest in a smooth move.

"And I think yer so excited to be spinning yer skirts that ye cannae see how bad I am." He chuckled at her enthusiasm.

The music slowed to a Scottish folk song, and he pulled her close, one arm firmly behind her back, the other holding her hand closely between them. "Now this is more to my liking."

"People are whispering about us and pointing. We have been dancing several songs." Anna gazed up to him.

"They are jealous I'm wi' the prettiest lassie in the room."

The blush on her cheeks was mild compared to the heat that coursed through her.

"Even sweeter when ye blush." He smiled affectionately at her discomfort.

Everett tapped on Joseph's shoulder, interrupting their tender moment. "Mind if I cut in?"

Joseph's grin turned to a scowl at the intrusion, but he maintained his manners as Anna expected he would. "As the lady wishes," he replied to Everett but nodded at Anna.

She wished to stay right where she was, dancing in Joseph's arms on the receiving end of his compliments, but etiquette for a recently widowed, foreign woman, dictated otherwise. She stepped back from Joseph and from the dance floor. "Joseph Hendrie this is Marcy Campbell's brother, Everett Rossi. Everett perhaps you already know Mr. Hendrie?"

"We have met," he mumbled as he briefly shook Joseph's offered hand.

"Good evening to ye, Mr. Rossi." He spoke clearly, over the now cowering Everett.

Anna took control of the situation to save Everett further embarrassment. "Of course, a dance would be lovely Everett." She smiled sweetly and allowed him to escort her to the dance floor.

After an awkwardly silent and physically distanced slow dance, Everett bowed to Anna. "I wonder if you would allow me to take you to dinner one night this week?"

Given the unease of their four-minutes on a dance floor, Anna could not imagine spending a whole dinner hour alone with this man, but she took pity on him and offered a vague reply. "Perhaps, later in the week or else I am sure we will see each other again at Sunday dinner with Ian and Marcy."

Anna stepped away intending to return to Joseph when Everett reached for her. Surprised, she glanced down where his hand firmly gripped her arm. "Was there something else?"

He pulled her hand through his arm forcing her off the dance floor in the direction opposite Joseph Hendrie. "I see your friend Elsie sitting alone at the table. I thought you might like to say hello."

Anna was happy to greet her friend from the library, but she was annoyed at Everett's boldness in forcing her direction. She pulled her hand back from his offered arm. "Thank you, Everett, that is a wonderful idea. I can find my way from here."

"I will call you about going for dinner," he said to her back.

She turned briefly, forced a smile, and nodded to him before retreating to her friend's table.

With a heavy sigh, Anna dropped into the vacant chair beside Elsie. "It's just as well. People were pointing and whispering behind their hands. I have received three separate notes like the one I showed you last week; all telling me I'm not welcome. Perhaps I should keep my distance from Joseph. I never imagined it would be so difficult to settle in."

"Nonsense. A few jealous spinsters do not represent the opinion of the whole town. Ignore them. If you give them attention, they will have won."

"I shouldn't have to be at battle anymore." Anna slumped in her chair. "I had visions of a different life in this beautiful country."

Elsie patted her hand and smiled. "And you shall have it, especially if it involves Joseph Hendrie." She wiggled her eyebrows up and down.

"Oh, Elsie. We have barely just met and here we are making a spectacle of ourselves on the dance floor. No wonder folks are chattering. But Everett need not have dragged me off the floor in the direction opposite Joseph."

"You were anything but a spectacle. You make a handsome couple. If people are gossiping, they are envious. Joseph Hendrie is an attractive, eligible bachelor, and he is—"

The man himself interrupted Elsie's compliments. "Good evening, Miss Blair."

"Oh, Joey, you know better than those formalities. Call me Elsie."

"Pleasure to see ye again." His smile was charming, and Anna could not stop the warmth that once again spread through her and blushed her cheeks.

"I came to see if ye ladies would care for a drink."

"I am fine. You two take off. Anna you are looking a little flushed, maybe some fresh air would be the thing." Elsie flicked her fingers dismissing the two, then winked at her friend when they exchanged smiles.

"She is right, 'tis too warm in here. Let's go out to my truck. I have a special dram of whiskey for ye to taste."

Anna was not innocent to his flirtation but was happy to accompany him and calm her nerves with a sip of something stronger than the virgin punch being served. They leaned against the side door of his truck, facing each other, relaxed in the cool air of the clear star-filled night.

"Yer dress truly is bonny." He reached under her open coat and ran his hands down the length of the boddice, stopping them to rest on her hips.

"Thank you," she whispered before stretching up on tip toes to meet his lips.

One hand stayed on her back while the other reached up and tangled into her hair. His kiss was gentle at first, but quickly grew deeper when she leaned into him and parted her lips on a soft moan.

Their tongues collided as his hands drifted downward and pulled her against the hard length of him. Her nipples pressed against the bulk of his chest, increasing her passion as they clung to each other both aching to be closer than the situation allowed.

"Let's get in the truck," he suggested, his voice deepened with desire.

"Mmm hmmm." She welcomed the private time knowing full well where it might lead.

"Anna, are you okay there?"

They jolted apart, Anna's head narrowly missing the side mirror. "Who's there?" she asked.

"It's me, Everett. I thought you might need some help."

She cleared her throat but did not step into the light. "I am fine thank you Everett. We were just getting some air."

"If you are sure." He stood, hands in his pockets, squinting toward them through the darkness.

"Quite sure, thank you again. I will be back inside shortly."

Stifling a giggle, Anna put her hand over her face and dropped her forehead to Joseph's chest. "We should have sat in the truck."

"On second thought, I should nae have suggested it. Yer new in town, ye have a reputation to uphold."

She glanced up at him. "You are a kind man. Thank you for looking out for me."

"Yer face is flushed. Stay here a moment wi' me." He held her hand as her heartbeat slowly returned to normal.

"I'm fine, I guess we should get back."

With a finger under her chin, he pulled her face to him once more and kissed her gently.

"That is not going to help me regain composure," Anna said, inches from his face, her smile confirming she did not mind the delay.

He grinned back. "Maybe ye will let me call on ye tomorrow for a drive up the coast where we wilnae have any interruptions."

"Well thank you Mr. Hendrie, I would be delighted for the outing."

He chuckled and motioned her before him through the door.

Back inside he stayed close and introduced her to new people every time she turned. He got her a cold fruity drink and they stood together at the side of the dance floor, never without someone to talk to, rarely more than a few inches away from each other. His random touches on her back and her arm felt intimate, and his smile and the occasional wink did things to her inside that made her ache with desire.

She was surprised by the number of his acquaintances given what she knew of his secluded accommodations in the woods and his handyman occupation. People spoke to him respectfully as if he were a town official and they were honoured to be in his presence.

Anna's gaze followed Joseph's when his eyes grew wide at a young woman's enthusiastic approach. No taller than

Anna, she looked to be in her mid twenties. Her plain, light blue dress, hung on her petite frame not unlike her lifeless blond hair hung straight from her head to just above her shoulders. Joseph dropped his hand from behind Anna's back and instinctively caught the woman when she made a running leap into his arms and encircled him with her arms and legs. "Joey, I am so happy you're back. I hoped to see you here."

He dropped her somewhat abruptly and pushed her back at arm's length, one hand remaining on each of her shoulders. "Nancy, what are ye doing here?"

She glanced to Anna with a frown, then turned a pout back to Joseph. "Hank at the Sunset told me you were home. I never thought I would see you again; I expected you to stay in Scotland with your cousins after the war. And here you are, at a dance even. You never dance. Ouu I am so excited we are finally reunited." She spun herself around, pushed Anna to the side, then linked her arm through Joseph's and attempted to pull him forward. "Come dance with me."

He stopped their progress, shoved her arm off his, took a step back and turned to Anna. "Nancy, I'm here wi' Anna. Anna Gordon, this is my old friend Nancy Clark."

"Old friend? Really, Joey, that's what we were?" Eyes wide, her head tilted abruptly.

He forced a smile. "We will have to catch up another time."

"That's not necessary. Please don't let me keep you." Anna extended her hand to their intruder. "Hello Nancy, nice to meet you."

Nancy shook Anna's hand quickly and nodded but didn't reply.

"I see Elsie waving me over. We can talk later." Anna ducked her head and left the two without looking back. Once again, she landed heavily in the chair beside her friend.

"You look miserable dear. Don't fret, you have nothing to worry about. He certainly doesn't care for her anymore," Elsie said.

Anna flopped her hand. "Miserable, no, I am not upset. He can see whomever he pleases."

"Mmm hmm, that is not what your glowering face tells me."

"Don't be ridiculous. He is a very nice man, and he has been kind to me, but I am sure he is pleasant to anyone in town who needs his help. He is a handyman by trade; that's what they do."

Elsie snorted and almost spit out her punch. "Handyman? Who told you that?"

"He came over to the Campbells just the other day to fix the steps. What has gotten into you?"

"Never mind that. I don't think you are just anyone to our Joey Hendrie. He has hardly been out the door since returning from the war. No one even expected him back. You got him out the door, to a social no less, and out on the floor doing the Lindy Hop."

"How would you or anyone else know if he has or has not been out the door?"

"It is a small town, and Maude Hendrie is a good friend of mine."

"He lives alone; how would she know when he comes and goes?"

"Because she is his mum. What would you know about where he lives? I thought this was your first date." Elsie's brow knit and she frowned at her friend. "What are you not telling me?"

Anna had withheld specific details of the night she met Joseph, unsure how staying the night in his cabin would be received. "Okay, stop. Are we talking about the same person? Firstly, it is not a date and I told you he picked me up and drove me to the library the night Ian attacked me."

"Yes, but you left out the part about how you got from that car ride to here." She pursed her lips and raised her eyebrows to Anna.

"I met up with him again at the Campbell's house; he came to do some repairs. He mentioned the dance, said it was a fun night, and a good way to meet people."

"He would not have mentioned it and he would not have come out unless he had a special interest in you. He has barely been an inch away from you since you walked in. I saw the way he looked at you on the dance floor when he pulled you close; not to mention the grin on your face when you snuck out for a sip of whisky and a kiss, I would bet. Why do you think people are talking? You two are adorable." She winked and Anna blushed.

"Well, now he is with Nancy, and I am sitting here with you so, there you go."

"Do you want to know who she is?" Elsie tilted her head.

"It's none of my business." Anna crossed her arms in front of her with a huff.

"Oh, pish posh, I know you're dying for details."

Anna chuckled at her friend. "Elsie, you are the best and I know you're the one dying to tell me."

She leaned in conspiratorially. "Nancy was his fiancé. She left him when he went off to war, told him if he enlisted, they were finished. She had no intention of sitting home alone pining for a letter from the frontline. No, she had bigger plans. Last I heard, she hitched a ride to Toronto, with Todd Lewis. Foolish girl. How could she leave a catch like Joseph Hendrie for someone like that?"

"Who is Todd Lewis?" Anna asked, resting her arms on the table, and moving closer.

"He was a bit of a shady businessman. He sold cars when people around these parts started buying, but last I heard, he planned to make it big in the city selling insurance. That Nancy thought the man could do no wrong. She was so charmed by his ambition, more like duped if you ask me. But off she went, saying small town life was not for her. She wanted to be in the city with him. I think she expected Todd to propose if she went along with him, but everyone knew he had other ideas. Her poor mother was devastated with worry; Nancy never wrote nor called. She came back around Christmas last year for a spell. I believe she had worked in the city in one of the munitions factories, but she never found her man or whatever else she was looking for. Now, I guess since the factory jobs have gone back to the men, she is back here living with her mother." Elsie shook her head.

"What is it? Why do you shake your head in disapproval? Not every woman is destined for settling down in a small town the minute they come of age. She did what she had to do and now maybe she is ready for marriage and a family." Anna smirked.

"Her life is no never mind to me. I am not shaking my head over her choices; but for his. Joseph better be wise to her shenanigans. She is a manipulative one and she comes from a family just like his. She had him convinced it was a good match once. She better not try again and then change her mind and leave him like she did before. I have no doubt that is exactly what she would do. You can't trust her as far as you could throw her."

"He was hurt then?" Anna asked.

"Honestly, no. His mother was more upset. The two families, the Hendries and the Clarks that is, had Joseph and Nancy married off shortly after they arrived in Canada a couple of years before the war."

"Family? I thought he lived alone."

Elsie drew back, her brow knit in confusion. "Who told you that?"

"No one, I, well, that is. Never mind, I must have misunderstood." Anna shook her head, frustrated now that she knew so little of this man, who everyone in town seemed to know personally.

"I don't know what someone else told you, but Joseph's family is quite well known in these parts as is Nancy's. It's not like he was devastated she broke off the engagement. He clearly had no mind to come back looking for her. There was even talk he might stay with kin in Scotland instead of returning to Kincardine. I would say you are a much better match for him than that—"

"Okay then, I think that is enough Nancy and Joseph story for me." Anna patted Elsie's hand, then stood. "In fact, I have had enough socializing for tonight. I am going to head home."

Elsie jerked back at the interruption and Anna's sudden change in mood. "Is Joseph taking you home?"

Anna turned and watched Joseph and Nancy walk side by side toward the back exit. Her heart sunk. "Clearly not, but no need to worry, I have Ian's car. Could I offer you a lift?"

"Oh, Anna, you are so clever. I never thought I would see the day when women drove themselves from place to place."

"Well, it's not my car; I will be a long way to affording one of my own. Ian allows me access to the family car, and I am glad of it. It's too cold to ride a bicycle now."

"Let me get my coat and tell Ruth I have a ride home. I came with her and her husband. I will be but a minute."

Anna waited by the front door for her friend, trying with all her willpower to avoid scanning the room, but failing miserably. She gasped when Elsie came up behind her and touched her arm. "You startled me. Are you ready to go?"

Elsie leaned closer and pointed to the corner of the room. "They are over by the refreshments, and he does not look happy. Are you sure you wouldn't prefer to stay, maybe take another spin around the dance floor?"

Anna followed Elsie's direction. Nancy stood by Joseph's side and placed her hand possessively on his forearm as they laughed at something another young man said. "He looks happy to me. Let's go."

She caught Joseph's brief glance before she turned to go. His laughter turned to a frown and his brow knit. She nodded to him, pulled up her hood and linked Elsie's arm through hers as they walked out into the cool night.

~

Frustration overtook Anna's ability to sleep. She tossed and turned, with lust for Joseph re-experiencing their kiss and his exploring hands. She was not a young inexperienced woman. She knew how things worked and her love for Graham had been real, their coupling satisfying, but she had never experienced the passion Joseph ignited. Added to that turmoil, was anger at what she realized was jealousy of his ex-fiancé and truly everyone in town who seemed to know him, and his family better than she did.

The only thing helping to erase her wanton thoughts was a bout of nerves that overcame her when she reviewed her presentation for what she knew may be her only chance at independence. Ian had agreed to introduce her and make recommendations on her behalf, but she knew better than to trust anything he did for her. Since returning to the house, Ian had behaved akin to a saint. While she wanted to think he felt remorse for his abhorrent behaviour and was legitimate in his offer to help her at the bank, her instinct told her that his benevolence somehow served to benefit him more than her independent future.

Anna so wanted to discuss the bank visit further with Joseph on their drive up the coast, but now she doubted he would come, doubted if she would see him at all on the level of confidante. She visualized his fiancé in his arms, tucked away cosily in his cabin, with a warm fire burning while they intimately celebrated their reunion.

"Stop it," Anna said to the empty room. "You're an idiot to trust him in the first place. He lied about his identity, who knows what else he lied about. Stop thinking about him and go to sleep." She pounded the pillow with her fists, followed by a thud with her head. Despite her self-deprecation, sleep did not come.

⁓

"What has you so miserable today?" Ian asked.

Anna glanced up from her book, a snarl her only reply. Her frustration that Joseph had not appeared for their drive as promised, nor called to cancel had initially brought on a private indulgence of tears. Now, anger had replaced her self-pity and the last thing she intended to do was discuss her lack luster love life with her brother-in-law.

Ian tossed an envelope in front of her on the table.

"For God's sake, not again." Anna's temptation was to toss the familiar note into the trash without even opening it, but a faint hope that it may be from Joseph had her turning the envelope in her hand. *Take the hint. Go back where you belong.* "Arrrrgh." She ripped the offensive message and tossed the pieces into the fireplace embers.

"Is there a problem?" Ian asked innocently.

She squinted at him suspiciously, again remaining silent, still hesitant to involve him in any of her personal business.

"There we are then." He held up both hands in surrender. "Could I challenge you to put a smile on for our dinner guest?"

"Dear God, who is coming this time?" Anna jumped to the window at the sound of a car door in front of the house.

"Not whomever you are expecting by the look of things."

She spun from the window, slammed her book on the table, and glared at her brother-in-law. "I asked a question."

"Everett is coming to dinner. We were trying to make up for the awkward visit last week."

"He is the awkward part and almost as boorish as you."

"It is Sunday dinner, a tradition in this house. I would appreciate your effort to be pleasant."

"I have no idea what you and Everett are scheming, but I will not have him forced upon me. I have no interest in the man." She stormed from the room, slamming the door on Ian's call for her to wait.

~

Anna returned to the living room almost an hour later, wearing the same khaki pants and dark blouse she had changed into after church. Her hair tumbled down her back in a messy disarray. She looked drawn and exhausted and knew she was inappropriately dressed for Sunday dinner but had decided her presence at all was better than what was expected. With a thud and a heavy sigh, she sat beside Marcy on the couch, the farthest possible seat from Everett.

"We would be happy to wait while you dress for dinner," Ian ventured.

She tilted her head and scowled at him. "And I would be happy to go back to my room and skip dinner."

Ian rolled his eyes and motioned them toward the dining room. "Shall we go sit then?"

Once again, Anna took the seat beside Marcy before Ian had the chance, forcing him to sit beside his brother-in-law.

"Did you have a lovely time at the fall fling last night? You and Joseph Hendrie made a handsome couple on the dance floor; everyone was saying so." Everett's smile appeared forced.

"Joseph Hendrie, the handyman? What the devil are you doing with someone like him?" Ian snarled.

"Dancing, taking refreshment and meeting new people, just as everyone else was doing," Anna snapped back while she kept her focus on her plate.

"You know exactly what I meant. He is hardly an appropriate suiter."

"For the love of God, Ian. She is a grown woman," Marcy defended, gaining a reproachful look from her husband.

"Thank you, Marcy for stating the obvious." Anna smirked.

"Do you mean Joseph Hendrie, of the Hendries of Tiverton?" Marcy asked, her enthusiasm drawing Anna's attention.

"Who are they? What are you on about?" Ian barked at her.

"The Hendries raise thoroughbreds. They are a well-to-do family; you know Howard and Maude. They have been in the area since long before the war. Why, one of their horses placed at The Prince of Wales Stakes in Leaside just this year. It was all over the news. How can you forget?"

"Yes, yes, of course I know Howard Hendrie, or at least I did before he passed earlier this year. This Joseph Hendrie cannot be their kin. His name is on the chit for the repairs this week. Pastor Simon recommended him as a handyman, said he is a Scottish bloke, lives alone in a shack in the woods."

"Well yes, they are Scottish, came from the Highlands, as did their beautiful horses. They have a few adult children who worked the farm and took the horses to the racetracks. There were at least two boys, maybe three, and I think one girl. I know one went off to war, but I don't remember his name." Marcy glanced upward in concentration.

"Well clearly, it cannot be the same man. Why would Pastor Simon say he lived alone in the woods at the north end of town, if he is a horse breeder in Tiverton? You are being ridiculous, Marcy."

"I do not think I am being ridiculous. I was simply taking part in the conversation. I know Maude Hendrie from the church restoration committee. I will ask next time we meet if this Joseph is her boy."

Thrilled to see Marcy finally speaking her own mind, Anna smiled at her and patted her hand. "That will not be necessary. At least, do not do any inquiring on my behalf. But I appreciate the offer." She softened her voice for Marcy's benefit.

"I can confirm, Joseph Hendrie is the son of the Hendries of Tiverton. We have crossed paths on occasion," Everett said quietly.

"Oh, right, you said you knew him when you cut in on the dance floor last night." Anna stared at Everett curious to hear what he would say about Joseph.

"You two were dancing. How splendid," Ian said.

"Well, we, I —"

"We danced one song, yes," Anna admitted.

"Would you be interested in attending the Christmas social at the hall? It is still several weeks away, but no harm in asking in advance." Everett stammered over the words and blushed profusely at Anna, although his squint suggested challenge not shyness.

"Oh, goodness. You have caught me off guard. You know, I have plans in the works to set up my own home with a shop to continue my parents' business. I think it will keep me quite occupied for the next several weeks up to the holidays."

"Yes, yes, of course, you are clearly very busy." He dabbed the corners of his mouth with his napkin, despite the absence of food, turned to smile at Ian and then returned to his plate once again.

"Let me see what I can arrange and let you know closer to the date, once I get settled." Anna offered vaguely.

Everett seemed to strain another smile making her squirm uncomfortably in her seat.

"Yes, Anna is meeting our bank manager tomorrow to discuss financing a jewellery shop," Ian piped up, wiggling his whole body as if the excitement of the business plan were his own.

Anna huffed and glared at her brother-in-law. "Ian as I have mentioned to you before, several times in fact, I would prefer if you would respect customer confidentiality and not discuss my finances or my business plan with others."

"Oh, don't be absurd. Everett is family and you just told him yourself that you intend to set up shop. You should be thrilled I am bragging about your potential instead of stating the obvious challenges you may face in your endeavor as a single woman."

"Everett is not my direct family and once again, I ask you to keep my financial business confidential as you would any other bank customer."

"I would be happy to help, if you need assistance."

"Thank you, Everett." Anna smiled sweetly. "I intend to finance the business on my own, in part with the funds my late husband and I set aside for the endeavor."

His eyes enlarged and his head shook quickly as he looked around the table. "Oh, heavens no, I did not mean financial assistance. I meant if you need to hire a carpenter to build your working space or such."

"Of course, thank you again. I will keep that in mind." She smiled slightly and he calmed himself.

Anna placed her hand gently on Marcy's arm, holding her in place, when Ian stood to walk Everett to the door after their dessert.

"What is it?"

"I wonder if you could shed any light on who may be sending me messages. If you recall, one awaited when I returned the morning after... well, last week. You tossed it in the trash in my room and dismissed the warning."

"I recall the note last week, but no I don't know where it or any others came from." Marcy's head drew back. "Are you suggesting I had something to do with it."

It was Anna's turn to flinch. "No, of course not; it never crossed my mind." She shook her head and thought *until now.* "I have received a handful of messages, all in the same vein, suggesting I leave town or go back from whence I came, written in a scrawling hand but on similar stationary. Each has simply my name on the front; no postage so they must be hand delivered."

"Oh my, that is disturbing."

"Your reference earlier to speak to your church group about Joseph had me thinking perhaps your women friends might shed some light on who, well, I suppose it could be the whole group behind it…" Anna dropped her head in her hands and propped her elbows on the table.

Marcy patted Anna's back. "There, there."

Anna sat back, not the least comforted by her sister-in-law. "You know what? Never mind. I will simply ignore them as I have been." She began to push herself back from the table, then stopped. "Don't you think it odd that Ian never sees who dropped off the notes?"

Marcy again seemed taken aback. "Are you accusing one of us of threatening you?"

"As I said, the thought never crossed my mind, but I must admit by your defensive reaction just now, I am beginning to wonder. Would you tell me if either of you had any knowledge of who may be sending the insulting messages?"

Marcy stared blankly and didn't reply. An awkward silence hung between the two when Ian stepped back into the room. "Are you two talking about me?"

Anna rolled her eyes and pushed herself from the table. "Excuse me."

"I will see you at the bank in the morning then. Good night, Anna." Ian spoke to her back as she closed the door on the two of them.

"What was that all about?"

"Nothing," Marcy spoke to her hands in her lap.

Ian leaned forward, his hands gripping the back of the dining chair. "Marcella, I insist. What has she said to you?"

Marcy rose slowly and came to stand face-to-face mere inches from her husband; the move so rare had Ian jolting back in surprise. "I said, it's nothing." She turned and left the room, leaving Ian blinking in disbelief.

Chapter Ten

The sun shone on the cool Monday morning as Anna walked up the wide front steps to the Bank of Canada ten minutes ahead of her scheduled eleven a.m. meeting. She held herself tall and confident despite the nerves that had her belly doing somersaults. "Good morning, Miss." The security guard held the door and greeted her with a smile and a tip of his hat.

"Good morning." She nodded in reply.

Tellers stood behind several glassed-in cubicles to her left where only two patrons were currently being served. The shining marble-floored foyer in the centre was devoid of any other customers. The large empty space coupled with the elaborate ceilings at least two stories above her head, made the establishment seem massive and more intimidating than she expected. Ian instantly appeared as she stood surveying the elaborate interior. She flinched and pulled her arm back when he touched her.

Drawing a stern look from the guard, Ian stepped aside and motioned Anna ahead of him toward a row of office enclosures. Attached to each other and devoid of ceilings, each meeting room had one glass wall and a single door which faced the public area. Before entering, Anna glanced to the other windowed offices with concern for the privacy of her business dealings. Ian stepped ahead of her and opened the door to the end unit, preceding her entry. The room was generic with a large oak desk in the centre, two chairs facing it, one larger wooden swivel chair behind it and two more chairs off to the side. A lamp with a golden pull cord stood at the top of the desk, which was otherwise clear of contents. No personal items adorned the side nor back walls. Anna thought the starkness of the area once again exuded intimidation where something softer would have been more welcoming and encouraged confidence among customers. *Perhaps bankers didn't want their customers to feel relaxed and confident.*

"Come in, come in Anna. I have organized your meeting with our senior officer. He takes care of all the businessmen in town. Anna, this is Mr. Lonsdale." Ian swept his hand in a grand gesture toward his superior.

Mr. Lonsdale was a tall heavy-set man, with salt and pepper hair that had thinned on top, necessitating an awkward combover. His welcoming smile exposed buck teeth that rounded extensively from his mouth drawing her attention immediately to it and reminding her of the donkey on Graham's parents' farm. The visual of the belligerent beast somehow calmed her so that she had to clear her throat to stifle a nervous giggle.

Anna returned the smile and extended her gloved hand. "It's Mrs. Gordon. I am pleased to meet you."

Ian sat in one of the chairs to the side of the desk adjacent his colleague, who remained standing until Anna had taken her seat in front of the desk. Mr. Lonsdale's obtrusive smile remained, as he sat in the swivel chair behind the desk. "Likewise, I am sure Mrs. Gordon. I thought you were Mr. Campbell's sister-in-law by his late brother Graham Campbell?"

"That is correct."

"Oh, I assumed you would be a Campbell as well."

"You assumed incorrectly. I retained my family name when we married."

A grimace replaced his smile. "My mistake, I apologize. I understand now."

"As the last member of my family with the Gordon name, and frankly with little time to do name changing paperwork before we both enlisted, it seemed easier to keep my own surname. Are we here to discuss my heritage or my finances?" She tilted her head to one side and forced a smile.

He held up one hand. "Oh, begging your pardon Ma'am; I meant no offence."

"None taken."

"Your brother-in-law speaks highly of you, and may I begin with my condolences on the loss of your husband; such tragic times for so many."

"Thank you." She kept her eyes on the senior officer as she tipped her head in Ian's direction. "I do not wish to have any further financial discussions with my brother-in-law present. I prefer he leave."

"But—"

Mr. Lonsdale held up a hand halting Ian's protest. "Mr. Campbell, as the customer wishes. Would you leave us please?"

Almost imperceptible nods exchanged between the two men before Ian left the room. Anna turned to the window to watch his retreat, waiting until he was out of earshot before returning her attention to the banker.

Mr. Lonsdale opened the desk drawer and pulled out paper and a silver and black fountain pen. With his hand poised over the notepad, he again smiled. "How can I help you today, Mrs. Gordon?"

"Firstly, for the record, I would like to be clear that this meeting is to be kept confidential. If that is not the case, I will take my business elsewhere."

"Of course; strictly confidential." He nodded curtly.

"I am here to borrow funds for a business venture." She leaned forward slightly and clasped her trembling hands together.

"That is lovely Mrs. Gordon. I would be delighted to review your business plan and discuss a loan toward the venture. What sort of shop were you thinking?"

She groaned inwardly, at the chauvinistic implication. "What makes you think my business plan involves a shop?"

His head jolted back, his eyes wide at her accusation. "My apologies for the assumption. Once again, I meant no offence."

"My family, that is my father and mother had a lucrative business in jewellery designs. We lived in Hatton Garden in England; perhaps you have heard of it."

"I'm afraid not. But, Kincardine could use a jewellery shop, excellent—" He began to write, but again flinched at her interruption.

"While my father commenced the business many years ago, I took over when he died a few years before the war. I have been told I have quite an instinct for gem quality. I am able to recognize superiority versus faux gemstones a trait that does not come naturally to many in the business. I bought jewellery at estate sales back home, refurbished some items and reset the stones of others into modern pieces which turned quite a profit."

"In your own name? That is astonishing." Mr. Lonsdale's wide-eyed expression showed his surprise before he returned to making notes.

"Well, no, the sales went through my father's company. I worked along side him learning the business until he and my mother could no longer keep it up, then I took over."

"And so, you managed the finances as a sole proprietor?" He glanced up to her from his notepad.

"Well, yes and no. I ran the storefront and balanced the accounts, but my da had a partner who was still alive and able to sign for me before women were entitled to handle their own financial transactions. I also evaluated the stones, created the settings, and kept the books independently. As I said, I have a recognized knack for the business. And I am certainly aware of what women prefer by design."

"What will you be using for collateral?" He glared at her; his pen again poised at an angle.

"I have a select few of the pieces I described to you and several raw jewels which were appraised in England before I came over. They are all I have left of my father's business. My husband and I liquidated all our assets before we both enlisted in the Royal Air Force. As a result of the liquidation, I have significant cash funds currently held in trust by my brother-in-law, Ian Campbell. Finally, I plan to buy a home with the loan and operate the shop out of my home, so the loan will also be secured by the house."

"So, your brother-in-law will be signing for your credit?" His pen remained still despite her detailed clarification.

"No, I would like the venture strictly independent of my brother-in-law. As I just explained, the jewels, my trust fund and the value of the house will serve as collateral and far outweigh the sum of the loan I am requesting. I am quite a wealthy woman; I see no need for a co-signer."

Mr. Lonsdale placed the pen on top of the notepad, slowly folded his hands and rested them on the desk in front of him. "I recognize your assets may outweigh the debt. The co-signer comes into play should you default on the loan."

"I understand the role of a co—

"My question is, how will you pay the loan if you are using profits from the jewellery to pay the bills of home ownership, and to make more jewellery?"

She huffed at his disrespectful interruption. "To be quite direct, once I have earned enough from the business to retain a lawyer, I plan to sue my brother-in-law for the return of the funds he is holding which are legally mine and as I mentioned, quite extensive."

Mr. Lonsdale's eyes enlarged once again, but he recovered himself quickly.

"I merely need cash up front to get the ball rolling, so to speak."

"I am dreadfully sorry, but I fear I am misunderstanding. Why do you not ask Mr. Campbell for an advance out of your trust fund to invest in your start up costs for inventory or equipment?"

His lack of note taking along with his placating smile told Anna she had already lost the battle. Her frustration mounted and the desire to expose Ian Campbell's true character was overwhelming, but she knew as a foreign woman, an angry rant about a colleague's personal indiscretions would only discredit her further. She took a deep breath and let it out slowly. "My brother-in-law currently holds the purse strings tightly on my account. He begrudgingly disburses only minimal advances at his own behest. I have no desire for him to have the same control over my business. His current allowance will cover the monthly payment of the loan. I am also certain the first few items I sell will set me up nicely as far as inventory. I need only a slight head start to set up my cottage and workshop on the premises. I intend to call it Castle Gordon." She waved her hand in front of her and sat up straight, proud at the prospect of carrying on where her mother and father had left off. He remained silent, so she continued her explanation, which now felt sadly like pleading. "I must have a work bench constructed, order pliers, metal stamps, needle files and so on. Many of these items come from overseas and can be a hefty initial investment."

"I understand start up costs, Mrs. Gordon, but—"

"Women are entitled to apply for business loans and mortgages, Mr. Lonsdale. Please tell me you will not deny me my legal right to do so."

He sat back fully and rubbed his hands back and forth on the arms of his chair, for several seconds, before he clasped them tightly once again and stamped them down on his desk. Leaning forward he offered another patronizing toothy grin before he spoke. "Perhaps in England things are somewhat more lenient, but here in Kincardine, my hands are tied by bank lending policies. I would love to help you and I have no doubt you are competent in business, but you must be aware a single woman, even a woman of means such as yourself, cannot sign for a mortgage or business credit without her husband's, or I should say, without—"

Already in a foul mood from the events of the last few days, and frustrated at the banker's response, despite awareness of the rules, her temper got the best of her. She stood and yanked the door open.

"Wait," he called after her.

One hand on the door, she glared at him over her shoulder. "Say no more. I do not know why I bothered to get my hopes up. I knew I had a miniscule chance against your prehistoric chauvinistic rules. I saw your nod to Ian Campbell before he left the room. You men sit back and let the money roll through your fingers at the expense of women's exhaustion. We work all day and then go home to wait on you hand and foot, keep your homes and raise your children single-handedly."

He stood behind the desk and raised his palms up. "Really, Mrs. Gordon—"

She spun back to him but stayed at the door. "The men who returned from the war have been offered free university and property to develop of their own. I too risked my life in service to the Royal Air Force, and I cannot so much as borrow a dollar in my own name. I am tired of being told what to do by men who have a fraction of my ambition. I will sell my jewels to make enough for a start up and I will sue my lecherous brother-in-law for the return of mine and my husband's money, and I will win. And, when I have my money back in my own hands, you can count on me taking my financial dealings to another bank."

He came from behind his desk and stepped toward her. "Mrs. Gordon, please wait. I meant no disrespect. If your brother-in-law is willing to co-sign, we can arrange a loan this very day."

"I told you, he has enough control over me and my money, which I assure you will not always be the case. I will not allow him the upper hand in any further dealings of mine."

"It is strictly bank policy. I am terribly sorry; I do not make the rules. If you have someone else, perhaps a silent partner who could sign and allow you free reign to run the business, I would be happy to discuss—"

"She's wi' me." His voice interrupted the banker and startled Anna.

"Mr. Hendrie?" Mr. Lonsdale's brow knit in confusion.

"Joseph?" Anna's expression mirrored the banker. She glanced around the corner to the empty waiting chairs outside the offices.

Joseph reached for her, drawing her arm through his. She glanced down at their linked arms and made a split-second decision to go along with his ruse.

"I, um, that is, won't you both come in." He motioned the two to join him in his office. "What brings you here Mr. Hendrie? I did not see you come in with Mrs. Gordon."

"We arrived separately. I merely waited outside to see if ye'd be equitable and allow her to sign on her own. As expected, yer stuck in the mirk ages like most bank managers and have no ability to see the way of the future."

"Mr. Hendrie, I assure you, I am simply following the rules. I mean, a woman as a sole proprietor, she is asking—"

"I ken what she is asking. I am fully aware of her business venture and yer a fool to turn her down. I will sign for her," Joseph said.

Anna glared at him. "You don't have to do that," she whispered.

He shook his head abruptly in return and she let him take the lead.

"We hoped ye'd be reasonable and allow her independent financing, given her collateral and her history in business but clearly, the banks are too narrow-minded to recognize a worthwhile investment when it bites them in the ass. Ye didn't even take the time to consider an appraisal of the gems in her possession. If 'tis the only way around yer asinine rules, so she can prove ye wrong, then we will do it yer way."

"Mr. Hendrie, your language in the lady's presence." He shook his head, frowning his disapproval.

"After five years in the service, the lassie has heard the word ass, I assure ye."

Anna smiled behind her gloved hand and stayed silent, praying she would not regret the decision to let this mysterious stranger into her life.

"Mr. Hendrie, you are a reputable man of business yourself. You must understand the policies the bank puts in place. My hands are tied."

She glanced at Joseph her brow puzzled, causing the banker to shift his gaze between them with equal confusion. "How do you two know each other?"

"He helped—"

Joseph shook his head quickly once again and she stayed silent. "I met her husband overseas and Anna and I discovered the connection when we met after her passage here to Kincardine."

"I see," he said, although he didn't appear to understand. "Might I be so bold as to ask your relationship?"

"No, you may not." Anna scowled at him.

He slumped in his chair with a sigh. "My apologies once again Mrs. Gordon. The problem is, unless Mr. Hendrie is a partner in your business, or family, more specifically, immediate family or your husband, our policy is he cannot act as co-signer, and as I have said, we cannot extend credit to you as a single woman or female sole proprietor."

"This is absolutely ridiculous." She jumped up. "We are done here, let's go Joseph."

Joseph tugged her arm and she landed hard in her chair, scowling in his direction.

Mr. Lonsdale smirked awkwardly, clearly confused. "Might I suggest you approach your brother-in-law once again to extend you an advance from your trust fund, or perhaps if you and Mr. Hendrie are closely acquainted, I might recommend that he extend you a personal loan."

"No, you may not suggest nor recommend. You are missing the point of my independent venture and frankly I have had enough of your chauvinistic dribble. I will sell my jewels and start on my own and you can all go to hell." She stood, glanced briefly at Joseph, and turned to leave.

"She is my fiancé. We will sign together as husband and wife."

Anna froze in her tracks and closed her eyes briefly. Going along with the ruse of a silent partner willing to co-sign was one thing but play-acting an engagement was going too far. Her lips pinched together in a grimace when she turned back from the door to face Joseph. "You don't need to tell him that. I will find another way."

He smiled and winked at her. She damned the warm glow that overtook her whole body in reaction to his intimate gesture. Seconds passed as she stood frozen to the spot mulling a decision that might change her life. Her barely perceptible nod had Joseph turning back to the banker with a smile.

"There ye have it."

Joseph patted the chair beside him and grinned at her discomposure. She hesitated, but returned to the chair, tucked her skirt under as she slowly lowered herself and faced the banker with a calm smile.

Joseph reached for her hand, and she let him hold it on her lap. "My Anna, I should say, my fiancé asked me nae to say anything. She has a wee stubborn streak as I am sure ye have clocked, and she wanted to be able to tackle this venture independently."

Mr. Lonsdale cleared his throat. "Well, I; that is, this is a most unusual meeting—"

Joseph held up his hand. "Never ye mind, no need to apologize, rules are rules."

"Mr. Hendrie, are you certain?" Mr. Lonsdale shook his head, his forehead creased in confusion.

"Are ye questioning my integrity or my financial ability to back this young lady's undertaking?"

"Neither of course Mr. Hendrie. Your accounts are in excellent standing as is your reputation. It is just that, I had no idea you two were, I …"

"'Tis nae yer business to ken. I would ask that ye extend Mrs. Gordon whatever sum she has discussed wi' ye, draw up the papers, and we will be back tomorrow morning to sign them together. The only condition being yer discretion. As ye pointed out, we have nae exactly made our relationship public. Her brother-in-law has been kept in the mirk and we are certainly nae ready to set a date nor publish bans. We have just recently committed ourselves to each other."

"I see." Again, his suspicious gaze shifted between the two. "She does not wear your ring."

It was a statement not a question, but Joseph shut him down once again. "I have seen her ring designs. They are spectacular. I believe she is the best jeweller in the province and soon others will ken it as well. There is no design I could select that would compare to her creations. We have agreed upon a mutually acceptable ring, and I have commissioned it. Once she has the equipment needed to set up her own shop, she will wear my ring. Any other questions?"

"I, no. No, Sir, of course not."

Joseph stood. "Then we are done here."

"Allow me to provide you with my card, Mrs. Gordon. My residential number is on the back. Please contact me at any time, even outside of banking hours, if you need my assistance."

She stood as well and fought the urge to roll her eyes in response to his enthusiastic offer as she took the card and placed it in her handbag. Instead, she smiled and nodded without response.

Joseph motioned Anna ahead of him out the door.

~

"Now you have us in a fine fix." Anna faced him outside the bank, her hands on firmly her hips.

"Thank ye might have been more appropriate."

She huffed in frustration and threw up her hands. "I appreciate the gesture, but what do you think is going to happen when the bank finds out you are marrying Nancy? They will call in the loan and I shall be in worse shape than I am now."

"Keep yer voice down." Joseph grabbed her arm and pulled her toward the truck parked down the street. He opened the passenger door and turned her toward it. "Are ye getting in?"

"Oh, now you want to spend time with me?"

"What the hell does that mean?" He threw his hand forward forcefully.

"I will get in, but only because it's freezing. I am not going anywhere with you." She clamored up to the seat and slammed the door, staring straight ahead while he climbed into the driver's seat.

He turned the keys in the ignition but didn't pull out into the road.

"Where do you think you are going?" she demanded.

He turned the truck off again and sat back against the driver door facing her. "Would ye please calm down and tell me what has ye in such a state."

"Need I state the obvious? You just told the bank manager that we are engaged when in fact you are intended to marry Nancy whatever her name is."

"Her name is Nancy Clark, and we are only friends."

"Well, she sure seemed to think otherwise. You left with her from the dance and didn't bother to call on me yesterday to drive up the coast like you said so I assumed you were busy with your, your …reunion." She flicked her hand at him, then turned to stare out the window attempting to ward off tears of frustration.

He chuckled. "Ye make a lot of assumptions. I didnae leave the dance wi' Nancy. We are nae engaged, and I left a note at yer house yesterday wi' that dastardly Ian because I had an emergency repair to do. Ye ken I dinnae have a phone at the cabin."

"Oh."

"Aye, oh. And might I point out that ye left the dance wi'out so much as a goodbye to yer date."

"I assumed—"

"Aye, yer good at that."

"Okay, but—" He cut her off again but this time by placing his finger on her lips to quiet her.

Anna glanced down at his lips. He moved just inches from her face, removed his finger and replaced it with a tender kiss. "But I'm charmed that ye'd be jealous."

Anna's head jolted back; the tender moment suddenly lost. "I am not jealous of that, that, ooooo, you men are all out to infuriate me today."

"Infuriating? I just saved yer bacon back there. Lonsdale was about to toss ye out on yer keister. Now ye will get yer funds to set up yer castle and make yer jewels to keep ye nicely until ye can sue yer eejit brother-in-law."

"You are right and I'm sorry." She smiled shyly. "I owe you a huge debt of gratitude, but I am still not sure we'll be able to pull it off."

"Ye can repay me by accompanying me for a drive."

"I am certain you didn't land in the bank to assist me. Do you not have business to attend to?"

"It can wait."

~

As they drove south along the highway, the dark blue lake in the distance to their right, the sun high in the lighter blue sky, Anna's negative assumptions about Joseph and her dashed hopes for the future quickly dissipated.

"Ye look much happier now than when I met ye at the bank."

"I am very much happier. You have helped give me hope for an independent future. You have no idea how much that means to me."

"Aye, I ken, more than ye think."

She was silent a moment before her curiosity got the best of her. "Why such a strong Scottish accent? I would have guessed you came straight from the highlands, not lived in Kincardine for years before the war."

"Someone been telling ye my story, have they?"

Anna blushed when he glanced to her with a raised brow. "Elsie started to and then Marcy said she knew your parents."

"I have nae seen much of Kincardine, little time to gain a Canadian accent like some. We, my family that is, came here from the highlands about two years before the war. Many folks here are Scottish, the accents mostly stuck. I enlisted early and I have only returned just this year."

"I heard the Hendries breed racehorses; they are a wealthy family. That can't be you."

"Well, aye and no."

"What does that mean?" Her frown returned. "I feel like such an outsider, unaware of what everyone else knows."

"'Tis nae a big secret. I am Joseph Hendrie of the Hendries of Tiverton, famous for excellent thoroughbreds. As I said, we came here in the late thirties; I was just gone twenty. I did all my schooling in the old country and never really wanted to emigrate. My da had big dreams for us. I enjoyed working wi' the horses, but I coudnae wait to enlist and go back overseas, do my part, ye ken?"

"Oh, I know."

He smiled and nodded, then continued. "I came home once during my service to surprise my wee sister on her wedding day. I had a falling out wi' my parents on that visit. Nae sure if yer aware, but horse racing had been banned during the war. I was embarrassed of my family. My da employed men who could have been serving in the war instead of working in track operations and gambling on races. Valuable resources like gas and tire rubber were consumed heavily in transporting horses to tracks while we were in desperate need overseas."

"I could see that would be upsetting having been on the front lines."

"It sure was, but they coudnae see my side of things and I coudnae see theirs. I left angry and returned to war. They sold my favourite horse to spite me and now my da is gone. I never got to see him again to reconcile our differences."

"That's awful, I am sorry." She reached across the seat and placed her hand on his arm.

He shook his head. "I have let it go and me mum is happy to have me back. She and my brother and my sister and her husband run the ranch and breed the horses. We all get along better now that da is nae there. He was quite wealthy, and his Will divided his estate amongst the four of us."

"So, you have a huge horse farm to work on as well as the means to buy your own house, but you chose to live in a little cabin on the edge of town. What is that all about?"

"I have nae decided when I will use the money. It feels wrong since it came from racing profits that I was so against."

"I can understand that." Anna nodded.

"The hard part is people in town ken my inheritance and a lot of them want a piece of it to help wi' this or that investment, including people like Mr. Lonsdale and my friend Nancy Clark. So, for now, I prefer my cabin, my privacy, and my money to stay in a regular bank account."

"And you work as a handyman?"

"No, I work for one of my da's friends, in constructing homes and stables mostly. But I go fix things for people when needed or when Pastor Simon requests it. I like to put in a full day's work, keeps my mind off the last several years and some of the not so admirable decisions I have made."

"Do I want to know what those might be?" She chuckled.

He shook his head. "Enough about me. Tell me more about yer adventures in England. Where did ye go to school and what was yer family like?"

She gazed at the horizon and smiled at the memories that came to mind. "Nothing too special. I was an only child, but everyone knew and loved my mum and da, so I was welcomed everywhere I went, and people were always happy to teach me things when my parents were busy. I spent plenty of time at their jewellery shop after school and on the summer breaks. When I got to the older grades in school, I declined the home economics class; I already knew how to sew and cook. I asked to take the auto mechanics with the boys. The teachers were aghast, but my da pushed for them to let me in. I was the only girl in the class and the boys made fun of me. That's where I learned my mechanics to help with the vehicles and planes in the war."

"See, ye had a knack for independence from the get-go."

"I wish my independence was more accepted around here. It seems people want to push away something they don't understand."

"I dinnae ken?"

"I have been receiving notes, threatening, well, not threatening, more like insulting. Each one on a single sheet of paper with only one line. 'Go back where you belong'; or,

'You're not welcome here'; that kind of thing." Anna smirked when he turned to her with anger in his eyes.

"Who would do such a thing?"

She shrugged. "I thought you might be able to shed light on that. Do you think your Nancy or maybe her mother from what I've heard, might prefer I were out of the way of the two of you?"

"Nonsense. I made it clear to her at the dance that I have no mind to see her again other than as a friend."

"Marcy said some women in town are put out by foreign women who show up and take the few remaining eligible bachelors off the market, or UK women who come back from the war on the arm of a previously single Canadian man."

His eyebrows raised. "I dinnae suppose I thought about it like that before."

"Nor did I."

"I would be happy to ask around." He glanced at her in question.

She smiled in return. "Thank you for being so welcoming. Without you and Elsie, I may well have turned and set sail back home. But please keep the notes to yourself. I don't want to make things worse. If I'm stepping on the toes of a woman who has a fancy for you, then you coming to my defence will only make matters worse."

Their conversation ended when Joseph pulled into a dead-end street, a wooded area in front of them, and a well-appointed inn off to their right. In typical Georgian style, the double two-story, clapboard building had a symmetrical arrangement of windows and doors on the front façade. The white picket fence enclosed a tastefully decorated patio with two small bistro tables and chairs in front. Neatly trimmed green hedges stood on either side and despite the lateness of autumn and several snow falls, the garden still held a variety of colourful fall mums, pansies, and violas. The name on the awning over the front door read, Port Albert Hotel. "This is lovely, where are we?"

"Port Albert."

Anna rolled her eyes. "I see that from the sign, but how, who—"

She shifted her attention from the hotel to Joseph who sat grinning at her. "Now I ken ye were an inquisitive child. Ye ask a lot of questions. Come on, fancy some dinner and a dram of whiskey?"

"A dram? Who serves whiskey around here?"

"More questions? Let's go."

He held her hand as they walked to the front of the hotel. She was reluctant to lose the warmth of him when he reached to open the door and motioned her before him. As soon as they stepped in, he once again took her arm and pulled it through his own. She shivered as his touch sent a tingle through her she hadn't experienced before.

"Hey Joey, take whatever's open. 'Tis quiet yet."

"Ta, Miriam." He held up two fingers and twisted his hand back and forth, receiving her nod in return.

"What does that mean?"

Joseph smiled at her curiosity as he pulled out her chair at the table closest the window.

"Ye will soon see."

Grey barnwood planks spanned the floor, the room warmed by a large wood stove in the centre. Several empty bar stools tucked under a bar top that spanned the length of the wall opposite the windows where they sat. Behind the counter, jars of preserves and non-perishables lined the shelves on either side of the entrance to the bright kitchen. A dark staircase started in the back corner of the room and disappeared to the left leading to what Anna presumed were hotel rooms. One other couple sat at a table near the wood stove and a group of three men occupied a booth in the corner behind Joseph. The men glanced her way when she sat, then nodded to Joseph, before they went back to their meals.

Miriam appeared within moments. Her hefty hips swayed in her navy-blue starched cotton dress. From waist up she was disproportionately small by comparison to her bottom half. Her hair was a mass of red curls, which contrasted the brighter red lipstick she wore. Her warm smile welcomed them both. "How are ye doing today?"

"Stoatin Miriam, nice to see ye again," Joseph answered with an equally warm smile, his accent stronger in the company of a fellow Scot.

She placed two mugs in front of them, surprising Anna when she glanced down to the contents.

"We have pure baked meat loaf wi' the bog gravy on special for dinner, comes wi' steamed neeps, buttered beets, and a split pea brose to start."

"Perfect, ta."

"Ye darling?" she asked Anna.

"Sounds delicious, I will have the same."

Anna smiled at Joseph when Miriam walked away. "Growing up in England, you would think I would be accustomed to the accents, so many there were between the Irish, the Welsh, and the Scottish. But wow, I feel at times like I am visiting my da's hometown around here."

"Which I hope is a good thing." He reached for her hand, and she turned it palm side up allowing him to entwine their fingers.

"Absolutely a fond memory. I loved visiting his family in Aberdeen. They had a beautiful home overlooking the North Sea. He met my mum in Edinburgh one summer. I think I told you, she was from Newcastle upon Tyne, in northeastern England."

He nodded. "Aye ye did, I ken it. Those towns are far apart. How did they connect in Edinburgh?"

"She went to work in Edinburgh as a nanny for friends of her family. My da was at Edinburgh University studying geology. He was in his final year when they met at a social. She went back to Newcastle, and he went back to Aberdeen.

They corresponded for almost a year before he finally went to her father and asked for her hand. They were married and managed to get a flat in Leeds. He worked in mapping but was always interested in the rare gems and minerals of the earth he learned about at university."

"Fascinating. Did he enlist in the first war?"

"Oh yes. He proved to be a great asset to the military. Geologists were used to guide extraction of groundwater, construct mine tunnels, dug outs and defences, and quarry resources to repair supply routes."

"An excellent use of his studies."

"Yes, the biggest challenge was for my mum. Unfortunately, she found out she was with child shortly after he left. She gave up their flat in Leeds and stayed with my grandparents back in Newcastle until he returned."

"I ken that happened a lot back then. How did ye all end up in London wi' a jewellery shop?"

Miriam silently placed their plates in front of them before Anna continued her story. "Like I said, my da was fascinated by rare gems. While in the war, he heard of Hatton Garden, a suburb of London, which had become more developed over the turn of the century and had gained a reputation as the area for jewellery and diamond production."

He glanced up from his food and shook his head. "I have nae heard of it."

"Part of the growth was brought on by The East India Trading Company, who imported the majority of the world's diamonds from India to Hatton Garden. Perhaps you have heard of the De Beers' mine, the most productive diamond mine in the world?"

Again, he shook his head.

She took a bite of food, then continued. "Ouu, this is so good. The mine was discovered in 1871. Then in 1888 De Beers merged their business with the London Diamond Syndicate, which was created by ten jewellers in Hatton Garden. Two years later, Hatton Garden secured its name in the diamond and gemstone industry. You see that deal meant Hatton Garden could utilise De Beers' domination of the diamond industry, giving them the opportunity to buy De Beers' entire supply of diamonds at a fixed price. That's why Hatton Garden in London is home to some of the world's finest jewellers to this day and I am proud to say, my da was one of them. He started off working at one of the shops and did so well, he was able to buy it after the owner retired. I learned my craft by working along side him."

"That is an incredible story. No wonder yer so keen to start over here and so knowledgeable in the business. I had no idea."

Anna smiled at his praise. "I feel it in my blood. I am meant to carry on where they left off and use the skills they taught me."

"So ye shall." He lifted his mug and tapped hers. "Cheers to Castle Gordon Fine Jewellery."

"I like that, thank you and thank you again for all your help. I would be lost here without you."

He grinned at the sentiment. "I dinnae ken about that, but I'm glad we met and I'm happy to help ye."

"Now maybe you can tell me how we are enjoying a dram of this fine whiskey in a dry town?"

He pressed his hand downward and snuck a glance at the other couple in the room. "Shhh. I suppose 'tis my turn for a history lesson then. During the war an air training base was built, and it operated nearby, just outside Port Albert. American, Australian, British, and Canadian airmen trained here."

"I knew the name sounded familiar. I remember now, one of the aviation technicians said he came from Port Albert." Anna continued eating while he explained.

"No doubt. Anyway, there has always been a ban on alcohol in Bruce County, but some of the aviators who were training here had a mind to indulge occasionally. So, a resourceful, independent woman just like yerself developed a wee drinking club." He spoke in a hushed tone and scanned the room once again.

"Why did she or the hotel not come under scrutiny by the law? Surely not everyone welcomed her."

"Ye cannae buy a drink here at the inn, but she sells memberships which entitle ye to a drink. Our girl Miriam kens the regulars and who to trust. My understanding is the supply of contraband arrives once a week at dusk from connections in Detroit. Her illegal drinking club has survived a few police raids thanks to those of us wi' a mind to forewarn her. For now…" He shrugged one shoulder.

~

"Come over closer," Joseph said when they clamored back into his truck. Alone in the secluded parking spot at the dead end of the road, warmth rose through Anna as she shuffled to his side, smiling up to him when he stretched his arm around her shoulders.

"Would ye like to take a walk?" He tipped his head toward the wooded area in front of them. "There is a lovely trail along the Nine Mile River just ahead of us. Or we could go over to the beach for a spell."

"I'm not sure I'll be warm enough. I dressed for only a bank visit today."

"Right, perhaps another time, then."

"I would like that. And I would also like to thank you for dinner; that food was delicious."

"Aye, they make a fine meal."

Anna hesitated, then continued. "And also thank you for the dance Saturday night since I was too pigheaded to trust you and stay long enough to thank you then. Also, my appreciation once again for helping me at the bank, and you can stop me any time here."

He pulled his arm from behind her shoulder and placed his hands on either side of her face. "Ye need nae thank me,

Anna. I am happy to help ye anytime. In fact, I am happy to be wi' ye anytime. I cannae seem to get enough of ye." Drawing her to him, he kissed her tenderly at first, then tangled his hand in her hair and pulled her closer, deepening the kiss.

A soft moan escaped her throat when his hand slid into her coat, massaging through her blouse to the hard nub of her breast. She leaned her head back allowing him access to trail kisses down her throat. His hands fumbled with her buttons allowing his tongue to replace his hand.

Anna tangled her fingers in his hair and pressed him to suck harder, her soft moan of pleasure all the encouragement he needed. He jolted up and pulled her across to his lap. Willingly, she hiked her skirt to straddle him, instinctively rocking herself against the hard length of him, aching for relief of her building passion. She kissed him deeply, tongues entangled, their breathing heavy and loud in the confines of his truck.

Hands on her face once again, he pulled back from her. His face was flushed, his gaze hungry with desire. "God, Anna, I want ye badly, but we cannae do this here in the parking lot. I apologize for getting carried away."

She dropped her forehead to his. "Joseph, you stir a passion in me that I have never felt before. You do not need to apologize; you have a willing partner in me."

He pulled her to his chest. "Mo chridhe, I feel the same passion."

Anna giggled. "I can tell." She climbed back to her seat but kept herself pressed against the side of him.

As he started the truck and backed from the parking lot, his hand possessively on her stockinged leg, she made no move to adjust her skirts over it.

In turn, her hand sat comfortably on his thigh, while her head rested on his shoulder. The drive back to Kincardine was over too fast for Anna. Their banter and his proximity comforted her, and she had no desire to leave him and return to the stress of the Campbell household.

He kissed her gently, his hesitancy to leave clearly equalling her own.

"Thank you again for all your help." Anna smiled as she reached for the door.

"No need to thank me. I will see ye soon and I will find a phone or reach ye in person instead of leaving a note wi' that worthless Campbell."

~

Still warm from Joseph's touch, Anna smiled to herself at the events of the day. Her happiness diminished when she passed the open door to Ian's office. She stopped, turned back, pressed her hands to the door frame, and leaned forward into his office.

"Why did you manage to pass along an anonymous insulting message yesterday, but somehow forget to pass along the note from Joseph Hendrie that was dropped off with specific direction to deliver it to me? You sat through dinner and acted like you had never heard of the man nor his family."

"Oh, I must have forgotten. Never mind that, come in and sit down. I have a proposition for you." He quickly cleared his desk of paperwork then circled his hand in front of him.

"I am not interested in anything you have to offer." She remained at the doorway.

"You are being ridiculous, Anna. I apologised to you for the drunken escapade and assured you nothing of the like will happen again. We have moved on."

She squinted; her lip turned up in disgust. "Perhaps you have moved on. I have not and will not until I am established in my own home miles away from your daily intrusions in my life."

He ignored the comment. "I presume you did not come to an amicable decision with Mr. Lonsdale today. I know the rules and you will need a male member of the family to sign on your behalf if you hope to get a loan and move out on your own." He pulled himself up straight and ran his hands along the arms of his office chair, mirroring the movements of his supervisor earlier in the day.

She rolled her eyes at the shared sentiment and gesture of the bankers, then grinned with satisfaction. "As a matter of fact—"

He held up his hand. "Let me finish; I am prepared to do us both a favour."

She dropped her arms from the door frame and slumped her shoulders, frustrated with this man's pompous attitude.

"Ms. McGavin informed us she is no longer able to act as the children's nanny and private tutor. She has accepted a position as a teacher in town and will be gone from the house two weeks hence. While Marcy has improved somewhat and insists she is capable of caring for the children herself, I prefer she have a companion to oversee her activities at least until I am convinced she has returned to full health."

"Are you done?"

"Do not be impertinent, it is so unbecoming. Tsk, tsk." He shook his head quickly.

Anna huffed in response and rolled her eyes once more.

"No, I am not done. My idea is this. You will accompany Marcy and the children on their outings and report to me if anything is amiss with my wife's behaviour. You shall receive room and board for free as well as your monthly allowance from the trust fund. As your next of kin, I will also graciously sign the loan you requested so that you can purchase your supplies or tools or whatever you need, and you shall be free to make your trinkets in your spare time. I will even arrange to have a workspace cleared in the spare room off the kitchen. There is a door to outside so people can do business with you, without coming through the main house. A brilliant idea that serves us all do you not agree?" He beamed with satisfaction at his thought-out proposal, clasped his hands together and thumped them on the desk.

These bankers are all exactly the same. "Now are you done?"

"You really should learn to be more respectful—"

"To whom, Ian? My elders? You are not one. My family? You are hanging on by a thread with that one too. You are the one who needs to learn about respect."

"Fine, go ahead. I know you will find holes in my plan. I honestly believe you pick a different route simply to disagree with me, not because it makes any better sense." He waved his hand at her and turned to stare off out the window.

Anna stepped into his office and leaned on her fingertips on his desk. He turned back to her with a curious glare. "What? How could you not like the plan? Graham would be pleased with my generosity."

"Firstly, where is the note that was addressed to me and delivered here yesterday?" She spoke slowly and enunciated each word.

"Really Anna, we get so much correspondence delivered to the house. I cannot be expected—

"You do not get mail delivered on Sundays."

He reached to a tray on the corner of his desk and re trieved a small stack of envelopes. "Oh, for heaven's sake, look at that. It's right here." He thrust it toward her.

Anna sat in front of his desk. "It has been opened. How dare you?"

"As long as you are living in my house, you will follow my rules. I have a right to know where you are and with whom." He tipped his head back and jutted his chin toward her.

"You have no right to direct me in any way. You are forbidden to interfere in my life and my business. How many times must I remind you?" She glared at him, awaiting his defence.

"What the devil do you want with a handyman anyway? Your husband is barely cold in the ground. And Marcy's brother—"

Anna jumped up, stuffed the envelope in the pocket of her skirt and once again leaned forward on Ian's desk. He recoiled in his chair putting distance between them. "Your less-than-brilliant idea is trash and serves no one but yourself, as usual. Clara and Thomas should be taking their lessons in school and making friends like all the other children in town. A private tutor is not necessary, and Marcy is more than capable of taking care of herself and of raising your children. The same cannot be said for you. Disbursing funds from my own account is not part of a well-thought-out plan; it is your legal obligation. You do not control me, and you will not control my money much longer. I have attained the loan by my own means, and I intend to start searching this week for a cottage that affords me the space and atmosphere appropriate to design and sell my jewellery creations."

"That is ludicrous. Mr. Lonsdale would not accommodate a business loan nor a home mortgage to a single woman. A female sole proprietor is unheard of." Ian blinked his eyes repeatedly.

"I have a co-signer and I will be leaving your wretched presence very soon. And once I have sold a few pieces, the first thing I will purchase with my own hard-earned money, is the services of a lawyer to sue you for the return of my own funds. Graham would not be proud of you, he would recognize you as the deceitful, self-centred imbecile you have become. He would, however, be proud of me and what I plan to do. By the time I am done with you, you will look foolish to every person in this town, and there is not a damn thing you can do about it. And lastly, if I find out you or Marcy has anything to do with the repeated notes I've received, I will make sure everyone in town knows you are jealous and insolent along with being fools." Anna turned and stormed from the room, once again leaving a gape mouthed Ian sitting stunned behind his desk.

Chapter Eleven

Anna grabbed Joseph's arm just before he entered The Sunset Diner at six the next afternoon. He flinched then glanced down where her hand held him in place. "Well, hello. This is a pleasant surprise. What has ye so excited?"

"Are you going in for supper? I have so much to tell you. I spent all day looking at cottages with Lee."

"Aye, of course. Please have supper wi' me, I would love it." He pulled the door and motioned her ahead of him.

"Get a table away from the gossip. I don't want everyone in town to know my business."

"Corner booth, my pleasure." He grinned and reached for her hand.

Ignoring the whispers when they entered together, they took a table farthest from the door. The corner was not particularly well lit which suited Anna just fine.

"Hello Joey; Miss. How's everybody doing?" The waitress wore the standard uniform, starched cotton dress in a pale-yellow colour, with the words Sunset Diner embroidered in forest green, on the chest pocket. Despite the stained apron covering the bottom half of the dress, it was clear her generous curves strained the buttons all the way down to her knees. Her hair pulled up in a clip sprouted errant dark curls that framed her friendly face.

Joseph returned her infectious smile before making introductions. "Fanny, this is Anna Gordon, she is new in town, and we are fine. I will have a tea and we will need supper menus."

"Coming up and what can I get for ye darlin?"

"I will have a cola, please."

Joseph's eyebrows raised. "I would have taken ye for a tea drinker."

"Please, I have been in the UK running with troops the last five years. I have had enough tea to float me to China."

"I suppose so." He placed his hand over hers on the table. "Tell me about yer day. Lee Porter is the realtor, correct?"

She turned her hand in his and linked their fingers. The intimate gesture felt natural. She patted her other hand over his and grinned from ear to ear as she began her story. "Yes, he helps people rent and buy houses and sells insurance. He has his hand in a lot of deals. But listen, I think I have found the perfect house, right on the shore, just this side of your cabin; almost directly behind the path where you found me the first night we met."

"Right on the shore, sounds inspiring." He chuckled at her enthusiasm.

"Oh, it is inspiring, a perfect, two-story cottage, with a solid stone foundation. There are windows all the top and bottom that face the lake, with a patio that goes into the yard so I can sit out overlooking the lake. On the side closest the laneway, there is a separate door that leads straight into a perfect sized space for my shop." She pulled her hands from his and splayed her fingers in front of her. "I can picture it now; I will put a sign over that door that says Castle Gordon Fine Jewellery. And it's close enough to walk into town until I can get myself a car and there is a rough road that comes down from Highway Twenty-One so I can put a sign at the top of the road and attract passersby."

He leaned over the table for a brief kiss. Despite their previous intimacy, Anna blushed at the public display of affection. "I'm happy for ye. Is it in yer price range? I can make up any difference."

"No, no, I want to do it myself. You have done enough by signing the loan. But listen to this, the woman who owns it is a war widow and she is moving in with her daughter. She is willing to leave most of the furnishings and she prefers it go to another woman who can enjoy the space as she did."

He chuckled again. "My goodness, ye are excited. That sounds perfect."

"Oh, I am certain it's going to work out. I can feel it. And it's a small cottage, another reason why I think I might get it. All the soldiers returning want three or four bedrooms for their families. This one is ideal for me. Lee is talking to the homeowner now. I am to meet him again tomorrow, hopefully to sign purchasing papers."

Anna dropped her hands into her lap when Fanny returned with their drinks and the one-page menu. "Hot chicken bridie on special."

"Ta, Fanny," Joseph said.

"What is wi' ye drawing back like that?" he asked after the waitress left them.

"I am not ready for the couple gossip. These odd notes telling me to leave town and then I get grief from Ian about going out with another man so soon after Graham passed. I don't want people to think I am disrespectful. Despite several months of mourning, I still feel… I don't know." She shook her head and glanced down to the menu.

"Yer nae the least disrespectful. Many people lost loved ones in the war. We can honour them by moving forward as they would have; does nae mean yer fond memories have left ye. Did ye have a rough time reading his note last night?"

Anna's excitement diminished instantly. She drew back with a frown. "Whose note?" She enunciated the two words separately.

"Damn it, nae again. I sent Jamie Thom over to deliver it to ye directly last night. He got to town a few days ago. I met him here for supper to discuss finding him work and he asked if I kent ye; said he had a note from yer Graham and was told to deliver it directly."

"Who is Jamie Thom?"

"I saw him sitting at the counter when we came in. Wait here." He left the table briefly, returning moments later alongside a young man looking remarkably like a taller, thinner version of Joseph himself.

"Jamie, this is Anna Gordon, Graham Campbell's wife. Anna, Lieutenant James Thomson." He waved a hand between the two before he retook his seat across from her. Jamie wore a longer beard but otherwise had identical compassionate blue eyes as his friend as well as the same dark red hair, cut shorter on the sides and combed over with gel from a side part.

He reached to shake Anna's extended hand. "Pleased to meet ye Ma'am. I'm glad I was able to get Soupie's note to ye, been carrying it around for several months now."

She smiled at the nickname. "Pleased to meet you as well Lieutenant. Gosh, you and Joseph could be brothers."

"We got that a lot overseas. But no, just friends. People, call me Jamie or Thom, no need for formalities among friends."

"Thank you, Jamie it is. Unfortunately, I did not get the note."

"I gave it to Soupie's brother. I told him I was requested to get it to ye directly, but he said he had taken charge of his brother's estate and ye were entrusted to his care. He assured me ye'd receive it."

"He makes a lot of assurances. I thank you for your trouble. I will be sure to track it down immediately on my return home."

"And I will be accompanying ye this time to make sure it happens." Joseph wore an angry snarl.

"Can I be of help to ye, Joey?"

"No, we will be fine. Would ye care to join us for a bite."

"No, I have eaten, but thank ye. See ye at work tomorrow. Pleasure to meet ye Mrs. Gordon."

"Call me Anna, please. I am sure we will see each other around town. And thank you again." She smiled sadly at Joseph's friend, then turned with a sigh back to Joseph.

"Well, that put a damper on yer excitement." Joseph squeezed her hand.

"I can't even eat. I've lost my appetite. Ian Campbell has gone too far." She shook her head slowly.

"Let's go." Joseph stood extended his hand to help her up and tossed a few coins on the table. "Fanny, keep a special warm for me. I will be back in half an hour."

She nodded and waved her hand over her head while she poured coffee into a customer's cup at the counter.

~

Ian flinched and bolted up straight when Anna and Joseph stormed through his office door. "Oh, a second gentleman caller, without so much as an invitation. Please sit down." Ian shook his head as he flicked a hand toward the chairs in front of his desk.

"Get yer head out of yer ass Campbell and give her the letter from her husband that was delivered last night by Lieutenant Thomson."

"The handyman telling me what to do in my own home. That is remarkable." Ian tipped his head and smirked.

"Where is the note from Graham?" Anna yelled.

Ian shrugged one shoulder in response.

She stepped closer to the desk and Joseph followed. "I also demand the original note he allegedly wrote to you to re-examine against his writing."

"You made the decision to vacate the premises against my better judgment and despite my generous offer. You stormed out of my office after threatening to ruin my fine reputation, not to mention, you are already cavorting with another man. Your mourning period is evidently long over. It was a frivolous poem that I knew would mean nothing to you, so I burned it."

"How dare ye?" Joseph side-stepped around the desk causing Ian to jump from his chair ready to dash.

Ian's gaze flicked nervously up and down the length of Joseph and then over to Anna, but he stayed silent.

"Ye bastard. How could ye disrespect yer own brother that way? I have never heard of such evil among kin. Ye should be ashamed of yerself. I have a mind to teach ye a lesson myself." Joseph's hands balled in fists at his side as he glared at Ian in disbelief.

"Never mind, he's not worth it. Let's go," Anna said.

Together on the front porch, Joseph pulled her into a hug which she gladly accepted. "What can I do to help?" he asked over her head.

She shook her head as it lay against his chest. Her hands still entwined behind his back, she gazed up at him and tried unsuccessfully to swallow her emotion. Tears pooled before she spoke. "There is nothing to be done now. He has taken Graham's final words to me and tossed them away like meaningless waste. Do you see what I am up against? He is evil and heartless."

"I never had a doubt about that."

"You should go get your supper. I am not good company anymore. I'm going to head up."

With a finger under her chin, he lifted her face to him for a tender kiss. "I will see ye soon. Please dinnae let him near ye."

~

Anna opened her bedroom door just a crack at the knock. "Oh, Clara, hello sweet pea. Should you not be getting ready for bed?" She drew the door back and Clara timidly stepped in.

"Are you crying?" The girl squinted up at her aunt.

Anna sat and patted the bed beside her. Clara jumped up and took her aunt's hand.

"My day didn't end so well, but I will be okay."

"I think I can help."

"You do help just by being here. Your company always makes me happier." Anna hugged the child to her.

"I have this." Clara held a singed envelope before her, unknowingly changing the life of her aunt.

Anna caught her breath when she turned it over and recognized Graham's handwriting. "Where did you get this?"

"Papa was screaming last night. I snuck down and peaked through the office door and called for my mama. Sometimes that gets him to stop yelling at her."

"You are very brave, but your mum can take care of herself. You should not get in the middle of them when they argue. You don't need to see that."

She shrugged in reply.

Anna shook her head sad in the knowledge that the child had witnessed enough arguments in her short life that they had become commonplace.

"I stepped into the office and went to Mama. That's when Papa tossed the envelope toward the hearth. I looked down and saw your name on the front. He screamed at me to leave, so I hid in the coat closet until he stormed out of the house and Mama went back upstairs. Then I snuck back in and pulled the envelope back with the poker."

"Oh, Clara, you could have been hurt."

"There were only embers in the hearth and the envelope landed to the side. It got a bit burned at the edges, but I think it came from your love. Will you read it to me?"

Anna slapped her hand over her mouth when she opened the letter and saw a full page of Graham's handwriting. "Come sit." She pulled herself up onto the pillows, sitting cross legged, bringing Clara up on her lap.

> *My darling, I write to you as I lay dying. They give me encouragement, but I know what they are told to say. I am the one who dictated the words intended to soothe soldiers in their final hours. I wish you were here so I could feel your soft lips on mine once more. My dearest Anna, I loved you so much from the start and we had such great plans to conquer the world with my farm and your jewellery creations. We had so little time together and alas you will have to go on without me. I know you will flourish as you always have.*

Anna retrieved a handkerchief from her pocket, to dry her eyes and wipe her nose. Through her tears, she smiled down at her niece, then continued reading out loud.

> *I could not track you for the last few weeks and I fear the worst, so while I am alive, I set our business affairs in order in keeping with our previous discussions. I have had my commander make some calls and wire funds to my brother's bank in Kincardine. Canada that is, not the Scottish Kincardine. I sent a brief note to Ian as well, explaining the situation. I offered to reimburse him to provide you shelter whilst you get settled but I am certain, he will decline remuneration and offer their gracious hospitality to you as long as you need. Please reiterate my appreciation to Ian and Marcy, and hug Clara and Thomas from their Uncle Graham. I regret never knowing them.*

Clara's eyes grew wide, then she covered her mouth with both her hands. Anna pulled her closer. "Yes, your Uncle

Graham was a kind, gentle man. He would have loved to meet you."

Tears sprung to the child's eyes morning the loss of a hero she never knew. Anna cried along with her as she read the remainder of the letter to herself.

Ian has my instructions to transfer all funds into an account in your name immediately upon your arrival so you can start your business venture when you are ready, like we planned. There is also a surprise in the crate we had stored… your favourites. I hope you have contacted Maeve in Hatton Garden and had it shipped by now and that everything arrived safely. Your designs are so beautiful, I know you will do well. If by some horrid twist of fate, we have met the same end, then my brother will inherit, as we discussed since he is the only living relative.

I also met a man a few weeks back. He knew of Kincardine but did not know Marcy and Ian personally. His family lived north of the town in an area called Tiverton. His name is Joseph Hendrie.

Anna gasped. "What is it?" Clara asked. "Tell me more what Uncle Graham said."

"It's nothing, just finances, adult stuff."

"Humph, adults always say that." The child wiped her face on her sleeve, then beamed up at her aunt.

Anna smiled again at Clara before returning to the note.

If you need anything that Ian cannot provide, do not hesitate to call on Joe. He is an honourable man, and you can trust him. Please remember me to him if you get there and cross paths. Tell him I almost made it; and tell him thank you for everything.

I hope this note finds you happy and healthy and that you have many years to enjoy life. I also hope you will find someone new to share your adventures. Make sure he loves you like I have.

My darling, until we meet again, my eternal love, Soupie xo

Anna hugged Clara once more, then tucked the note back into the envelope and stashed it in her own pants pocket before she scooted back to the side of the bed. "You have changed my life by saving this note for me. You have no idea how much it means to me. Thank you so much."

"Do you miss him?"

"Yes, of course I do, but losing someone in war is a bit different than losing someone you spend every day with. It was like I lost a part of him as soon as we signed up to serve. Some days I feel I hardly got the chance to know him well and that makes me sad too."

"Are you going to leave us?" Clara cringed, and her tears pooled once more.

"I am, but I will not be far away. You and Thomas can come and see me at my house, and we can play on the beach, and you can maybe stay over sometimes, just the three of us. Won't that be fun."

She jumped at the idea and clapped her hands. "Oh yes, please."

"For now, off to wash up for bed, young lady before you get us both into trouble."

Chapter Twelve

Having lain awake analysing every one of Graham's last words, questioning Joseph's sincerity and running scenarios about the men's connection, Anna awoke Wednesday morning with puffy eyes, still exhausted and confused. She struggled to dress and get herself to her meeting with the realtor on time.

Her emotions were a roller coaster mess as she tried to focus on Mr. Porter's advice. Graham's loving words tugged at her heart while anger consumed her at her brother-in-law's proven lies. The satisfaction of hard evidence against Ian along with her excitement to purchase her dream home, had been dampened by the knowledge that Joseph kept his relationship with Graham a secret. Adding further confusion, her body betrayed her with wanton cravings for Joseph's passionate kisses, while her guilt warned her to respect her mourning period.

The seller accepted Anna's offer without negotiation, and the house purchase was completed in mere minutes. She should have been ecstatic at the generosity of the previous owner and the ease of the transaction, but she returned dazed and frustrated to her bedroom. Sun filtered through the window as Anna tried to concentrate on her book. She slammed it shut after reading the same page several times. Stomping down the stairs, donning her boots and coat for a walk in the crisp fall air, she hesitated when the phone rang. "Anna," Ian hollered from his office.

She glanced around the office door. His head was tilted, and he wore a look of disdain as he held the receiver in her direction. "Your beau."

She shook her head quickly. "I am on my way out," she whispered.

"She went out," he stated, then dropped the phone back into its cradle without the courtesy of taking a message.

~

A knock on the bedroom door startled her from another bout of insomnia. She opened the door a crack, scowled at Ian's appearance in the hallway, then slammed the door and slid the lock, her heart racing at the prospect of another attack.

He knocked again. "Anna, please; I need to talk to you."

"You are not coming into my room," she yelled through the door.

"Will you come down to the office please. I can have Marcy attend with us if you prefer."

"Give me five minutes."

She dressed fully and went to his office but remained by the door. "What do you want?"

"Please come in and sit down."

She glanced at the minimal remnants of brandy in the glass near his right hand, then back to his face. "No. Everyone has gone to their rooms; I prefer to keep distance between us. What do you want?"

"Fine, I wanted to apologize."

"I am listening." She crossed her arms in front of her and leaned against the door frame, a tight-lipped frown on her face.

"I was angry that you dismissed my idea to work from our home and I will admit the idea of gentlemen callers caught me off guard. I expected a period of mourning."

"For God's sake, Ian, it's been several months, and you have no idea what it's like to lose loved ones to war. You are in no position to judge me. More importantly, for the hundredth time, my life choices are none of your business. What is your point?"

"Well, I beg you to reconsider." He stood and came from behind his desk.

Anna opened the door fully to the wall behind it. "The door stays open. Do not come any further."

He ignored her plea and stepped closer. "Anna please."

She held up her hand keeping him an arm's length away as she took a step back toward the foyer. "What is the matter with you? I have made my intentions quite clear. You have your own family, and even if you did not, you disgust me. I do not want you in my life."

He lunged at her, grabbed her arms, and yanked her back into the office before she had a chance to turn and run. "You must stay. You have no idea what's at stake. You will stay in this house." He shook her as he spoke.

She was ready for him this time and so angry after reading Graham's letter that murder was not far from her thoughts. She brought her knee up forcefully between his legs and slammed dead centre on her target. He doubled over in pain, moaning on his way to a crumpled heap on the office floor. She pulled her leg back and swung it forward with all her strength, the tip of her shoe landing direct centre of his face, causing a satisfying crack of his nose. Blood poured onto the carpet in front of him. He struggled to clamp his gushing face with one had while he clutched his injured groin with the other. She slammed the office door and left him for dead behind her.

Chapter Thirteen

"Did you see that, Jack?"

"Huh?"

"That angry man just tossed a screaming woman into the ice-cold brink."

"Mind yer business Roy, and hand me that flask. We don't need the copper down here again now that we landed ourselves a good spot to shelter."

"It was a woman, left for dead. We can't let her float away. C'mon." Roy scooped his arm through the air.

"Yer on yer own mate, I ain't seen nothin'," Jack said.

"A real gentleman you are. More like a gentleman's arse."

Jack waved his hand at his friend and rolled closer to his makeshift bed by the fire.

Roy went alone to the end of the pier and glanced over the edge into blackness. "Damn it. Where did she go?"

He walked back to the site of the commotion and again gazed into a calm lake, blackened by the dark cloudy sky. "I can't see a God damn thing. Jack, get over here and help me look."

"Sod off. I have no mind to draw attention."

"Here." Barely a croak of a plea before a splash on the opposite side of the pier from where she had been thrown.

He dashed to the sound, lay flat out on the cold, wet pier and stretched himself toward the white arm barely visible above the water. "Reach my hand darlin, I got ya."

"I cannae reach." Barely a whisper again before she sunk under the water once more.

Without a second thought, Roy dove into the frigid water, flailing his arms in circles until he connected with the coat of the fallen lady. Following the coat tail to her waist and then her shoulders, he linked his arm around her neck and dragged her lifeless body back to the pier. Climbing the slippery rocks to gain the top of the walkway was impossible so he swam with all his might the fifty yards back to shore, knowing if stopped, they would both be dead within seconds in the freezing water.

"What have ye gotten yerself into now? Draggin' a dead body to our doorstep. Who in the name of Jesus do ye think they will blame?" Jack scoffed but he stretched out to help his friend and the lifeless woman from the water.

"Shut your hole and help me drag her up near the fire."

Before they reached the fire, she came to, coughing and moaning, instantly thrashing at her rescuers. "Easy now, you're safe," Roy held an arm around her back to help her sit up.

Fully awake her eyes were huge. Blood dripped down the side of her face, from a gash on her head.

"I'm going to take your coat and hang in on the branch there by the fire," Roy explained.

She stood and helped as best she could to shrug out of the sodden coat.

"Get her a blanket," Roy demanded.

"I will nae give up me only warmth," Jack spat back.

"I will be fine," she said, her voice hoarse and weak. "Let me sit by yer fire a spell."

Roy kept his arm securely behind her as she stumbled toward the fire and landed hard on the ground beside it. He stood and motioned for her to stay where she was, not that she seemed in any hurry to leave. Returning seconds later, he wrapped a well-worn woolen blanket around her and handed her a flask. "Have a sip to warm ya darlin. You're going to be okay."

She nodded and accepted the flask but did not speak.

"Have ye a name?" Jack leaned into the firelight to take a closer look at her.

She shook her head slowly, then reached to remove her shoes and place them in front of her before she slumped down to rest in front of the warm flames.

Roy woke with a start at the light of dawn, an empty space where his damsel had lain, her shoes and coat gone. Jack snored loudly beside the now extinguished fire, oblivious to the situation. Muttering as he relieved himself against a tree, Roy stretched his hand to investigate a crumpling in his pants pocket.

"We're rich!" he yelled into the darkness gaining a gruff sputtering from his friend.

"What ye be hollering about at this ungodly hour ye dumb ass?"

"The lady I rescued left me a wad a cash, lookie here." Roy unfolded several damp paper bills.

Jack shook his head and smirked at his friend. "Great, now ye will be accused of stealing as well as accosting the woman."

"You are a fool, and I am happy to keep the reward for meself since you had no mind to take part in the rescue." He huffed.

"Well, I didnae say—"

"Enough." Roy held up his hand. "You made your position clear, and I accept." He trotted away, wiggling with satisfaction, leaving his friend sputtering his disagreement behind him.

Chapter Fourteen

Navigating her way through the cold of night down the somewhat familiar path to Joseph was easier this time. Anna had dressed appropriately in winter boots, coat, hat and wool mitts over her day gloves, but still she struggled against the cold wind, taking over an hour to make the three-mile trek.

Disappointment overwhelmed her when Joseph did not answer her knock. "Now what do I do?"

She expected the door would be unlocked, no reason to be otherwise in his secluded hideaway. She let herself in and stoked the fire that had almost burned itself out. Before long the small space took on a warm glow and her temperature returned to normal. Joseph gasped when he entered and saw her sitting on the rug in front of his fireplace.

"Made it here myself this time," she said.

"So I see." He bent and pulled her up from under her arms, drawing her into a hug once she was standing. "Are ye all right?"

"No." She stood stiff, her arms straight down at her sides.

He pushed her back at arm's length and blinked at her gloomy expression. "What has happened?"

"You knew Graham. I asked you specifically and you blew me off." It was a statement, but she expected a reply.

He blew out a long slow breath and dropped his hands from her shoulders. "How did ye find out?"

She held out Graham's letter. "Clara recovered it from the hearth in Ian's office. You lied to me."

He ignored the accusation and turned to read the letter by the light of the fire.

His tears dripped onto the page, immediately softening Anna's misgivings. "Why are you upset? What happened between you and Graham?" She stepped forward, tilting her head to his level to gain his focus.

"Don't worry; it does nae matter." He stared into the fire, ignoring her hand on his shoulder. "War was difficult, the thing is…" He squeezed his eyes tightly for a long moment before he wiped his face with the back of his hand and turned to her.

She took the offered letter, folded it, and returned it to her pocket then reached for both his hands. Her brow knit and her frown remained, while she waited for him to continue.

"He died because of me. A few good men died that day, all comrades."

"Oh, Joe, so many people died in the war. It wasn't your fault."

"Come sit."

She followed him to the small table where he pulled out the chair for her, then took his own seat directly across from her. "Yer Graham and I and Jamie and a few others oversaw a transfer that day. We had to get the chutes ready quickly and get moving."

"Oh no." Anna covered her mouth, tears briming, knowing what was coming.

"Aye, I'm afraid we didnae have time to check all the packs. I mean, others packed them, but they are supposed to be double checked before loading. I reminded Graham and he brushed it off. We just didnae have time. We had about a dozen on board when we took off. Soupie was flying and Jamie Thom was co-pilot when we took a hit only a few miles to our destination. We all had chutes and we had time to jump before the plane hit thanks to yer Graham's maneuvering, but three out of the group, didnae open. To make it worse, we took on enemy fire after we landed. The three died on impact who didnae have proper chutes. Graham felt responsible since he brushed off the double checking and he felt 'twas his duty to go check on them. 'Twas nae his job to be out in the field, 'twas mine. 'Tis the medic's job to pronounce the dead."

"Dear God." Anna slowly shook her head. She reached for his hand, but he yanked it away, stood and raked his fingers through his hair while he paced.

"I took Jamie Thom's word that the three were gone, and I didnae go back to check. If I had, I would have taken the hit, nae Graham." He hesitated, leaned an arm on the fireplace mantle and took a deep breath before he started again. "I saw yer Graham go into the field and I started to run after him. Jamie tried to stop me and drag me to cover. He told me to leave Soupie that we would all die if I ran back out to the field."

"You went back for him, didn't you?" Anna left her tears unchecked as they rolled down her cheeks.

Joseph nodded. "He had been hit and he was in bad shape. I threw him over my shoulder and zig zagged back for cover narrowly missing us all getting shot. Soup, that is, yer Graham was unconscious by the time we got to the tree line. I tried. I'm so sorry."

"How did he get to the field hospital?" she whispered the question.

"I carried him the few miles, had to rest from time to time; the others told me to leave him, but I had seen enough injured men to ken he had a wee chance. I got him as far as the military hospital and I'm sorry I had to leave him there. We had a lot of guys to evacuate from the base. I never saw him again after that day, but Jamie did. He went back to deliver supplies to the hospital a few weeks later. That's when he got this note and made a promise to Graham to come find ye. He kept the note wi' him all these months."

She focused on her hands in her lap, confused by emotions of guilt and sadness, unable to look at him.

He mistook her silence for anger. "I'm guessing ye will be wanting a ride back now?"

She stood and went to him, once again reaching for both his hands and forcing his focus to her. "It was not your fault. He died because the plane took a hit and troops shot at you on the ground. You had no control over enemy fire."

"I should have—"

She yanked his hands with both of hers, stopping him short. "There are too many things we think we should have done, too many things we wish we had done differently, but we all did what we must to survive each day in the circumstances. He died in a comfortable bed with food in his belly and comrades around him, instead of bleeding to death alone in a field. He said in his letter he thought you were an honourable man and I agree."

"I didnae expect yer forgiveness, but I appreciate yer understanding."

"I understand the front lines as well as you do. Enemy fire is to blame, there is nothing to forgive you for. What I do not understand is why you didn't you tell me sooner?"

He dropped her hands and blew out a breath. "I was going to tell ye, the first day when I let ye out behind the library, then ye put yer finger on my lips and I melted inside. Yer so beautiful and ye were in trouble. From that first night when I carried ye unconscious through the woods, before I kent ye were Graham's Anna, I wanted to wrap ye up and protect ye from that tyrant Ian. Ye were the first person I could talk to since returning from the front lines. I was comfortable wi' ye from the start, but once I kent who ye were, I didnae want to betray Graham nor take advantage of his loss or yer circumstances."

"Oh, Joseph, you should have spoken up. I hate lies. Maybe not the first day we met, but you've had plenty of opportunity to tell me since then."

He ran his finger from her ear to her jaw. "I feel responsible or that I could have at least done more, and I worried ye'd blame me for Graham's death and rightly so."

"I wouldn't—"

"Anna, I have fallen for ye. I didnae tell ye about Soupie for selfish reasons. I didnae want ye to leave me."

She wanted to stay cautious, and to sort out what had happened that fateful day, to talk long enough to establish his intentions, but his loving words and gentle touch did things to her that she couldn't deny. Heat coursed through her from between her legs. Without any regret, she melted into his kisses, her fingers tangled in his hair, his hands gripped her hips and pulled her against him.

He lifted her and carried her to the bed, their lips locked. Aching against his touch, she moaned when he trailed kisses down from her neck as he undid the buttons of her blouse and released her aching breasts from her bra. His tongue circled her hardened nipple, her hands in his hair forcing him to deepen his sucking torture.

She reached for his belt as his tongue switched attention to her other aching breast. Her moan was all the invitation he needed to bat her hands away and tug her pants off before he tossed his own jeans aside. Positioned between her legs, his naked body loomed over hers while he ran a finger down the length of her.

"Ye are so beautiful."

She pulled up on her elbows and reached for him, stroking her hand up and down his pulsing shaft. He crushed his mouth on hers and swallowed her moan of pleasure as their tongues collided.

He sat back on his heals. "Turn over," he said.

She obeyed, stretching a leg on either side of him.

He dropped kisses down the length of her back.

"Joseph, I need you," she begged when he reached her tailbone.

He reached his hand around her waist and pulled her up to straddle him, while he massaged her breasts from behind her. Grinding against each other, she cried out when he reached his hand down to circle her. "Oh, God, don't stop."

She pulsed around him as he dropped them both to the bed, driving deeply into her with one last thrust before he withdrew, catching is own release in the sheet of the bed before he dropped down beside her.

"I'm sorry, mo ghràdh." He brushed the hair off her face, while she caught her breath.

She lifted her head, then crawled up to rest her face on his chest. "You have nothing to apologize for. I believe I mentioned before that you have a willing partner in me. I am not an innocent virgin. You do things to my insides that I cannot seem to resist. I have never felt such passion."

He winced but drew her up with him to lean against the head of the bed. "I still feel, well, we hardly ken each other and yer Graham's—"

"Stop." She placed a finger over his lips, then replaced her hand with a kiss. "No more talk of war or of those we have lost, at least for tonight. Let us admit, we have been drawn together from the start and make no apologies to each other or to ourselves."

"Yer a clever lass, the likes I have never met."

"I will take that as a compliment. And you are a man who intrigues me and stirs me the likes I have never met."

His grin returned, drawing a smile from Anna in return. "That is more like it."

"Talk to me about yer house. Did ye get the deal?"

Her excitement rose, she pulled out of his embrace, reached to the bottom of the bed for his discarded t-shirt, slipped into it, then sat cross legged facing him. "I signed the papers and then waited in Mr. Porter's car while he presented the offer. The woman signed them back immediately without even negotiating my offer. Not only did I get the house, but she is leaving the furnishings and she has a reasonably new ice box and cook top. I am so excited to get moved in and make it my own. I cannot even describe how much I want to be there, to make it, I don't know what. I don't even know how to explain what I am feeling."

"Hiraeth is the word."

Her brow knit and she tipped her head. "I have never heard that. What does it mean?"

"'Tis a Welsh word, that some interpret to mean homesickness tinged wi' nostalgia over the lost or departed, but unlike homesickness, hiraeth can be felt for a place one has never been to. I interpret the word to be a sort of a spiritual longing for home, or for a person, or a time that ye cannae get back to; and perhaps a desire to belong to something greater than a spot on a map."

"Yes, that's it, that is it exactly. Since I left Hatton Garden and my parents died, I have longed for a place to call home. Graham and I didn't get the chance to establish anything to call our own and certainly there is nothing homey on the front lines. Since coming here, I have been very displaced. This house, my Castle Gordon house, will change all that. Yes, hiraeth, that is exactly it."

"I ken the feeling well. That is why so many expected me to stay in the highlands wi' my cousins after the war. I have never felt at home here wi' my da and his farm. I mean I worked hard, and I made the best of things before I enlisted, but I think a big part of joining the reserves was my desire to be back in the old country."

"Do you wish you were there now, that you had stayed?" She held her breath afraid of his answer.

"I wish to be right where I am beside ye." He reached for her, and she gladly returned to the comfort of his embrace, stretching her body long against the side of him and resting her head in the centre of his chest.

"This right here, what I am feeling right now, feels the most like home, I have felt in many years," she said.

He kissed the top of her head. She smiled and pulled herself tightly against him.

"I'm sorry m'eudail, the letter, that is Graham…"

"You have beaten yourself up long enough. I said we were going to let it go for now. I need time to think on what you have told me, to process my own guilt and sadness. But for now, let's think good thoughts and not dwell on the past." Anna gazed up and he nodded his reply.

"Ye have yer ammunition against that bastard Ian now at least. I cannae believe he is Graham's flesh and blood."

Anna pulled herself up to lean on the headboard beside him. She cringed when she turned to him.

"What now?" he asked.

"I might have injured Ian. He lunged at me again and told me I had to stay at their house. It was an odd exchange, like he was begging and threatening at the same time. He is such an angry man, and he doesn't even know I have Graham's letter. I cannot betray Clara; I will have to say I found it myself."

"Aye ye will. What have ye done to him?"

"I was ready for his attack this time. I kicked him between the legs and then in the face. Blood was pooling on the floor, and I left him for dead."

"No more than he deserved. I would have liked to see that wi' my own eyes." He chuckled. "Remind me nae to make ye mad." He pulled her to him, and she rested her head on his shoulder.

"I see red when it comes to that man; the opposite of how I feel when I am with you." She twirled her finger on his chest, then looked up to him for a kiss. "Where did you get to tonight? Supper at the Sunset again?"

He looked away.

"Is something wrong?"

"No, I, that is supper was fine. Would have been nicer wi' yer company, but I'm used to eating alone. I sat in the truck wi' Jamie Thom after I ate; we had a whiskey together. I told him about Ian and the whole letter fiasco, and we were rehashing war stories."

"I thought you didn't like talking about it?"

"Jamie's different, we experienced some things that only he and I would ken. Yer full of questions tonight. Finish telling me about yer new set up. I ken yer anxious to get moved into yer own cottage but tell me about yer business, how 'tis going to run. Certainly, Kincardine is a step away from the fancy shops in London that yer used to."

"Of course, it will be downscale, but the work will be the same. I bought from estate sales and auctions and some new stones from mines like DeBeers I told you about, and I set them into new creations. The trick will be getting the word out and making sales to people in the bigger cities. What are you grinning at?"

"Ye, yer enthusiasm makes me smile. When ye talk about yer work, ye get a happy glow. I have never met a woman so ambitious as ye. I barely ken ye and I'm proud of ye."

She climbed on top and straddled him as they kissed, his hands pulling at her hips to draw her over him once again.

"Yer asking for trouble if ye keep that up."

Her hands gripped the headboard above him, and she grinned down at him. "What kind of trouble?"

"Holy, hell, Anna, what ye do to me."

She rode him slowly this time, heightening her pleasure. Just as she cried out her release, he grabbed her arms, flipped her to her back, and drove her fast while she pulsed around him, drawing his simultaneous climax.

"Damn it."

Again, she pulled herself up on his chest, weakened now by a second round of passionate sex.

"I didn't, we… I released my seed in ye."

"Graham and I were never able to… That is, I am not sure if I can conceive. I don't think you need to worry is what I am trying to say." She spoke without looking up at him.

He pulled her tightly against him. They lay quietly for what seemed a long time.

"Why dinnae ye let me help ye set up; ye dinnea need to deal wi' the likes of Lonsdale and the others at the bank. I have the means."

His voice startled her. "I thought you had nodded off. Why are you still worrying about the loan? I also have means and now with Graham's letter, Ian will have no choice but to release my funds. I know how much Graham and I had in the Bank of England before we enlisted. I may not even need the loan or not in its entirety. Thank you for offering, but I suppose part of my determination to go it on my own, is my inability to trust others."

"Ye dinnae trust me?" He pouted when she pushed herself up to face him.

"Yes, I do, surprisingly, in a very short time. At least, I am trying to. I mean, I guess I haven't given myself the opportunity to get to know many people in much of my adult life, that is, really get to know people enough to rely on them fully, men in particular."

"Then marry me."

Her head jolted back and although she could not help a surprised smile, she glared at him wide eyed. "How can you propose marriage while you relax back, arm behind your head like you just asked me about the weather."

"We would make a good team." His mischievous smile returned.

She hesitated to speak, a confused crease of her brow letting him know she was unsure of his true feelings. He extended his hand, and she met it, rubbing her thumb across his fingers, but remaining silent.

"Are ye nae ready to let go of yer Graham?"

"It's not that. I have realized over the last few months that although we loved each other, I never had much chance to get to know Graham. I certainly wept when I got word he died and I'm sad for what he missed out on and what we might have become, but I can come to terms with my own loss. We buried so many, I fear my heart grew a bit cold."

He pulled another pillow behind him and drew her closer. She naturally curled against him once again and nestled under his arm, her face resting on his chest. "I worry you don't understand me. As in, understand my nature, the big picture that is. You have barely known me a fortnight. I am an unconventional woman and I have plans. I don't fit into most men's vision of a dutiful wife."

"I ken ye just fine m'eudail. Yer stubborn and independent like most Scottish women. Just when folks think they have seen all ye can throw at them, ye turn and smile and say 'ye ain't seen nothing yet'. Yer stunning but nae vain; yer hard like a rock when someone crosses ye or someone ye love, and yer as soft as the lake breeze when someone needs ye. Ye will do just fine in life, and I would like to be a part of it."

He looked down and pulled her chin up to face him. "Are ye crying, mo ghràdh?"

"Maybe a little." She swiped at a tear with the back of her hand. "I am going to have to let you know."

"Fair enough, I will wait."

They lay silent a few moments, each lost in their thoughts, until they eventually fell asleep comfortably wrapped in each other's embrace.

Chapter Fifteen

"Good morning," Anna said, as Joseph tried to slip quietly from the bed.

He crawled back on top of her, the thin sheet the only barrier between her and his obvious desire. "Good morning to ye, my bonny lassie."

His kiss deepened as his hand pulled at the sheet. He sat back, lifted the t-shirt she still wore, and tossed it beside them.

Anna tangled her hand in his hair and pulled him back, moaning her pleasure as he trailed kisses down her neck.

A loud bang at the door, startled an instant break to their passion.

Joseph jumped from the bed and reached to the floor for his jeans. Anna pulled the t-shirt back over her and clutched the covers to her neck as he opened the door to their intruders.

Shock was an understatement, at the appearance of the chief of police and his deputy at the door.

"What is it? Is someone hurt? Is me mum okay?"

"Your family is fine Mr. Hendrie; we need to ask you a few questions."

"What's wi' the Mr. Hendrie, Derek? We have been friends long enough to be on a first name basis. What is going on?"

"May we come in?"

"Well, I have company. Give us a minute."

He closed the door and turned to Anna. "Can ye change in the loo, they want to come in."

"Of course." Anna returned moments later, her face washed, and her hair brushed, fully clothed as if she had just arrived.

The officers leaned against the kitchen counter, both holding small notepads in hand. "What has happened, Joseph?" She moved to his side.

"Anna, this is Police Chief Derek Bane, and his assistant Officer Oakley. Gentlemen, this is Anna Gordon."

"Pardon the interruption, Miss." The senior officer removed his hat and nodded in her direction. Tall and slim, he appeared too young to be chief of police, perhaps only a few years older than Joseph. His full head of hair was dark, as were his eyes which now stared at her a moment longer than seemed necessary.

Joseph pulled out a chair at the small table. "Sit, I'm nae sure what's going on. Fanny from the diner is missing and I gave her a ride home, so they have some questions."

Anna shook her head but did not speak. The scrutiny of the officers felt more due to the obvious reason she was at Joseph's cabin this early in the morning, than to any wrongdoing connected to the waitress' disappearance.

"Mr...., Joe, you were the last to see Frances Burnsley. Reg at the diner told us you left with her after her shift last night. You were drinking in your truck with one ..." he glanced at his notepad.

"Lieutenant Thomson; he goes by Jamie Thom. We were in the service together. Aye, I had my supper at the Sunset and a drink wi' Jamie in the truck and then I drove Fanny home after her shift. I got here before eight and Anna was here waiting."

"Mrs. Gordon is that true?"

"Yes, absolutely," she replied too quickly.

"What time did he get here?" the young officer asked.

"I, um, do not remember exactly. Like he said before eight. I did not get here myself until a few minutes before," she said, wide eyed and nervous at being drawn into the inquisition.

"Joe, you are going to have to come to the station with us," the chief said firmly.

"On what grounds? I gave Fanny a ride home, which I have done in the past. I dropped her right to her front door and left to come back here. I have been here wi' Mrs. Gordon all night."

Anna dropped her gaze to her hands, hoping to hide her blush.

The police chief tilted his head and squinted suspiciously. "Fanny's husband reported her missing and since you were the last to see her, we have some more formal questioning. I know we go way back, but we need to go by the books."

Joseph looked pleadingly toward Anna.

"I will be fine; go answer their questions. We can talk later." She smiled and tried for a reassuring nod.

~

Anna straightened the bed, a lone tear rolling down her cheek at the sweet memory of sleeping in Joseph's arms. Sitting alone on the side of the bed, her thoughts rushed in circles. She wanted to trust this man who offered to help her, who listened to her, confided in her, made passionate love to her and who proposed marriage. But then she reminded herself, he kept his identity from her as well as his relationship with Graham. Now he lied to police about the time he arrived at the cabin. She recalled his vague answer about his whereabouts the prior evening and now she had lied to police to protect him. Was it possible he was not all he seemed? Could he be involved with Fanny's disappearance? He was equally as obliging as he was mysteriously aloof. Her aching heart conflicted her common sense that told her to back away.

Unsure how long he would be and at a loss what else to do, Anna made the hour long walk back to the Campbell's home, the trek made slightly tolerable by the warm morning sun shining through the trees. Already cold and confused on her arrival, Ian's appearance added to her misery the minute she stepped in the door. He had dark black circles under both eyes and a scabbed over cut across the bridge of his nose.

"Your boyfriend has been arrested."

His sneer along with the tip of his smug chin had Anna wishing she could punch his face again. "You don't know what you're talking about, and I am in no mood for another confrontation with you. Get out of my way before I make your face look worse than it already does."

"I saw the police at the coffee shop this morning before I went to work. They were questioning the owner, Walter Burnsley. He is the husband of Frances Burnsley. She's a waitress at the—"

She spun back toward him after shoving her cloak into the front hall closet. "I know who Fanny—"

He took a step toward her and jammed his fists on his hips. "Well then perhaps you also know your man and Walter's wife have been having an affair. Reg, the owner of the Sunset was there as well this morning. He confirmed it. He saw your handyman take her in his truck after work and she has not been seen since. Fanny left with that Joseph Hendrie, and witnesses say it is not the first time. He was drunk after sitting out back in the parking lot with his army buddy for hours and then he grabbed that poor young woman after her shift and hauled her God knows where."

"Your friends have fed you a line I am afraid. Step out of my way and let me pass. I will not hear another word from you."

He did not move from her path, nor did he stop talking. "He lives in a Godforsaken shack back in the woods, the preacher told me. He probably took her there and murdered her. I told the police as much."

Anna dropped her head on a loud sigh. "Why can you not mind your own damn business? Joseph did not kill any-one, and he was not drunk. He dropped the girl off at her home down near the harbour, so she didn't have to walk home from work in the cold. Then he went home, and it is a comfortable cabin just off Lake Road, not a shack back in the woods. I know because I was there with him."

"You were with a murderer?" His eyes enlarged and his fingers covered his mouth.

"You are an absolutely ridiculous man who listens to idle gossip and exaggerates rumors at the expense of innocent citizens. I am not having this conversation with you." Anna pushed his arm forcing him to step aside so she could pass.

"You need to stay away from that man. You will be safe indoors here with Marcy and me," Ian called to her back.

She stopped on the bottom step and turned slowly to face him. "Even if he were a murderer, which I know for a fact he is not, I would still be safer staying with him than you and for the last time, I am not remaining in this house." She turned back to the steps, stormed off to her room and began packing her suitcase.

～

"I need to go away for a little while, but I will be back for you, and we are going to work things out for you and Thomas," Anna said. She folded her clothes into the suitcase, occasionally checking over her shoulder for Ian's intrusion to stop her hasty departure.

Clara sat on the bed, her hands neatly folded in her lap, her feet dangling over the side not meeting the floor. Tears flowed down her cheeks, but she forced a smile when Anna looked her way. "Where will you be? Can I come and see you?"

"I will be at The Walker House until my house purchase closes. I only need a few days to sort some things out and then we will visit, I promise."

After an emotional goodbye with her niece, Anna managed to sneak out the door unnoticed just before noon.

Barely moments later, as Clara retreated to the kitchen, she heard a knock at the front door. "Auntie Anna," she ran through the foyer in hopes of her aunt's return.

She yanked open the door and gasped at the tall man standing on the other side of the screen. His smile seemed friendly, and Clara smiled in return but did not move to open the screen door between them. Although she guessed who he may be, she waited for the stranger to speak first.

"Hello, ye must be Clara."

She pushed on the screen door allowing him entrance. "Hello. Are you Joseph? My Auntie Anna talks about you a lot."

"That I am. Pleased to make yer acquaintance. She talks about ye and yer brother a lot to." He crouched down to Clara's level and shook her small hand. "Is she home?"

Clara shook her head. "She's not here. She said she had to go away."

"Do ye ken where she went?"

"The Walker House." Clara tilted her head after answering and stared, mesmerized even at such a young age by this beautiful man. "She said your eyes are the colour of sapphires. She is teaching me about gemstones, but she doesn't have any sapphires." Clara's eyes widened and she brought her hand quickly to her mouth.

"What ails ye lassie?" His brow creased, curious at her reaction.

"I told Auntie Anna I would keep her jewels a secret."

He placed a hand on her shoulder and smiled. "Yer secret is safe wi' me, Clara."

"Step away from that man." Ian's voice boomed through the hallway, causing Clara to leap back and Joseph to draw himself up to full height.

Ian reached them at the front door and roughly shoved his daughter back with a hand on her chest. "Go to your room." He yelled at her but fixed a squint at Joseph.

Clara watched Joseph over her shoulder as she walked slowly through the foyer. He leaned past Ian, winked at the child, and mouthed "thank ye". She stopped at the kitchen door, smiled, and wiggled her fingers back at him.

"How dare you come to my home?" Ian demanded.

"I am looking for Anna and dinnae get me going on how dare ye. Ye would be a fine one to talk."

"I will certainly not give you any information on her whereabouts," Ian said.

"I dinnae need yer help and I have no intention to fight wi' ye. Like Anna said, yer nae worth the trouble."

"Trouble? I think you are in enough trouble with your violent temper. It is only a matter of time before you are arrested for murder and sent to jail. Everyone in town knows you and Fanny have had at each other and you were the last one to see her alive. Your hard-working father will roll over in his grave at the scoundrel you have become. Honestly, violating a young woman like Anna when her husband is barely dead in the ground. Then when she is not enough for you, you snatch another innocent off the street and God knows what you did to her. Get out of this house and do not ever come around my family again."

Joseph drew back his arm for momentum and punched Ian square across the jaw so that he stumbled back, tripped over the umbrella stand and landed hard on his backside.

"That one was for Anna. If ye ever touch her again, ye will answer to me."

~

Joseph's next stop was the boarding house where his friend Jamie Thom was staying. Miss Jackson sat on the front porch of the two-story white clapboard country home. Wrapped in a hooded woolen cloak, with her head tipped back and her eyes closed, she rocked herself slowly in the cushioned wooden chair. She jolted up at the sound of his truck and scurried down the two front steps to meet Joseph on the front lawn. "You caught me in a rare moment of re-laxing."

"Well deserved to be sure, Miss Jackson. Sorry to interrupt ye. Is Jamie Thomson in the house?"

"He went to work this morning like he has each day he has been here."

His forehead creased questioning how Jamie got to work when Joseph was his usual ride. "Are ye certain?"

"Well, yes, I'm sure of it. A black truck, just like yours came and picked him up. I didn't check who was driving. I thought it was you to be honest. Is something wrong? Shall I leave him a message for you?" Her brow knit with concern.

"No, everything is fine. I thank ye for yer time." He turned to leave but stopped short of his truck and faced her again. "Did ye happen to see a lady friend wi' him when he left this morning?"

"Oh, heavens no. I do not allow boarders to have overnight visitors in my rooms."

"If ye… never mind. I thank ye again."

She smiled and nodded to him then went back in the house.

Chapter Sixteen

"You may go up, Sir. She is in room 12."

Joseph knocked quietly, unsure how he would be received.

Anna opened the door and waved an arm in invitation but did not make eye contact nor speak. He closed the door behind him and stood just inside the room while she crossed to stare out the window at the harbour.

"Can we talk for a few minutes?" he asked to her back.

Anna shook her head. "I am not sure what to make of our relationship, Joseph. I am honestly not sure I can trust you."

"I never lied to ye, Anna."

She scoffed and turned to him wide eyed. "You lied from the start about who you are and about knowing Graham. You lied to the police and said you got home before eight, when you did not come in until after nine and I'm not entirely sure about what you were doing up until then. Then you tell me you are falling for me and ask me to marry you when you barely know me. When the police took you away this morning, I was as heartbroken as I was confused."

Joseph ran his fingers through his hair and blew out a long breath to the ceiling before he sat in the chair beside her perch on the windowsill. "Please let me explain."

"I hardly know you, Joseph. Graham told me to trust you and my initial instinct was to do so. I want to believe you are not involved in Fanny's disappearance. And I would really like to allow you time to heal from the war and what happened the day Graham was gunned down, but I am having a rough time thinking things through. Trusting people is not my best suit, especially after what I have been through with Ian since arriving in Canada."

"I didnae lie about my family, nor about my friendship wi' Soupie. I simply never got the chance to explain it to ye. And I certainly didnae lie about my feelings for ye."

Anna blew out a sigh and moved over to sit on the edge of the bed. "Okay, that aside, what happened to Fanny and why did you lie to the police about what time you came home?"

He cringed, then clasped his hands and leaned forward in the chair. "Fanny is married to Walter Burnsley. He is the owner of the coffee shop. The truth is her husband is an ass. He is ten years her senior and he treats her poorly. She does nae care for him much and frankly she is a bit loose if ye ken my meaning. She has been taking up wi' Jamie Thom since he arrived in town."

"So, she was with him last night?"

He nodded. "I'm getting there. Fanny sometimes tells Walter she is working late at the diner until eight or nine and that she will get a ride home, because Walter cannae stay up past seven since he does the coffee shop early in the morning. Then she finishes around seven and takes off wi' Jamie for a wee… visit." He smirked at Anna and shrugged. "I'm nae saying I agree wi' what they are doing, but it has been a long time alone for Jamie and well, Fanny is an enthusiastic partner."

"So, Jamie was the last to see her? Did you tell the police that?"

"No, I was the last to see her. Jamie does nae have a car. I had my supper wi' him like I told ye and we had a nip of whiskey while he waited for Fanny. We made it look like she left wi' me, but she went wi' Jamie. I stayed in the truck about a half mile from, well they have a place to go, it does nae matter where. I nodded off for an hour or so to be honest and then I went and fetched them both. I dropped Jamie off first because he was closest. He boards wi' Miss Jackson out by the highway. I came back through town and dropped Fanny home at her front door; they live just past the harbor. Ye can almost see her house from here." He pointed out the window.

Anna glanced up to the window but stayed where she was.

"She hopped out of the truck, waved to me from their front step, and I left. That is the God's honest truth of it, I swear on my father's grave."

"But you lied to the police about what time you dropped her off? Why did you not tell them what really happened, tell them she was with Jamie, and you dropped her closer to nine."

"A man does nae betray his brother. We have an honour to uphold."

"Oh, for heaven's sake, he is not going to go to jail for having a quick tumble with another man's wife. If Walter heard her come in, or someone saw her get dropped off, now you look guilty of some wrongdoing."

"I didnae want to get Jamie nor Fanny in trouble. Walter would have been asleep whether I dropped her at eight or ten. The likelihood someone saw her leave work after seven was higher than someone seeing her get dropped off so, it made more sense to say that was when I dropped her off and got to the cabin around eight."

"What happened to her then? What if Walter found out about Jamie and Fanny and he has done her some harm?"

"I wish I kent what has happened. She would have had her tips from the day of work, mayhap one of the vagrant workers knew her routine and took the opportunity to jump her for her loot."

"But then what? Even if someone robbed her, you said she was right at her front door. She could have screamed for Walter or handed over her cash and fled inside." Anna stood once again and stared from her window across the water.

"Maybe Walter scared her out of town, and he is trying to make it look like someone else did something to her," Joseph suggested.

"Have you seen Jamie? Is he not concerned that she's missing? Did it cross your mind that Fanny may have gone back to him?"

"I tried to check wi' him just now, but Miss Jackson said he left for work this morning and she does nae allow guests in the rooms, so Fanny coudnae have gone back to Jamie. The odd part is that Miss Jackson said he left this morning in a black truck like mine. But the only one who has a truck like mine is Steve and I dinnea ken how he would ken that I coudnae pick up Jamie."

"The whole town knew you had been taken to the police station." She raised her eyebrows and tipped her head.

"Aye, I suppose yer right. But it is odd that Jamie would go off to work if he kent Fanny was missing and I had been taken for questions."

"So, that's it?" She threw her hands up in front of her.

"What do ye mean?"

"Well, you just admitted, it would be odd for him to go to work in the circumstances. Did you go see him at work? Maybe he knows where she is."

Joseph frowned and shook his head. "'Tis impossible."

"Not from where I am standing. If you tell the police she was with him, perhaps they can weed out of him where she may be."

"No, I didnae mean 'tis impossible he may ken where she is. I mean, 'tis impossible to go see him at work. Well nae impossible, but time consuming and nae an easy drive if the snow is blowing. The men left today for a job in Tobermory, more than a hundred miles north of here. They will nae be back for a few days. Besides that, I cannae send the police sniffing in Jamie's direction."

"I don't know what to think anymore. You cannot stand accused for something you did not do just to protect a friend."

"There is no indication that anyone has been accused of any crime. She may have left Walter of her own accord and be hiding out. 'Tis the gossipy small town that is making it into something 'tis nae. I have ejits like yer Ian Campbell calling my integrity into question and telling everyone who will listen that I was the last to see her and I'm a murderer."

"Why would he say she was murdered? No one has suggested that."

"I didnae think of that. I dinnae ken why he would say it."

"When did you see Ian?"

"Before I checked wi' Miss Jackson for Jamie, I went to the Campbells' house to find ye. I'm sorry to say, I may have sucker punched him good, but he deserved it. I will say he was already bruised and cut from yer kick last night. If ye didnae break something in his face yesterday, then I may have today."

"This situation could get difficult. You have no idea what he is capable of."

"Ye believe me, don't ye?"

She hesitated before answering. "Yes."

He huffed a breath and his shoulders slumped.

"He is about to get another punch in the not so literal sense. I have been to see a lawyer and he will be serving Ian with a motion to release my funds."

"That is some bit of good news in this mess." He stood and went to her at the window, pulling her into a hug and stroking her hair when she rested her face on his chest. "And the part about falling for ye and wanting to spend my time wi' ye is nae a lie, Anna. It pained me to be taken away this morning and I let Chief Derek Bane hear about it. Ye were all I could think about."

She glanced up to him and accepted a brief kiss. "It pained me too, but it gave me some time to clear my head. I want to believe you, Joseph. I have never felt so drawn to anyone else before, certainly not so quickly, and that scares me more than working on the front lines."

He dropped his lips to her. "Ye can trust me wi' yer life, mo ghràdh. Me and my sapphire eyes." He waggled his brow up and down.

"What?!"

"I met yer wee Clara. She said yer teaching her about gemstones and using my eyes for comparison."

"You even managed to charm the ten-year-old, did you?" She couldn't hold back a grin.

His mischievous smile had returned causing an ache within her.

"Why am I not surprised?" She wove her hand into his hair, drawing him closer and deepening their kiss. "It has been a long war for us too."

~

"Good morning, beautiful." Joseph touched her face when she opened her eyes.

"Here we are again." Her smile matched his own, at once tender and mischievous. His hand wandered lower beneath the sheets, cupping a bare breast as she stretched languidly, raised her leg over his hip and shimmied herself closer. A moan escaped her as his mouth replaced his hand.

The knock once again startled them both from the tender moment.

"I cannae believe it, two days in a row." Joseph snarled as he threw back the sheets.

Anna gasped and pulled the sheet back to her chest, sitting up alert before calling to their intruder. "One moment."

The key turned in the lock before Anna had a chance to scramble from the bed. The hotel keeper stepped aside allowing the uniformed officer to enter first. Joseph reached for his pants from the floor and held them in front of his naked self as he stood at attention. "Gentlemen, I demand ye turn yerselves away from my lady, until she is decent."

Despite the situation, the officer and the hotel keep had the decency to turn while Anna jumped from the bed, donned a house robe, and knotted the belt firmly. She came from behind the bed to stand at Joseph's side within seconds of their intrusion. Joseph had taken the opportunity to jump into his pants and now reached an arm around Anna's shoulders pulling her closer to him.

"How dare you enter my room unannounced?" Anna glared at the hotel keeper demanding an answer.

"Police business, Ma'am; I had no choice." He glanced briefly at her then dropped his gaze to the floor.

The officer spoke for the first time since entering the room. "Begging your pardon, Ma'am but I asked Mr. Webber to lead me to Mr. Hendrie on a matter of some urgency."

"I hardly think you need to come barging into a private room of a single woman, in the absence of a distress call or a fleeing criminal. Unacceptable behaviour, both of you." Anna shook her head quickly.

"State yer business, Officer Oakley. Where is Chief Bane?" Joseph demanded.

"You are correct, and I apologize. The tip we received led us to believe Mr. Hendrie was in this room and perhaps you were here with him against your will," the officer explained.

Anna encircled Joseph's waist and pulled herself tighter to his side. "Do I appear to be in danger? And did it cross your mind to ask me if I were in harm's way prior to forcing entry?"

"Again, beg your pardon, Ma'am. Joe, you will need to come with me."

"On what grounds? I answered all yer questions yesterday and as Mrs. Gordon stated, we are both here of our own free will and prefer nae to be disturbed."

"Aside from the anonymous call, we also received information from Mr. Burnsley that raised more questions in regard to the disappearance of Mrs. Frances Burnsley."

Anna tipped her head and snarled. "Let me guess, the tip came from Ian Campbell? The man will stop at nothing to—"

"The anonymous tip came from a female. I will wait in the hallway, if you would kindly come along voluntarily so we don't need to make this situation any worse than it is."

The men left the room, closing the door quietly behind them. Joseph drew Anna to him and kissed her gently on the forehead. "I'm sorry, m'eudail."

A lone tear escaped and ran down her cheek. Her hands still linked behind him, she leaned back to see his face, wishing she could read his thoughts, gauge his true emotions. "This cannot be happening. Again."

"I'm sure 'tis more misunderstanding. I have done nothing wrong. I will answer their questions and be back to ye soon, that is a promise."

He left the room without looking back. Anna picked up the pillow and threw it at the headboard, then allowed herself the luxury of a bout of tears.

"Nothing is solved by crying in bed all day." She raised her head from her hands and stared out the window at the overcast sky. "Graham, Mum, anyone up there listening?

Give me a sign. Tell me who to trust and what to do. I'm starting to think I should heed the mysterious notes and go back to Hatton Garden."

She drew a bath and lay in it until it grew cold; then slowly dressed for the day. All her movements felt like slow motion, all her thoughts felt like doom. It was late morning by the time she called to the kitchen for egg and toast and coffee. Unsure how much time passed as she stared at the busy street below her room, her coffee grown cold in her hands, she flinched when the phone rang in her silent room.

"Good morning, Mrs. Gordon. How are you managing on this gloomy fall day?"

"I have been better, Mr. Lonsdale, what can I do for you?"

"I, ah, that is I have a couple of things we need to discuss. Would you mind coming into the bank?"

"I have no mind to go out today. Is there a problem with my loan? We are meant to be closing the house purchase next Friday."

"Yes, well, that is the thing. As Mr. Hendrie was your co-signer and as he has unfortunately, um. Well, the thing is, despite his accounts being in good standing, your co-signer needs to be gainfully employed and, not in jail to be precise."

She huffed into the phone. "Mr. Hendrie is gainfully employed, and he is not in jail. This conversation is a waste of both our time."

"I am sorry to be the bearer of bad news, but I heard directly from a customer, whose husband spoke to Police Chief Bane, just this morning, that Mr. Hendrie had been arrested and may be charged in the disappearance—"

"He is not being charged with anything. They took Mr. Hendrie for questioning since he was the last to see Fanny, only because he was kind enough to give her a ride home from work. Perhaps she left her husband for a lover or went to visit a friend. No one has proven any wrongdoing. This is ridiculous."

"I am merely acting on information given to me from a valid source, and I am sorry to say we cannot release any funds when the borrower or the co-signer is facing criminal charges or incarcerated as the case may be. It is stated in the rules."

"The only thing more ludicrous than your rules is your sense of propriety. A reputable businessperson such as yourself should get his facts straight before spreading rumors around town and cancelling loans based on idle gossip."

"I am sorry, Mrs. Gordon, your loan is pending, ah indefinitely."

"In all likelihood, I will not need the loan in any event. I also have information from a legitimate source that will allow me full access to the funds currently held in trust in my name. My lawyer will be in touch with you later today. I have commenced legal proceedings against your own teller, Mr. Ian Campbell to return my trust account into my name alone."

"I am sorry again Mrs. Gordon. That is the second thing I needed to discuss. Mr. Dunlop, your lawyer has been in touch, and we are aware of the proceedings. He has requested a full audit of the account and although we have provided him access, the initial perusal of the transactions through the account seems to have produced more questions."

"How so?"

"I am afraid I am not at liberty to discuss the matter, as it may also involve some criminal activity. Suffice to say, the account has been frozen until further notice and neither you nor Mr. Campbell will have access to it until the matter is resolved."

"That is ridiculous. It is my only source of income."

"Please understand, Mrs. Gordon, you are a valued customer, and we will be happy to sort it all out for you once the courts have made a decision. In the meantime, I invite you to use my personal line should you need my services at any time of day."

"I highly doubt that will be necessary since you have frozen my account and are unwilling to accommodate my business loan."

"You have my card. I wish you a good day, Mrs. Gordon."

Anna slammed the phone in the cradle, picked it up and slammed it again for good measure.

After a few deep breaths to digest the reality of her situation, she dialed Mr. Dunlop with the faint hope he would have an answer for a way out of her newfound poverty.

"Yes, I have had discussions with Mr. Lonsdale. Ian Campbell appears to have been using your account to hide funds from illicit activities. What we expected to be a straightforward audit, and transfer of estate funds, has caused more questions than answers. We will get to the bottom of it."

"What shall I do in the meantime?" She scoffed. "Ian held the entirety of mine and Graham's savings in that account. That was my only source of income and now my loan is pending to buy my house because my co-signer gave a woman a ride home from work. I am a wealthy woman from a well-known family and a successful marriage and now I am essentially destitute."

"I am sorry I do not have better news for you. We have sent a process server out with the papers to sue Mr. Campbell. With the handwritten proof that your husband provided, and the fact your Bank of England account was joint between you and Mr. Graham Campbell, I have no doubt the money will come back to you in its entirety, but these things can unfortunately take time."

"Damn it. Now I have to go back to that ghastly house until I can sort this out."

"Could you stay with a friend?"

"Yes, I will have to make alternate arrangements. I simply cannot be near that vile man for a day longer."

"Please stay in touch."

Anna called Mr. Porter the realtor next to give him a summarized version of the events that had taken place since signing her papers. She stopped twice to pinch the bridge of nose, lest she fall to sobbing on the phone. "I am sorry, but you will have to put the deal on hold until I can sell some of my jewellery pieces or sort out these money issues with the bank."

"Mrs. Gravitz is insistent that we sell to no one but you. I think we shall have some leeway even if we need to extend the closing. Let's just let things lie as they are until you have a chance to find out what's what. Where can I reach you?"

"Thank you, Lee, that does offer me some hope. I will unfortunately be heading back to the Campbells' this afternoon. I suppose I will be there for the next couple of days until I can sort out other accommodations. I will leave word with your office if I relocate."

Chapter Seventeen

Joseph sat in front of the police chief's desk, in an office full of clutter. The papers on his desk were coffee stained, the bulletin board behind him so full of tacked up notices as to become indecipherable, and the trash bin beside his desk overflowed with balled up papers and leftover food which emitted an unpleasant smell of rot.

Joseph curled his lip. "Do ye ever clean my man?"

The police chief waved his hand in reply. "We had someone, but she…" He scratched his head and shuffled a few papers around until he reached a blank note pad; then drew a pen from the drawer, touched the tip to paper to check for ink, then finally glanced up to Joseph. "Okay then."

"Derek what is this all about?"

He laid the pen down and leaned back in his wooden swivel chair, raised his hands and linked them behind his head, then slowly swivelled back and forth as he spoke. "Reg saw Fanny get in your truck after work at seven-fifteen."

"I ken, we went through all that yesterday. I dropped her home. What is the problem now?"

He came forward abruptly, his arms landing on his desk with a thud. "Well, Reg talked to Walter and convinced him to come and talk to us. He is certain he heard her come in closer to nine. He is also certain you and Fanny have something going on as in a romantic something and he said Fanny told him—"

Joseph shook his head quickly and waved his hands in front of him. "Told who? Who is certain? Reg or Walter? I cannae even ken the gossip; how can ye believe a word of it?"

The police chief took a deep breath and splayed his hands before starting again. "Fanny told her husband, Walter that she was interested in someone else and that she had a mind to run away with him."

"So, what has that to do wi' me? I'm sitting right here, and Fanny is nae wi' me." He threw his hands up in front of him.

"Walter is certain, you are the someone and you know where she is, or you have done her some harm when you decided you were done with her."

"'Tis a damn lie. Walter likely had words wi' her when she came home late and he ran her off or did some harm himself and now, he wants to lay the blame on me."

"I thought you dropped her right after work?"

"I meant, perhaps he heard her later on and thought she came in late and that is when they fought. I dinnae ken what time they had words. Yesterday, ye said Walter never heard her come in at all."

"Well, that is the discrepancy. I am not entirely sure if he is giving me the real story or if he wants revenge for you cuckolding him." The chief shook his head, got up and paced behind his desk.

"I have enough damn women in this town on me and ye keep taking me away from the one I want to be wi'. I certainly have no interest to take up wi' another man's wife."

"He was fairly adamant the two of you are having an affair. And then I have this damn Ian Campbell breathing down my neck again today, insisting you are violent, and that you threatened and assaulted him recently. He had multiple bruises on his face that he said were your doing."

"Ian Campbell is a lecherous fool. He forced himself on to his sister-in-law, who has become a close friend of mine and he is trying to steal her money. 'Tis him ye should be investigating. Anna hit him when he tried to rape her nae only once, but a second time. I sucker punched him and told him to stay away from her."

"I wish you hadn't admitted that. That is assault, Joe."

"'Tis less than what he deserved and if ye were nae the law in town, ye would have done the same thing to protect yer lady. We have known each other for years, Derek. I'm nae a violent person and ye ken it well. I would nae take up wi' another man's wife and I would nae harm a fellow man unless in protection of an innocent woman or child. That is why I joined the medics in the war. I coudnae afflict pain on another human if my life depended on it."

"I have to keep you at least until I get a chance to question Burnsley another time. I am sorry, Joe. I want to take your word but there are too many fingers pointing at you."

"Absolutely, as farfetched as it gets. This town owns ye, Derek; ye need to grow some balls and tell them to mind their own business. Do yer job, man and investigate the right people."

"Are you sure there is nothing else you want to tell me about that night?"

Drawing suspicion on his friend was not an option. Joseph shook his head without reply and motioned the officer ahead of him to the cells. "Take me away then."

"Damn it." The police chief reached for his keys to the holding cell.

~

"Anna, you have returned. How pleasant. Will you be joining us for dinner?"

"I know you are behind this mess with Joseph and trust me when I find out how, you will wish we never met."

Ian had the audacity to chuckle at her threat. "Tsk, tsk, you must calm yourself. At the risk of raising that vile temper of yours further, I will say, I told you not to mix with the likes of that handyman. Now that he is in jail for murder, perhaps you will be more inclined to take my advice. You must learn to be a better judge of character if you intend to go it on your own in a new country."

She squinted at him and clutched her hand tightly around the handle of her suitcase. "Oh, I will go it on my own, the minute the courts throw you and your false reputation out into the streets for withholding funds that do not belong to you."

"Nonsense, that will never happen."

"It will and sooner than you think. I know you read Graham's note, which I'm happy to say now comprises the evidence I needed to sue you for return of my money." She smiled smugly at his puzzled expression.

As if mentioning the claim summoned the server, the knock at the door held Ian's retort.

"Mr. Ian Campbell."

"Yes, I am he. What is the meaning of this?"

"Sign here please." The process server held a clip board while Ian signed for the envelope. "Thank you, Sir. Have a wonderful day." He tipped his hat toward Anna, turned, and skipped back down the porch stairs.

"Humph." Ian turned from the door without reply; opened the envelope and quickly scanned the enclosed documents. He glanced up from the papers, an angry snarl on his face. "How dare you?" he asked through clenched teeth.

"How dare I? Really, Ian; how dare you? Now the account is frozen while it is in audit so neither of us can get at it."

His mouth dropped open, and his eyes bulged. "No! No," he screamed, before he ran to his office and slammed the door behind him.

Anna stormed up the stairs to her bedroom, slammed her own door and tossed her suitcase across the room. Her emotions spilled out like the contents of her suitcase before she collapsed onto her bed and indulged in sobs of tears.

Despite her lack of sleep the night before and the emotional turmoil of the day, Anna lay awake staring at the canopy of her bed. She wanted to trust Joseph. The passion he ignited had her craving even the sight of him. They had connected instantly and each time she had seen him they talked like they had known each other a lifetime. His words were sincere, but his actions drew her suspicion. He was right, he had not exactly lied to her. "Evasion is a form of lying too." She spoke to the empty room, reiterating her mother's words from long ago.

Anger having replaced her tears, she rejected the idea of resting, forced herself from the bed, and bent to retrieve her suitcase and the clothing that had fallen on the floor in her tantrum. Refolding her clothes and placing them back in drawers only added to her frustration. "I will never get away from this absurd household and make it on my own."

Her brow knit as she reached for the final item of clothing and saw a book peeking out of the suitcase pocket beneath. Realizing she had not checked the inside flaps of the case when she initially unpacked her overseas trunk, she felt within the folds and recovered a second book and a large manilla envelope. Anna smiled for the first time since she woke in Joseph's arms.

Taking the items over to her bed, she pulled herself up against the head of the bed allowing herself time to indulge in sweet memories from her past. Inside the suitcase pockets

Graham had hidden the copy of Gone with the Wind that Anna had received on her eighteenth birthday from her mother. The other book, Rebecca, by her favourite English author, Daphne du Maurier, had been given to Anna before she and Graham enlisted. "In case you have some spare time to read," he had said. She smiled at the recollections of receiving both gifts, feeling the loving sentiments as if they happened just days before.

Her curiosity peaked as she lifted the flap on the large envelope. She retrieved a flat box wrapped in what appeared to be another handwritten note. She caught her breath, her hand instinctively covering her mouth when she recognized Graham's handwriting once again.

If you are opening this without me, the worst has happened. Although we agreed to liquidate everything and transfer our joint funds via the Bank of Canada, I fear I do not know my brother nor his family well enough to trust him with conveying the entirety of our estate. Keeping this nest egg back seemed like the sensible thing to do. I hope this is enough to get you started against the possibility that Ian has not come through for you or the transfer went somehow awry.

Also, I could not bring myself to sell your favourites at a reduced price. I am certain you will want to re-read your two much-loved books; but more importantly, your priceless gems, the ones you created with a piece of your heart and soul. Know that you are more precious than any of these stones and you deserve the world.

Yours, Graham xo

P.S. To: Mauve, if Anna has not returned, and you are unpacking her trunk, please accept this note as legal transfer of the enclosed for you and you alone with our gratitude for years of your kind friendship.

"You think of everything, Graham." Anna smiled remembering his meticulous attention to details during the short time they had together. She opened the small box, a tentative smile building until she squealed and thumped her feet on the bed at the sight of the exquisite jewellery sitting on top of a bed of British notes in various pound denominations. Holding it delicately as if it would break, Anna raised her beloved alexandrite ring to the window. Like the sign she ached for, the late day sun broke through the clouds for the first time all day and shone brilliantly in a stream through her window and across the bottom of her bed. She watched in breathless awe as the stone changed from dark crimson to pale green when the sunlight touched it.

The stone brought on a flood of emotion at Graham's kindness saving her favourites and her relief that they had arrived unscathed. At first tears sprung with nostalgia for better days working in her family's business, but as the gravity of her situation sunk in, she smiled a satisfied grin, then started to laugh. She laughed so hard, her angry tears were replaced by tears of amusement at the irony of her circumstances. The bank notes more than covered the cost of her down payment while the alexandrite's value surpassed that of her entire house purchase and more.

Chapter Eighteen

Satisfied she was in a much better position financially, Anna wanted nothing more than to relax and stay out of sight until her house deal closed in a matter of days. She wanted to scream off the rooftops about her discovery but was skeptical her good luck would somehow backfire, and she would be lost and alone once again. What she truly wanted was to talk to Joseph, to find out what happened at the police station and tell him about her newfound wealth.

Following her breakfast alone in the kitchen, she strode purposely to Ian's office, intent on demanding her messages. She was certain if Joseph had called, Ian would have kept the information from her. Shuffling through correspondence on the corner of his desk, she found nothing addressed to herself. Her shoulders slumped in disappointment. She wanted desperately to share her news with Joseph and get an update on Fanny's disappearance. Marcy entered the office quietly just as Anna was about to retreat. Anna jolted back, startled by her appearance.

"What are you doing here?" Marcy's brow furrowed suspiciously over red rimmed eyes.

"I was checking for messages. Ian tends to keep things from me." Anna smirked.

"I meant, here in the house. I thought you were staying at a hotel." Marcy's withdrawn expression and monotone voice gave no indication whether she was pleased or troubled that Anna had returned.

"I had to come back. The bank froze the trust fund, and this month's allowance is almost at an end. Ian has apparently been using my account to cover up his own illicit activities. I am sorry Marcy. I appear to have brought strain upon your family, but had Ian behaved appropriately from the start, none of this would have happened. I will be leaving once the house transaction is complete."

"How will you pay for that?"

Marcy's question held accusation and had Anna feeling suddenly uneasy. "I am not sure I want to discuss finances right now. Suffice to say, I have found another way. Are you well? You look upset."

"I am fine. Better than ever." Her smile looked forced before she turned her back to Anna and fussed with the coffee tray on Ian's credenza.

Her sister-in-law's angry tone had Anna concerned but she didn't have the time nor emotion to deal with Marcy's insecurities today. "Where is Ian?"

"At work."

"On a Saturday? The bank is closed."

Marcy turned back to Anna and raised her hands. "I don't know. He goes into the office sometimes to catch up paperwork."

"Since he is not here, I would like to use the telephone if you will excuse me."

Marcy hesitated drawing Anna's sympathy. "Again, I am sorry Marcy. I know Ian is involved in some shady business and I would love to allow time to discuss it, but I have some urgent banking to take care of before I lose my house deal.

Can we speak later? Perhaps we could have tea this afternoon if Ian is still out."

"I would like that, thank you." Marcy retreated, closing the door softly behind her.

⁓

"Mr. Lonsdale, I apologize for bothering you on a Saturday at home, but since you gave me your card, I hoped you might be able to take care of some urgent business at the bank this morning."

"What a pleasant surprise. I would be delighted to assist you Mrs. Gordon."

An hour later Mr. Lonsdale was all pleasantries as he unlocked the bank doors, then turned to lock the two of them inside.

Seated in the same generic office, Anna felt anything but intimidated this visit. "I will be needing an account in my own name as well as the use of a safety deposit box. It seems the bulk of my funds and the more valuable part of my jewellery collection were held back by my sensible late husband who knew better than to trust his deceitful brother." Anna opened the satchel she had carefully guarded under her coat and revealed the jewels and pound notes to the banker.

His jaw dropped momentarily before he recovered himself. "Of course, Mrs. Gordon. What a wonderful turn of events."

She pushed the stack of bills toward him. "I trust you can have these pound notes exchanged for Canadian currency and deposited into an account in my name alone prior to my house closing date next Friday."

"Of course, yes, of course. Anything you need." His protuberant smile emerged as he nodded profusely.

Anna stifled a giggle at his enthusiasm in the sight of her newfound wealth. "And you can audit the account in Ian Campbell's name all you like. Once that matter is settled my lawyer will also provide you with an order to transfer those funds into my independent account."

"Indeed, Mrs. Gordon. I appreciate you trusting your business to our establishment."

～

"Where have you been this morning?" Marcy asked. She sat alone on the couch in the living room, looking suddenly as frail as she had on their first meeting so many weeks before.

"I had Mr. Lonsdale meet me at the bank. I had money to deposit and items to place in a safety deposit box until I am ready to set up my business. Surprisingly, Graham had the forethought to ship a nest egg within my items in the trunk, which fortunately I discovered when I most needed it. You had to see that Mr. Lonsdale today. He was all, yes Mrs. Gordon, of course Mrs. Gordon, indeed Mrs. Gordon. I had to hold back laughing at his ardent attentiveness."

"I am delighted for you," Marcy muttered.

"Are you? You seem like something is bothering you. Did Ian come home? He wasn't at the bank. No one else was there."

She shook her head quickly and the forced smile returned. "He must have gone to the city early this morning. He tells me these things and I tend to forget"

Marcy flinched when Nellie opened the living room door, Clara and Thomas following into the room behind her. "I will be leaving shortly for my afternoon off, Mrs. Campbell."

"Oh, dear heavens. Mr. Campbell did not mention it. Are you sure it needs to be today?"

Nellie twisted her hands in front of her and exhaled loudly on a sigh. "I would stay but I made arrangements for this evening out quite some time ago."

"No need to worry, Nellie, we will manage." Anna smiled.

Nellie retreated without waiting to be told twice.

Marcy dropped her head to her hand.

"I was just thinking we should go to town for ice cream. What do you think?" Anna asked hoping to alleviate Marcy's stress at the necessity of parenting.

"But, but, it's November," Clara stated the obvious.

"Nonsense, all the better to keep the ice cream from dripping. Come on Marcy. It will be fun. I would love to meet your lighthouse keeper. Are you up for it?"

She nodded briefly but did not smile as the children reached for their aunt's hands when they left the room.

~

"Hello Mr. Eastman, this is Mrs. Anna Gordon, my husband's sister-in-law, by her late husband."

"Pleased to make yer acquaintance Mrs. Gordon and I offer ye my condolences." Despite the pipe in his mouth, his smile reached his eyes, and she knew straight away his kindness was genuine.

She shook his offered hand. "Call me Anna, please."

"If ye will call me Daniel. Ye'd be new to town then?"

She beamed at his warm welcome and nodded in answer.

"I will tell my Judy to have ye round for tea. She loves to meet newcomers and show them around."

"I would like that."

"Tell Anna the story of the sky people, Mr. Dan," Clara pleaded.

"The what?"

"The piper, the one you always tell."

"Aye, of course. If ye've a mind for a wee Scottish folklore, Miss Anna."

"My favourite kind of story." She smiled at the kind man. Clara took Anna's hand in both her own as he began.

"According to legend, back in 1856, on a cold October day, a small vessel left the Port of Goderich, that's about thirty miles south of here. The family onboard was originally from the Isle of Skye, Scotland. The boat got lost in a storm as it neared Kincardine. 'Twas still kent by the native name of Penetangore back then, which meant the river wi' the sand on one side. That was the year they built the parallel piers to straighten the curve of the river and control the flow into Lake Huron. We didnae even have a lighthouse yet."

"Tell about the lost family, Mr. Dan." Clara wiggled with excitement and pulled on Anna's hand. "You will love this Auntie Anna."

Mr. Eastman smiled at the child's enthusiasm, then continued. "Aboard the boat, Donald Sinclair, fearing for his family, fetched his pipes and began playing a lament. The sound carried across to land where another piper heard and played a lament in return. The captain of the boat, hearing the drone of the pipes, headed for the sound on the shore and they arrived safely."

"Incredible." Anna shook her head slowly.

"See, I told you. Is that not the best story you have ever heard?" Clara whispered.

The keeper laughed at the child. "Clara, ye must be a true descendent of the Scots to feel the heart of that story."

"I have no doubt this one is a romantic at heart." Marcy smiled proudly at her daughter.

"Glad to see ye made it out of the cold the other night. What the heck had ye and Mr. Campbell so interested that ye'd be walking the pier after dark? Were ye looking for a lost ship?" The lightkeeper chuckled.

"Pardon me?" Marcy's smile turned to an annoyed snarl; her forehead creased in confusion.

"I saw ye and Mr. Campbell on the north pier the other night, Wednesday past. Then the splash. What were ye throwing rocks? 'Twas so loud; I ran down to see if one of ye had landed in the brink, but ye were both gone. He must have got ye back home in a hurry. 'Twas a cold one. Ye should be more careful, there's already ice on the pier."

"It was not me. Clearly you must be mistaken about the gentleman as well." Marcy shook her head quickly and stood to leave.

"Oh, no Ma'am, I'm used to seeing in the dark. Tis my job. 'Twas Mr. Campbell for certain; the light shone right on him. Although yes, the woman did have her back to me. I only assumed 'twas ye wi' him. She was the likeness of ye, yer ah, size and so forth and a dark cloak and hood just like the one yer wearing." His blush and sudden jump to his feet confirmed his realization that Ian had been out walking with another woman. He cleared his throat and turned away quickly. "Yer likely right and I was mistaken. If it weren't ye, then it must have been a different man as well. My mistake."

"No harm done. Let's go children." Marcy kept her head down as she shoed the children ahead of her.

"Bye Mr. Eastman," Clara called over her shoulder and Thomas followed suit.

Anna turned to see the man wave, his brow knit and his head shaking slowly. "Bye children, come back soon," he called after them.

"He must have seen Joseph with Fanny on the pier before he threw her over like people are saying. Ian told me your man was the last to see her before she disappeared. I will go talk to the police tomorrow and tell them what Daniel said. They will need to speak to him."

"Don't be ridiculous, Joseph looks nothing like Ian. There's almost a foot difference in their height alone; no way Mr. Eastman could confuse the two. And you will not start rumours about Joseph Hendrie. He dropped Fanny home to her front door, they were nowhere near the pier. You would be smart to keep your tales to yourself. If Mr. Eastman is the honest man he appears to be, he will be telling them it was your Ian down on the dock with Fanny, then he will have some answering to do himself."

~

"Ian is still not home?" Anna asked after they removed their coats and sent the children off to play.

"Um, now that you mention it, I am certain I remember him telling me he had business in Goderich Monday morning, and he would be heading down this weekend to get a head start."

"Mr. Lonsdale did not appear to know anything about it. I asked if Ian came in to work this weekend and he said he did not expect him until Monday. That would imply he is expected at the bank Monday not in Goderich."

Marcy flicked her hand over her shoulder as she headed to the stairs. "I need to rest. The walk has tired me. Can you ask Lorna to feed the children? I will make an effort to attend them before bed."

"No need, I can oversee the children's supper and get them ready for bed later."

Marcy's dash up the stairs indicated anything but lethargy. Anna stood alone in the foyer, squinting after her sister-in law. "What are you up to?"

~

Anna had plenty of reasons to be overwhelmed by happiness having discovered her most treasured alexandrite; independently organized her finances; confirmed with the realtor her purchase could go through and caused Ian such distress with her lawsuit that he seemed to have gone into hiding. Instead, tension consumed her, and she was desperate to talk to Joseph. Without word directly from him, she feared the worst, that he got himself arrested by covering for Jamie or worse yet, they found some proof that he was involved in Fanny's disappearance.

Another sleepless night had her vowing to take the matter into her own hands the following day and tell the police about Mr. Eastman's admission as well as have them investigate Jamie Thom's involvement despite the men's brotherhood code.

Chapter Nineteen

Early Sunday Marcy barged into the dining room, startling Anna. "What has you so excited and awake so early? I have spilled my darn tea." Anna chuckled as she wiped at the tea on her blouse.

"Anna, you have to help me." Marcy's eyes were wide with shock and red-rimmed from lack of sleep. Her hair was disheveled, and she still wore her nightgown and robe.

"What's wrong? Is it the children?" Anna sat alert, ready to jump to their aid.

Marcy flipped her hand, dismissing the concern. "It's Ian."

Anna's shoulders slumped and she rolled her eyes. "I am not interested in helping him. Can one of his staff not intervene with his problem when the bank opens tomorrow morning? I am on my way out to the police station as soon as it opens. I cannot sit idly by without knowing what has happened to Joseph."

Marcy shook her head quickly, tears pooling. "No, please you can't do that."

"What is it? Where is Ian? Did he come home last night?"

"No, I have barely slept for the last two nights for fear he would come in and I would have to face him."

Anna stood, went to Marcy and held both her hands in her own. "What has he done?"

"I truthfully do not know." She choked on a sob before she continued. "Daniel Eastman was correct. Ian was on the pier on Wednesday night. We had argued earlier in the week. I caught him reading a letter from your husband and insisted he give it to you, but he refused. He stormed out, like he often does, and we barely spoke for the next two days. I keep my distance when he's in that kind of mood."

"Okay, so what about Wednesday?"

"I had been in bed for some time. I heard the two of you arguing and then the front door when you left. Not long after that, the door slammed again. It had to have been him. He came home about an hour later, scratched, and wet, with blood on his hands and his shirt and sand on his shoes. He said he got in a scruff with a dog, and he was wet because he had been caught in the rain, but I did not hear any rain. Initially, I feared he had chased after you and done you harm, but then you came back the next day, so I didn't know what to think. But then I heard about Fanny and, oh God… What if he killed her?"

"Dear heaven, Marcy. You have to tell the police. They have had Joseph Hendrie in custody going on two days now. They think he has something to do with Fanny's disappearance."

"I can't do that. I cannot turn evidence on my own husband. They will think I knew all along and he will be arrested, and I shall be destitute, and, and the children will be taken away from us—"

"Joseph is in jail. You can't let him face charges for something your husband may have done. They may not even have evidence against Ian. Maybe there was an accident, and it can all be explained away but you must at least tell them he was out that night to alleviate suspicion against Joseph."

"There was no accident." She pulled her hands from Anna and ran her fingers through her unruly hair.

"What are you saying? Were you there?"

"No, I just know him. He is, well, that is he has been, in the past, that is—"

"Marcy, spit it out. What are you trying to say?"

She hung her head, then took a deep breath. "He is some kind of deviant. He likes to do different things, in the bedroom that is."

Anna guided Marcy to a chair at the table and then sat beside her sister-in-law, once again drawing one of her hands into her own. "Not all men are equally as considerate when it comes to, well, how they like coupling. Some like to be dominant, without much care for being gentle during the throws of passion. And it doesn't help that you have never had a true love match."

She winced before she replied. "He ties me to things and has his way, in well, in unnatural ways. He shoves himself into holes where it does not belong if you know what I mean, and sometimes he uses his belt on me. He talks when he is you know, taking what he needs, and he has called me by other names, even yours."

Anna forced herself to remain calm, despite the bile rising in her throat. "Did he say Fanny's name."

Marcy stared at her and did not reply.

"Marcy!" Anna's impatience mounted despite her sympathy.

"I, he…"

Anna patted her hand. "Tell me what he did and what he said that night."

Marcy put her head in her hand.

"Please, you have to tell me."

"He came home, and I saw him in the light from the hall. I pretended to be asleep because then he sometimes leaves me alone; but I saw him when he came closer. He had blood on his shirt front, and he was drenched wet, clothes and all, not just like he had been caught in a rain shower."

"Then what?"

"He went over to his dresser, and I could tell he was angry because he was slamming things around. Then he came and yanked me out of bed and that is when I saw the scratches on his hands and his face. They were still bleeding. I asked what had happened and he gave me the story about the dog, and how he threw it in the lake, and it splashed him."

"Did you ask what he was doing at the lake?"

"Dear God, no. I never speak back to him when he's in a temper. Then that is when he, well he…that is, he forced me down on my knees and his man part was…" She choked on another sob.

"What has he done to you?"

"He says it is natural, between a man and a woman," she defended quickly through her tears. "He had his, well, I was on my knees, and he told me to keep my hands on the floor or he would tie me up, and he had himself in my mouth and I was choking, and he kept pulling me toward him by my hair. When I tried to pull away for breath, he shoved himself in me further and he called me another name as he was pounding at me like that and he said, I know you like it rough." Her voice elevated with each bit of the description.

"Dear God." Anna reached her arm around Marcy's shoulder and let her cry. "Did he say Fanny's name?"

She sat back and shook her head slowly. "No, I couldn't understand him. I was sobbing and he moans with his release. It sounded like, ma'am. I cannot say with certainty that he had something going on with this woman, but it would not be the first time I have had my suspicions about him with someone else. He seems to have an enthusiastic appetite for, well, for that, on a daily basis and if I do not perform my wifely duties, I would imagine like most men, he finds a willing partner elsewhere."

"Marcy, it is all well and healthy to have an active physical relationship with your spouse and if you both like to spice things up, that is fine too, but it is not healthy for a man to force himself on you to the point of harm, especially when you are so averse to it. And no, most men are not like that. Rarely, some may take their needs outside the home on occasion, but most married men are respectful and considerate of their wife's feelings."

"He insists it is the least I can do for all he has done for me."

Anna shook her head in disgust. "He does nothing for you Marcy, other than abuse you. He extorted money from your father and disrespected your wishes, not to mention he took you away from the love of your life. You must not stand for it. I will help you and the children get away from him."

Marcy squeezed her eyes shut before she jumped from the chair and began pacing the dining room, her breath coming in short, sharp gasps. "What to do? What to do?"

"What to do? How can you even question what to do?"

Marcy leaned her forehead on the door frame and motioned downward behind her.

"I will tell you what we will do. We will go to the police and tell them your husband is a rapist and he has been abusing you and tried to violate me and likely tried to rape Fanny and ended up tossing her in the lake when she tried to fight him off."

"Oh, dear heavens, no. We cannot do that."

Anna remained seated and spoke with a calmness she did not feel. "If you do not, I will. Wait, it was you. You made the anonymous call to the police to have Joseph arrested, didn't you? Officer Oakley said it was a woman."

After one terrified glance back in Anna's direction, Marcy left the room as aggressively as she had entered.

"Marcy wait," Anna called after her, but it was too late.

~

Anna soon gave up her hunt after storming through the house, opening and closing doors to all the usual rooms Marcy would inhabit. Instead, she re-focussed her search for the children.

"Nellie, thank goodness."

The nanny and both children looked up as Anna entered the playroom. "Is everything okay?"

"No, not really. I need you to pack up the children's things and take them somewhere safe, to the Eastmans' at the lighthouse, or to Elsie at the library. Stay with them until you hear from me."

Nellie stood; her eyes wide with concern. "May I speak with you in the hallway, Mrs..... Anna?" Out of earshot of the children, Nellie got right to the point. "What is happening?"

"You need to trust me," Anna pleaded. "Mr. Campbell may have been the one to kill Fanny Burnsley. Marcy confided in me this morning and I fear she may have now run off to save having to face him or testify against him; I am not sure. She is like a scared animal that has been beaten all its life. She needs help, but I can't find her. I need to take the information she gave me to the police. So please, take the children to safety until I know Mr. Campbell will not be returning and until I know Marcy is level-headed enough to take care of her children."

"Of course, I will not let them out of my sight; you can count on me."

Anna placed her hand on Nellie's arm. "I know I can. Wish me luck."

Anna quickly scanned the downstairs rooms once more before donning her coat and boots. As she reached for her gloves, the roll-top desk against the wall opposite, drew her attention. Sitting unused in the front foyer since her arrival, the lid had always remained closed, an opaque vase centred on top of it. Anna presumed it an ornamental antique and had never thought to open the lid and scan the contents. Today the vase had be placed on the floor beneath the desk and the lid had been rolled back. She lowered her head and investigated the various slots in the back. Her previous suspicions were confirmed. The largest space in the middle held a variety of stationery and envelopes identical to those that had been delivered to her starting the morning after Ian violated her. "Why would she want to send me away? I was the only one being kind to her?"

Chapter Twenty

"Mrs. Gordon, please come in."

She stepped into the police chief's office, and clenched her hands together in front of her, unsure why they trembled. "Could I enquire as to Mr. Hendrie's condition."

"He has been released; no charges laid." He closed the door behind him and motioned to the chair in front of his desk.

"Oh, thank God." She sat down and released a pent-up breath. "He had nothing to do with any of this, I assure you. I came to tell you I have had a confession from Marcy Campbell, that is Ian Campbell's wife and I have information from my conversation with Daniel Eastman at the lighthouse yesterday. He saw Mr. Campbell on the pier with another woman and Marcy said Ian came home wet and bleeding from a violent encounter."

The police chief sat behind his desk, clasped his hands firmly and leaned forward on his desk. "We have statements from both parties. I have also spoken to Mr. Lonsdale from the bank and your lawyer Mr. Dunlop about Mr. Campbell's potentially fraudulent behaviour in relation to your husband's bequeath."

"Oh." Anna blinked back her surprise. "I did not expect them to speak with you so quickly. That is. Oh. Then I suppose you don't need me." Unsure what to do, she stood looked toward the door, then back to the officer.

"Please sit down. I do need to talk to you." He again motioned to the chair.

Relief, fear, and exhaustion overwhelmed her all at once. Tears pooled as she returned to her seat. She ran a finger under each eye and forced her composure. "I am so sorry. I don't know what has come over me."

"This is an incredible situation you have landed in since your arrival to town. There is absolutely no need to apology." He opened his top drawer, withdrew a handkerchief, and extended it toward her.

She waved it away. "Oh, no thank you. I am fine, truly."

"Mrs. Gordon, why did you lie the night we came to the cabin? You told us Mr. Hendrie arrived before eight that night, when in fact he allegedly dropped Frances Burnsley off closer to nine."

"I, that is, the question caught me off guard and I was so upset about escaping the circumstances at the Campbell household that I scarce knew what time I had arrived. I am sorry. You do believe him don't you, that he dropped Fanny off at her home."

"Yes, we do and in fact, we are not even sure it was Fanny Burnsley down at the pier with Mr. Campbell. Walter Burnsley has given us cause to question his original statement that his wife never came home. And Mr. Hendrie has held firm that he dropped Fanny off directly from work, but now you have admitted that perhaps that was not the case. I also have evidence that you attacked Mr. Campbell the night of Fanny's disappearance. Therefore, we have some discrepancy whether the injuries Mrs. Campbell witnessed, are a result of that incident or something that may or may not have happened on the pier that night."

"Oh no. No, no. She said he was scratched and bleeding from the hands and face; and he was wet and had sand on his shoes. I merely kicked him in the, that is, I… oh my." Her suddenly dry mouth prevented her from swallowing the lump in her throat. "Ah, I'm not sure—"

He dismissed her discomfort with a flick of his hand. "That aside, now that Mrs. Campbell has stepped forward with detailed information about her husband's chronic violence and his adulterous behaviour, he has become our primary suspect in the disappearance of Mrs. Burnsley. Although the police rarely become involved in such domestic matters, her description of his behaviour over the years, leads us to believe he may be deranged and prone to violence with women other than his wife."

"Oh, thank God." She sighed on her answer. "Perhaps it's not relevant, but I should also point out that someone has been sending me anonymous handwritten notes suggesting I'm not welcome in this town, and should go home, meaning, back to the UK. I did see stationery in Marcy's desk similar to the notes, but I'm at my wits end why she would send them when I have scarcely just arrived, and I've been nothing but kind to her. My next guess would be that they came from Ian himself."

"Generally, folks in Kincardine are a welcoming bunch, especially to fellow emigrants from the UK. In my experience, I have seen domestic violence affect people in various ways. Strangely, as farfetched as it may seem, Mrs. Campbell may have somehow found you a threat to her. Some women believe even a difficult marriage is better than no marriage at all. By your appearance, the Campbells' differences have come to light, come to public knowledge in fact. I assume they will divorce on the grounds of cruelty or adultery."

"Yes. I suppose you are right. What will happen to them now?"

"We have moved Mrs. Campbell into a safe home where she will stay until we find Mr. Campbell. I am concerned for your safety and that of their children as well. None of you should be staying at the Campbell home."

"The children are with their nanny. I will be staying at The Walker House until my house purchase closes. I plan to move myself and the children to my new home on Lake Road at that time. To my knowledge Ian does not know the address. I believe we will be safe there."

"I ask that you check in with me on a daily—"

A brief knock on his office door interrupted them, followed by the appearance of his assistant, Officer Oakley. "Oakley I am in conference, do you mind."

"It's urgent Sir, Mrs. Frances Burnsley is in the waiting room."

"What?!" He jumped from behind his desk. "Excuse me, Mrs. Gordon."

Anna bolted out the door behind him.

"Mrs. Burnsley, you are alive and well." His shocked expression matched all those in the room, who awaited her explanation.

"Aye, Sir." She cringed and twisted her hands in front of her, her gaze darting between the officers and Anna. "I am terribly sorry for all the confusion. It all comes down to a marital dispute between me and Mr. Burnsley. We had words and I was trying to teach him a lesson by running off for a few days."

"Confusion? We launched a potential murder investigation after your disappearance. You have some explaining to do as does Mr. Burnsley." Chief Bane snarled at her.

"If she wasn't fighting at the pier with Mr. Campbell, then who was?" Anna asked the obvious question to the room.

Chief Bane nodded. "That is a very good question and I have a mind to speak with Mrs. Campbell again to see if perhaps she is not the victim we assume her to be."

"Oh dear, no. You don't know the half of what Ian Campbell is capable of." Anna glanced to Fanny, unsure how much to reveal in front of someone who served the whole town at the diner. "Could I speak with you privately a moment, Chief?"

"Do not move. I have plenty of questions for you." He pointed a finger at Fanny. She nodded and slowly lowered herself to the bench at the front of the office. He turned to his deputy. "Tie her down if you must. I'll be right back." He motioned Anna ahead of him back into his office.

They barely sat down when she started in a rush. "You cannot doubt Marcy's statement. She has been abused in that house for years and Ian Campbell extorted his way into their lives from the get-go. I was witness to his tirades, not to mention him trying to violate me as well, which by the way is why I attacked him, strictly defending myself as best I could."

"That is irrelevant now." He waved her defence away. "And, as I mentioned previously, the police rarely involve themselves in matters of discipline between a man and his wife. If this is merely—"

"Discipline?" Anna huffed. "No, no wait. What he does to women goes far beyond the upper hand treatment some men rule over their wives. I need to explain. Marcy is not strong enough to fight him physically or emotionally as I did. He came home after some kind of quarrel with another woman on the pier and he raped his own wife. Mr. Eastman witnessed Mr. Campbell there that night and I am certain he was with someone other than Marcy."

"Well Mr. Eastman said he witnessed Mr. Campbell on the pier with someone and then heard a splash. He did not see fighting and he thought the person on the pier was Mrs. Campbell. If Mrs. Burnsley was not out there that night and Mrs. Campbell is alive and well, as you just brought up, then who would you suggest it was?"

"I daresay that is your job to figure out, but I assure you it was not Mrs. Campbell. I can vouch for her."

"Just as you vouched for Mr. Hendrie?" He tilted his head at her, his lips set in a straight line. "You were allegedly with Mr. Hendrie at the time in question. How could you vouch for what was happening in the Campbell household?"

Suddenly overcome with fear, Anna's words again came out in a tumbled rush. "Right, well, I, that is. I was at Joseph's cabin. But what I mean is I can vouch for Marcy's honesty, and I can attest to Ian Campbell's abuse and sexually deviant behaviours. You must believe me. Whatever Ian was up to on the pier that brought him home bloody and soaking wet had nothing to do with Joseph Hendrie nor Marcy Campbell. You must believe me." Her voice escalated with each statement.

He motioned downward with his hand. "Settle down, I am of the same mind, and I certainly have more questions for Mr. Campbell than Mrs. but he seems to have disappeared, and Mrs. Burnsley has reappeared. Now all I am left with is a deranged runaway, a scared wife, a confused lightkeeper, no missing person and apparently no crime."

Anna stood, shaking her head at the sudden turn of events. "Will you keep me up to date? That is, at least with relation to Mr. Campbell. There is still the matters of his disappearance and the freeze on my account. Not to mention, in the absence of a capable next-of-kin. I will need to take over care of their children until Mrs. Campbell is able to do so."

"Of course. I will be in touch in the next few days."

~

Once again Anna packed her clothes into the suitcase she had so recently unpacked. Every creak of the floor had her jumping to scan the hallway. Her mind raced with emotions, fear that Ian would return, concern for Marcy and the children, embarrassment that Chief Bane had caught her in a lie, but worst of all confusion about Joseph. Why had he not come to see her after being released from the police station? Why had she put so much faith in such a brief tumultuous relationship? Surely, she would meet someone else in town who was more stable, more trustworthy. "I do not want someone else, damn it." She scolded the empty room as she punched the closures on the case. Turning to leave, after hefting the large suitcase off her bed, she screamed when Lorna approached her doorway.

"Sorry, Miss, didnae mean to startle ye."

"I am fine Lorna, a little jumpy is all."

"Ye'll be leaving us again?"

Anna placed the suitcase down and reached for the cook's hand. "You must go as well. Mrs. Campbell has been taken into protective care and Mr. Campbell is still missing and under suspicion for a number of misdeeds."

"A nefarious greedy fool, if ever I met one."

Anna chuckled at her assessment and nodded. "Unfortunately, you are right."

"Where are the weans?"

"Safe with Nellie for now. They will come and stay with me once I close my house purchase later in the week until we can sort Marcy out."

"Thank the good Lord for yer arrival Miss Anna, I dinnae ken what might have happened had ye nae come when ye did."

"Anna!" Joseph called from the front foyer.

"Oh, deary me. I came to tell ye, yer Joey is here to see ye."

"Thank you. I will be in touch and let you know when Marcy and the children are able to return. Do you have somewhere to stay?"

Anna caught her breath as Joseph approached behind the cook. Awash with relief, longing and fear, tears pooled against her will. Their gaze locked for several seconds.

"I will leave ye two." Lorna turned to go.

"No, Lorna. I heard Anna ask if ye have a place to go."

"I will be fine Joey, never ye mind. I've a brother in Tiverton. Nae my favourite kin, but under the circumstances, I'm sure I can bade wi' his family." She dropped her head and shook it slowly as she aimed to pass Joseph.

"No need. Pack up yer belongings and I will take ye to the Hendries. Ye've ken our family for years from the kirk. Me mum's been harping for someone to help her in the kitchen, and I ken she would love to have ye. There is a team of farm hands need feeding three times a day. Ye'll have yer hands full, but they will welcome ye like kin. And whatever Ian Campbell's been paying ye, I will double it."

She perked up straight, a grin on the side of her mouth, the only emotion she showed. "I thank ye for yer generosity, Mr. Hendrie."

He chuckled. "Ye never called me anything but Joey. No need to change that now. Get on wi' ye."

He turned back to Anna and extended his arms. She gladly went to him and allowed herself the luxury of his comforting embrace. He leaned back, bringing one hand between them to tilt her face to his. He kissed her tenderly at first, then tangled his fingers in her hair and pulled her harder against him. She melted into his caresses at first but then stepped back abruptly, causing Joseph to jolt back eye's wide. "What ails ye?"

"I am only, that is, I don't know my own mind. I am so relieved you are here, but I am still unsure what is happening and who I can trust. If Fanny was not at the pier, then who was? I found the writing paper matching my mysterious notes in Marcy's desk. Has she been lying to me all along and she and Ian had another violent argument and that's all there is to this? I feel like I am in the middle of a nightmare, and I can't wake up."

"Yer overthinking."

He extended a hand to reach for her, but she retreated a step and shook her head. "No, I am not. You lied for Jamie. You lied about knowing Graham. I am certain of my physical wanting for you, and I have ached to talk to you, but I am unsure I know you as well as I think I do."

"I didnae lie—"

"You were not forthcoming. It is the same thing. I lied to the police for you and Chief Bane asked me about it. I have never been in that kind of situation before, and it was unnerving. I cannot help wondering what else you are keeping from me. And I certainly cannot trust either of the Campbells."

"What are ye saying?"

She threw her hands up and shrugged. "I don't know what I am saying. I so wanted to carry out my plans here in Kincardine, but now I'm of half a mind to go back to London. I am confused."

He shoved his hands in his pockets and stared back at her, unsure how to respond.

"I will be at The Walker House until the transaction goes through for my new home." Anna broke their silence.

"I can help. Ye can stay wi' me." His head tilted slightly to the side.

"I don't need the loan anymore. I only need some time to think things through."

"Will ye meet me at the diner after I drop Lorna off at my mum's?"

"I'll see, maybe tomorrow."

His shoulders sunk and his expression crossed between anger and pain, piercing her heart.

"I don't mean to hurt you, Joseph. I am truly glad you're okay."

Without reply, he turned, head down and walked away, without looking back.

Anna slid down the wall until she sat on the floor beside her suitcase. She pulled her legs to her chest and dropped her head to her knees. "What have I done?"

Chapter Twenty-One

Once her eyes adjusted to the darkness of the diner, Anna found Joseph eating at a booth. "Mind if I join you for breakfast?"

He gestured to the empty bench across from him. "Please do."

Anna shook her head when Fanny approached. "I can't believe you are here. That is, I'm glad you're alive and well, but—"

"I'm sorry, Mrs. Gordon."

"Call me Anna, I lied to police for you. You best be using my first name."

"I'm so sorry to have put ye both through so much." She wiggled into the booth beside Anna, startling her. "Ye see, I'm in love wi' yer Jamie and we have promised ourselves to each other."

"Yer a married woman, Fanny. Ye don't go promising yerselves after a few nights of passion." Joseph stated the obvious then continued to spear his eggs with toast.

"Shhh. 'Twas the best four days of my life." She gazed off dreamily, a beaming smile on her face.

"I wilnae shush. Ye and Jamie got me in enough of a fix. Derek locked me in the cells while ye were out making love and half the town thinks I'm the one ye have a fancy for."

His loud voice drew her back to reality and she had the audacity to giggle at his recap. "I'm sorry Joey. Jamie didn't want ye to have to lie for him. If it makes ye feel any better, I convinced him nae to tell ye we were running off. We never would have stayed away so long had we kent ye were in the lockup."

"Mmm hmmm."

"Ye ken what real love is? I cannae stay wi' that horrid Walter." She glanced between Joseph and Anna seeking sympathy.

Joseph looked to Anna before he replied. "Aye, I ken love well enough, but ye best be discussing things wi' yer Walter before ye go promising yerself to another man."

She pushed herself up from the booth, took his empty plate, leaned over, and kissed him on the cheek. "Luv ye, Joey."

He chuckled despite his sour mood. "Cheekie lass, get off wi' ye. Yer customers are waiting on their breaky."

He turned to Anna and reached for her hands. She let him hold them. "So, they were together after all." She smirked.

"Aye, Fanny fought wi' Walter and ran off to her sister's that night. She used their truck to get Jamie in the morning knowing everyone would believe he had gone off to work, myself included. They stayed in their love making loft. 'Tis a cabin similar to mine off the highway near Tiverton."

"And you did not think to look there?"

He shook his head. "Miss Jackson said he left for work. I thought he must have used her phone to ask Steve to pick him up and he was in Tobermory wi' the men."

"Well timed that your men were on their way out of town."

"Ill timed more like. See what I mean about this small town?" She nodded and he continued. "Thanks to some well-placed doubts from Reg and Walter's lying gossip, even though Fanny is alive and well, the whole town, including ye, it appears, questions my integrity."

She shook her head, unable to address his accusation, still stunned by Fanny's reappearance. "If Fanny was off on a tryst with Jamie, then who was at the pier?"

"I spoke to Derek this morning. Mr. Eastman insisted 'twas Ian Campbell, but he didnae ken who was wi' him. He thought 'twas Marcy until Fanny went missing, but now she's back, he is saying he is nae even sure 'twas Ian."

They were silent while Fanny put Anna's plate down and refilled both coffee cups.

"And why does Jamie get to lie to you about Fanny's whereabouts while you went to jail to protect him? I thought you had the brother code. Does it not work both ways?"

Joseph chuckled. "Aye it does. Like Fanny said, he never would have left if he kent what was happening. They took off before he heard anything about all the police business. Then he was so busy making love wi' his woman, he never came out of the cabin. He has apologized many times for it."

Silence hung awkwardly between them as Anna pushed her food around her plate. "I believed you," she finally said.

"It does nae seem like it, ye didnae even enquire when I was locked up. I poured out my heart at the cabin, we made love many times and I kent ye felt something too." His voice was hushed, and his eyes pleaded for a comforting response.

She hesitated, then looked down at her lap before she reached to hold his hand. He yanked it away. "Don't be stubborn. I had no way to enquire, and I was in the middle of, that is, the things Marcy said." She stopped and shook her head at the memory. "My main concern had to be for the children. I have not even had the chance to tell you about all that, nor the bank issues."

"I'm sorry, yer right. The bairns are the main concern." He pinched his lips in a straight line and wrapped his hands tightly around his coffee mug.

"Why are you angry? I don't understand."

He stared into his coffee as if weighing his answer. "Are ye safe?" he asked instead.

"They have not found Ian, but I am safe at The Walker House until my purchase closes this week. Ian doesn't know the new house and I doubt anyone will tell him my address now that rumors have started about him. The children will stay with me as next of kin since Marcy's brother, Everett is unable, well, unwilling more like. Nellie offered to help as well if I need it, but I don't think I will."

He stood, tossed coins on the table, then stared at Anna for a brief few seconds. "I will see ye around town then."

"But wait, I have so much to tell you." She reached her hand to his arm.

He glanced down where she held him, shook his head, and turned to leave, taking a piece of her heart with him.

Chapter Twenty-Two

Anna swelled with pride the day she took sole possession of her new house. The police had accompanied Nellie and Anna to the Campbells to retrieve the remainder of all their personal belongings, almost filling the truck Anna had hired for the move. One of the two upstairs bedrooms in her new house, had a single bed and a small dresser for each of the children, while the slightly larger bedroom had a double bed, dresser and an oversized chair that faced the floor to ceiling window looking out over the water. The two women along with the children rearranged furnishings and their few household items in the kitchen and living space downstairs. They cleaned the whole house until they were comfortably exhausted. Although Clara and Thomas cried when they had to say goodbye to their nanny, they were thrilled to be reunited with their aunt. No one spoke of Marcy or Ian Campbell.

Three days later Lorna arrived with baskets of baked goods, and jarred preserves. "Come in, come in. Children, look who's here."

They ran to their beloved cook and wrapped themselves around her generous skirts. "Aye, my wee bairns, I missed ye too. I brought ye some treats."

"Can you come in for a visit? I'll put on some tea."

"I would love to bade for tea. Thank ye."

The children talked non-stop to Lorna entertaining her with stories of their moving adventures from place to place, while Anna arranged the goodies on the plate and made tea.

After Anna placed the plate on the kitchen table, Lorna handed her a long package wrapped in brown paper and tied with a string. "I brought ye this."

"Ouuu, what is it? I love surprises." Anna smiled at the children and took her own seat at the table to unwrap the package.

She unsuccessfully tried to swallow the lump in her throat. Her tears flowed as she ran her fingers over the beautifully carved, gently sanded wooden sign. A chain pulled taught across the top screwed into each end to allow fastening it to her front door. Carved and burned into the front in beautiful English scroll were the words

Castle Gordon Fine Jewellery.

"From yer Joey," Lorna said quietly.

Anna nodded, unable to speak through her tears.

"He misses ye too." She reached to hug Anna, then turned to the children. "Clara, Thomas, can ye each take a biscuit into the front room and give me a minute wi' yer auntie."

Anna swiped at her face with the napkin from the tea tray. "I am so emotional these days. The children are a God send and I love them like my own. But I wish I had someone to share all my excitement and my fears."

"That someone should be yer Joey." She patted Anna's hand.

"I do miss him Lorna, but he seemed so angry. He walked away from me. I wasn't sure he even wanted to see me again."

"He's a stubborn Scot like the rest of us, yerself included it would seem. I doubt he will make the first move. If ye cannae trust him, he feels unworthy of yer love."

"I don't know who to trust anymore. I pictured things much differently when I sailed overseas after the war. I had no idea what I was walking into. I expected much more from Graham's family and then—"

"Joey Hendrie is nae like them? I ken ye see that as will as I do."

"I know that, of course. Ian Campbell is evil, and Joseph Hendrie is, well, he is incredible." She smiled thinking of him. "Can you tell him for me—"

Lorna shook her finger in front of Anna. "Oh, no, ye need to talk to him yerself."

Anna chuckled. "I will soon. I will be getting a phone installed in the house in the next week and I will call the Hendrie house and ask him over. But please tell him thank you for this lovely gift. I will hang it over my door with pride."

She nodded, then stood to leave. "I will tell him ye will be in touch."

"You are such a romantic." Anna hugged her when they stood. "Thank you again for all the treats. Please come again, we are all so happy to see you."

~

Their days were busy. Anna still had no phone and had not received any updates from the police about the Campbell family, nor had any contact from Joseph. Unable to register for school without one of their parents' consent and unwilling to put them in the path of Ian Campbell should he return, the children took their lessons daily with Anna who followed the notes Nellie had written out for her. A week into their new routine, in the middle of one of their reading lessons, a knock finally came at the door.

Disappointment overcame her when Anna saw the police chief instead of Joseph. She sent the children up to their room to read to themselves, then welcomed her guest into the kitchen.

"Can I get you tea or a cold drink?"

"No thank you; please come and sit. I came because I am concerned for your safety and that of the children."

"Ian has been gone for two weeks now. Do you really think he will come back to the area?" Anna sat at the kitchen table across from the officer.

"We do not believe he would have any way of knowing, but there is now a warrant out for his arrest."

Anna's breath hitched. "Do you have new information? Is it the bank fraud? Is Marcy safe?"

He nodded to each of her questions. "Given what we now know and having received Mrs. Campbell's detailed statement of repeated violence, we agree with her assessment that he may try to kill her if he returns, so we have advised her to remain where she is until we find him."

"If you speak to her, please let her know the children are safe."

"Gladly, thank you. So, what I came to tell you is, it was Miriam Cooper who was pushed from the pier into the frigid water and left for dead."

"Why does that name sound familiar?" Anna squinted.

"Have you been to the Port Albert Hotel?"

Her eyes widened with recognition, and she nodded. "Right, Miriam. She served us lunch a few weeks back. Is she alive?"

"Yes, she will be fine. We have reason to believe Ian Campbell was involved with her in a liquor or, I should say, bootlegging arrangement. The account at the bank was set up in your name long before you arrived. He made regular withdrawals on the dates the liquor ran into Port Albert and then large deposits a few days later. People think we can't find out about smuggling transactions if they hide them in cash or barter or deposit into another person's name, but truly, we have always known about the liquor run, we just turn the other cheek, pick the important battles if you know what I mean."

"Yes, yes, I understand. How did you find out about Ian's involvement with Miriam?"

"It took a while and the town gossip pointing us at the Burnsleys' domestic issues and Joseph Hendrie's involvement threw us off. Unfortunately, Kincardine Township does not share missing persons' information with the police in Ashfield, Colborne, Wawanosh Township. We didn't hear anything about Miriam's story until just yesterday. She had been reported missing and then found unconscious outside of town over a week ago. She only recovered enough to make a statement as of yesterday. Their police came to me with a warrant for Ian Campbell. "

"What happened?"

"Ian and Miriam fought that night on the pier almost a fortnight gone now. She refused to give him the money from the liquor run, said she was keeping it and leaving town. She did her best to fight him off, hence the scratches on his hands and his face and his bloodied shirt. She took a nasty blow to the head, and he threw her in the lake. She almost pulled him in with her, but he landed on the rocks and pulled himself out. He left her for dead. One of the shoremen saw the whole thing and pulled her to safety from the other side of the pier. A lot of the shipyard workers have a bit of a past themselves, so I imagine he had no mind to come to police, nor involve himself in what he likely thought was a couple arguing."

Anna shook her head slowly. "Is she okay?"

"She will be. She trudged her way back toward Port Albert on foot if you can imagine."

"That's got to be twenty miles."

"Yes, over that. She walked for days, and she almost froze to death. Lost a few toes as it were to frostbite."

"Dear God. Why did she not come to you that night and turn Ian in to police?"

"It would be hard to explain their connection without incriminating herself in the liquor distribution, so she set out on foot thinking she could just leave town and all their dealings behind her. I don't think she cared about having him charged, she just wanted to be rid of him."

"I can appreciate that." Anna nodded.

"The owner of the Port Albert Hotel reported her missing, but we were not aware. As I said, she was found unconscious in a ditch, by one of the locals, still several miles from the inn. She was incoherent, suffering from the cold temperatures and lack of food. They nursed her back to health; they love her like family at the hotel. In any event, the local police finally got her story and came to me with a warrant for Ian Campbell's arrest for attempted murder along with a number of other sundry charges."

"The poor woman. She's lucky to be alive," Anna said.

"Thank goodness she is, or we would not have anything on Mr. Campbell. After Fanny reappeared and since Ian vanished after you served him with the court papers, we were thinking he fled simply to avoid being caught with the liquor money. We had no idea he was involved this deeply."

"How so?"

"When we spoke to Miriam, we found out not only was he behind the bootlegging of the liquor, but he had a, um side business relationship if you know what I mean." The officer winced.

"He paid her for sex."

He took a deep breath and blew it out slowly, then glanced briefly out the window before he turned back to Anna, "I'm dreadfully sorry to bring up such a topic in mixed company, but in a nutshell, yes, although often other women or men were involved. More of a mistress of sorts although she admitted he liked to pay extra for an audience and enjoyed taking unnatural liberties shall we say."

"I can't say I'm surprised. Will he be charged?" Anna shook her head.

"Those kinds of charges are hard to make stick in the absence of witnesses, and since she accepted his money, well." The officer shrugged. "That aside, once all the soldier trainees had left, and the Royal Air Force navigation school dismantled, Miriam was ready to move on. He insisted she stay and run liquor for him and threatened to turn her in to police as a bootlegger and a prostitute if she didn't. She in turn tried to blackmail him, threatening to disclose their affair to his wife and his sexual preferences to the community."

"He said her name."

"Pardon me?" Chief Bane tipped his head.

"Marcy said when he returned wet and scratched, he raped her and said another name as he, ah, finished." Anna rolled her eyes and blushed.

"Are you comfortable speaking of such details?" He reached in his pocket for a notepad and a pencil.

She waved off his concern. "I am fine, it's Marcy's story which I understood she passed on to you already."

"Only that he came home wet and bleeding from an apparent fight. The rest of her accusations were with respect to previous incidents."

"Well, she told me the bit about him being wet and bleeding, but also that he then forced himself on her which he had done before and that he often called out another name. That night in particular, she was sobbing, and she thought he said ma'am, but he must have said Miriam."

He shook his head but noted her statement on the small pad. "Well thank you for that additional information and again, my apologies for the necessity of such an inappropriate conversation."

"No offense truly. I only want to see Mr. Campbell brought to justice."

"We will have plenty to charge him and detain him, now that Miriam has confessed, but Mrs. Campbell's claims will add to it. Mr. Lonsdale has also been co-operative in releasing bank account details and assured us neither you nor Mr. Hendrie had any connection, despite him agreeing to co-sign the loan with you."

"I can explain all that and how I came into the bulk of my husband's money."

"That will not be necessary, and your finances are none of my business. You have a fine man in Mr. Hendrie if you are a couple or even just friends. He is to be trusted which we knew all along. Unfortunately, circumstances prevailed that required we question him. Some people in the community can be quite pressing if they feel we are not doing our job if you catch my meaning."

"Thank you for saying that. I believe Joseph and I are still friends, but no, we are not a couple. I own this house and soon to be Castle Gordon Jewellery independently and the children are safe here with me as long as they need to be."

"That is what concerns me. I know you are a self reliant woman and I respect that, but with Mr. Campbell on the loose, I fear for your safety out here all alone. If there is any chance Mr. Hendrie could be convinced to stay with you, at least until we find Mr. Campbell, I would feel you were much better protected. I cannot be everywhere to protect everyone at the same time." He tilted his head, expectant of a reply.

Anna shivered but forced a confident smile. "I appreciate your concern, but I do not need a man's protection. I have considered the dangers myself if Ian were to seek me out. I keep the doors and windows locked when we retire. I cannot kennel the children all day. We need to go out and about and to town for food and the library and so on. I am trying to educate them myself until Ian is detained, and I can get

Marcy's consent to enroll them in school; and I am in the midst of setting up my business."

"I understand all that, and I believe Ian has likely left town if he knows what is good for him, but there is still a chance he may be unaware of what he is up against and may resurface, especially if he finds the whereabouts of his children."

"He has never cared much for his children, trust me. Audrey Nelson a few doors down has a telephone. I am expecting installation of one myself very soon. We will call your office if there are any sightings of him."

"That is the best we can do then. Please keep me up to date."

"And you also. Thank you for stopping by."

That night once the children were upstairs sleeping, Anna sat reading in her living room, the only sound the crackling of the fire in her fireplace. She tipped her head against the high back of the chair and felt herself nodding off. A crash outside startled her abruptly awake.

Chapter Twenty-Three

Anna jumped from her seat, her book dropping to the floor with a thud. Suddenly dizzy as she bent to retrieve it, she held the back of the chair until she regained her strength. "What is wrong with me?" She pulled the cord on the table lamp, leaving the room in darkness, to better see outside. Her heart beating rapidly, barely tamping down nausea, she peered through the curtain opening, and sighed with relief at the sight of two coyotes nosing through the wood pile to find their next feast.

"Good doggies; thanks for keeping the mice away." She chuckled as she walked to the washroom. Wiping her face with a cool cloth, she pulled it down her neck next and berated her drawn reflection in the bathroom mirror. "You told everyone you are independent and capable. You need to stop losing sleep over Joseph Hendrie and get on with your own life." She trudged to her bed and slept soundly until the children came pouncing on her bed with the first light.

~

Her visit with Detective Bane the week before and random noises of animals or blustery weather had Anna jumpier than she liked. Despite frazzled nerves and insomnia causing her nausea and exhaustion, Anna kept to routine with the children and made every effort to dismiss her yearning for Joseph. Not only was the officer correct, she would feel safer with him nearby, but she longed for his touch, his laughter at her quirks, and mostly his companionship to discuss all the challenges she faced. Her smile for the children was sincere but in the confines of her lonely nights of solitude, she still pondered how to mend things with Joseph or if she should even try.

Saturday morning came; the children took a break from lessons, so Anna allowed herself a break from her chores and business set-up as well. The sky was clear and the sun warm for late November. Thomas drew Anna's attention by pulling on her hat string then pointing down the beach. "Auntie Anna." He crawled onto her lap but kept his focus on the man walking toward them.

Clara stood proudly. "That's Auntie Anna's friend, Joseph Hendrie." She waved her arm wildly in welcome.

As he approached, Anna stood holding Thomas in front of her. She appeared more reluctant than her welcoming niece. "How have you been?"

"I didnae ken if ye'd welcome the company after I was so stubborn." He tipped his head to the back of her house. "It looks like a lovely home."

"A lot has happened in the last few weeks, but yes, I managed to close the deal and get moved in, along with my two favourite house guests." She smiled down at the children.

"Hello Miss Clara, lovely to see ye again." He smiled at the beaming girl and received a shy "hello" in return. Next, he crouched and extended his hand forward. "Ye must be Thomas. I'm Joe."

Thomas shook Joseph's hand enthusiastically and smiled in return. "I'm six."

"A strapping young man wi' a strong grip; pleasure to meet ye Master Thomas."

He stood and turned a tortured gaze at Anna. "Mind if I visit a while? I would like to hear how ye have been."

Warmth overtook her at the sight of him, all her misgivings instantly forgotten. *Stay for the rest of your life if you like.* "Of course, please join us. We have been digging tunnels and making forts out of rock piles."

"I'm an expert at that." He sat on the edge of Anna's blanket and immediately joined fort making.

"Children, did you know Joseph used to live in a castle in Scotland."

"Well, maybe nae a big castle the like ye see in yer books, but 'twas a big stone building, wi' a courtyard and a turret and water around the outside."

"You had a moat?!" Thomas glared with worship at their new friend.

"Did you have horses too?" Clara asked.

"Aye, we had a huge barn wi' some of the most beautiful horses ever to roam the earth."

"Whooa," Clara exclaimed on long breath.

"I have horses nae far from here. I would be happy to take ye all riding one day if yer auntie says its okay."

"Can we, can we?" Both children chimed excitedly.

She smiled and nodded at their excitement. "Of course, you may."

"Joseph, I—"

"I'm sorry, Anna—"

"Ye go first," he said. "Tell me how ye managed to pull this off." He waved his hand in the direction of the house. "I found out Mr. Lonsdale pulled our joint loan. He heard from me about it, but I dinnae imagine that helped ye when ye needed it."

"Turns out I did not need it. You are not going to believe it, but Graham had hidden away my most precious gems and a hefty portion of our liquidated funds in my trunk before he even enlisted. When I read his first note, you know the one that Jamie delivered, Graham had said something about saving my favourites."

Joseph nodded. "And?"

"And I thought he meant the few jewellery pieces I found in the box in the trunk. But he kept some of my best raw stones and creations from my parents' business along with a couple of my favourite books and a clump of cash hidden. If I had not tossed my suitcase across the room in anger, the day they arrested you, the day Mr. Lonsdale denied the loan; well, I may never have found it or certainly not found it in time to purchase the house. The trust fund Ian had locked up, is just a fraction of what we had liquidated. I had my own means all along."

"Mr. Lonsdale said something about the account being frozen. He would nae give me any details though. Of course, he assumed we were no longer a couple."

"Somehow, I think he assumed that all along. As you can well imagine, he now treats me like a queen."

Joseph chuckled and nodded. "No doubt."

"I'm waiting to hear about the audit, but it appears Ian was using the account to hide money from smuggling liquor. It's no wonder he was dead set against closing the account and releasing funds to me. It was a perfect cover for him, or at least he thought it was a perfect cover."

"If Ian was involved, we should have kent it would be something crooked."

"I will get the balance owed to me eventually once they have determined what came from the UK account and what came from illegal means."

"At least there is no urgency now. I suppose ye heard about Miriam?"

"Yes, Chief Bane came by last week. Terrifying ordeal for her," Anna said.

"She's safe now. And ye have yer lovely home and all on yer own as ye planned."

"Well, yes, but thank you for all you did to help me and thank you for the beautiful sign for my door."

"My pleasure, truly."

Their gaze locked and Anna ached to reach out and touch him. Instead, she turned away and looked out over the water.

"If Graham had not had the forethought that Ian may try to keep my money, I never would have closed the house. I am not sure where the children and I would have gone."

"Ye could have come to me."

She smiled, unsure how to accept his kindness after struggling endless nights over her doubts. "And how have you been?"

"No harm done. I have been keeping to myself mostly. My involvement will blow over and I will be old news soon enough. 'Tis like that in these small communities. As soon as someone needs me or my money, I will be a local hero again, and that's okay wi' me." He smiled and shrugged one shoulder.

"You never stopped being my hero, Joseph. God knows what could have happened if I hadn't met you that first night on the trail."

They both focused on the children navigating the large rocks in their mittened hands while they filled their pails with water for their moat.

"Anna, look at me," he requested quietly.

She fixed her gaze on his once again. He touched her face, and she leaned her cheek into his hand.

"I missed you," she said.

"I came to order a ring. I want blue stones the colour of yer eyes. I dream about them every night. They remind me of the ocean off the Isle of Skye, one of my favourite places in the world. And I want ye to wear my ring because being wi' ye has become my new favourite place in the world." He turned himself around from sitting to kneeling in front of her, holding her gloved fingers in his hands. "No pretending for the bank, no hiding from the locals. I want us to be married for real, mo chridhe. I want to love ye for the rest of my days. Will ye have me Anna Castle Gordon?"

"You are my heart as well." She wiped a tear with the back of her hand before he stood and pulled her up to him. "What took you so long?"

Pain shot through her chest when he crushed her to him, the first embrace she had experienced since she had last been with him. The realization of the cause of the tenderness in her breasts had her mind spinning with dates and her heart racing with emotion. He stepped back and held her at arm's length. "What is it mo ghràdh; have I hurt ye?"

"I am… that is… I did not think I could… I think we are," she stammered then backed away and retched in the bushes.

His eyes wide with fear, he rubbed her back until she was able to stand firmly in front of him once again.

"Auntie Anna, are you okay?" Clara asked as both children stood by, frozen with concern, pails held tightly at their sides.

"Why did she cough into the bush?" Thomas asked.

"Aye, Auntie Anna, are ye okay? And why did ye cough into the bush?" Joseph enunciated slowly as he mimicked the children's concerns.

She glanced up at him, a smile growing, her hand gently rubbing across her belly. "I believe you may be getting more than you bargained for in your proposal. Does the offer still stand?"

His eyes enlarged with realization. He glanced down at her belly, then over to the children who now wore puzzled expressions, then back to lock eyes with Anna. "Are ye saying what I think yer saying?"

Her brow raised and she smiled up at him. "I believe I am."

"Woohoo!" He threw his arms up in the air. "I'm going to be a da!" He crushed his lips on hers and she kissed him back amidst her laughter.

"Ooou kissy, kissy." Thomas giggled.

Clara smacked his arm causing the water in his bucket to slosh onto his leg. "Hush, Thomas."

"Are ye laughing at me young man?" Joseph side glanced the boy.

Thomas dropped his bucket, his eyes wide, nervous at first.

Snatching Thomas by the waist, Joseph stretched his arms up and held the boy high in the air, then tickled his sides until he giggled with excitement.

Clara stood speechless staring in awe at the friendly interaction between Thomas and Joseph before turning to her aunt. "Did he propose marriage to you?"

"Yes, I believe he did." Anna swiped a tear that threatened to fall.

Clara's mouth fell open drawing a chuckle from Anna. She ruffled the girl's hair and decided to save the remaining news until she had time to sit with the children and answer the technical questions that were bound to arise.

"Make sure he doesn't throw Thomas in the cold lake. I will go make us some hot chocolate and a plate of treats. We shall have a celebration feast inside by the fire. I am getting cold and now that Thomas has slopped his bucket of water on his pants, we best go in before they freeze onto him."

Anna was over the moon, her grin beaming from ear to ear. Humming to herself, she gently rubbed her hand across her belly. *Could it be true?* "I think I need to pinch myself." She giggled as she skipped into the kitchen from the back entrance then froze in her tracks. Her heartbeat doubled time and her mind raced with her options to flee and protect the children.

Ian Campbell stood opposite her just inside the front door of the house. Apart from his very presence, Ian's disheveled appearance was the biggest shock. Given his unshaven face, hair clearly in need of wash and wrinkled layers of clothing, Anna wondered if he had been on foot in the weeks since his disappearance. "Where have you been and how did you find me?" She fought for control in her voice despite her terror and disgust.

He ignored her questions and raised a gun with an unsteady hand. "You ruined me with your blasted lawsuit. You brought an investigation into my accounts and drew attention to my private dealings. You ruined my life and now you are going to pay."

Even with the generous space between them, his offensive body odor filled the room. She raised one hand to her face to fight back the sudden wave of nausea and held the other in front of her in defence. "I only wanted what was mine Ian. We can sort this out."

"It's too late. You have the police on me, and I have lost my position at the bank as well as the respect of everyone in town." He took a full step into the kitchen, toward her.

"I had nothing to do with that."

His gaze darted the room, then he jumped and spun back scanning the living room.

Anna took the opportunity to glance quickly behind her. From the corner of her vision, she glimpsed Clara running toward the house. She backed herself to the window to block Ian's view of the child and prayed Clara would notice her hand waving her off.

"I will come with you, just leave the children alone," Anna said.

"I do not care about the damn children. They are with their delusional mother and that is where they can stay."

Anna was pinned against the window as Ian took another step into the kitchen. Outside, Clara stopped in her tracks at Anna's warning. Crouching below the windowsill, she crawled on her knees, peered around the open curtain, and gasped at the sight of her father holding a gun.

Slithering to the edge of the patio, she bolted full speed back to the beach, then cowered behind Joseph and pulled on his sleeve.

"What is it Clara?" He smiled down at her.

"Papa," she whispered and pointed to the house. "He has Anna."

"Watch yer brother," he demanded before charging to the house.

Joseph's military training served him well as he crept unnoticed through the back entrance, hiding behind the pantry door that allowed him a clear view to the Ian Campbell side of the standoff. His focus jumped instantly to what he recognized as a British issue Smith and Wesson military revolver, now aimed directly at his fiancé of five minutes. Joseph's reaction escalated from anger to sheer terror of losing Anna now that he finally got her back in his life. Out of her view, he had no way to gauge Anna's exact location nor her response to the intrusion.

Striding into the kitchen, appearing more confident than he felt, Joseph quickly scanned the room and placed himself between the two in just a few steps. "Drop it Campbell before someone gets hurt."

Squinting displeasure quickly replaced Ian's initial shock at the intrusion. "She is mine; the money is all mine. Marcy has been dealt with and Anna is coming with me. Get out of the way Joseph Hendrie. You will soon be in jail for two murders and there is nothing you can do about it."

Anna gasped, drawing Ian's attention back on her once again. "What do you mean Marcy has been dealt with?"

"Neither here nor there." Ian flicked his gun haphazardly between his two hostages.

"Anna, step outside," Joseph spoke quietly but his command was clear.

"She will not leave, or I will shoot you both."

One step back brought Joseph close enough to act as a body shield. Anna clutched his shirt with both hands and momentarily dropped her forehead to his back. "Dear God," she whispered.

He tapped the side of her leg in reassurance.

"Ye have no way to come out of this clean, Campbell. Drop the gun before ye cause yerself more jail time."

Joseph made tiny shifts of his feet, creeping painfully slowly toward the pantry door, bringing Anna along with him.

"Do not move another inch," Ian said through clenched teeth.

The front door sprung open with a loud bang against the inside wall, drawing Ian's attention and allowing Joseph mere seconds to shove Anna through the pantry door before he leapt forward on top of their assailant.

The gun fired, Anna screamed and dashed back into the room. Chief of Police Bane entered the room from the front simultaneously. Both Ian and Joseph lay motionless, blood trickling along the floor beside them.

Chapter Twenty-Four

"Ian Campbell, you are under arrest, get up."

Anna bolted across the room and drew Joseph off Ian.

Joseph's eyes closed as Anna rolled him over, a groan escaping his mouth as she lay him gently on his back. "Joseph," she whispered through her tears.

"I'm okay." His jaw clamped tightly as he attempted to sit up and reach the wound in his upper thigh.

Anna pulled his arm then knelt behind him to support his upright position. She ran her fingers through his hair and kissed the side of his face. "Dear God, please be okay."

He reached back to pat her hand. "I'm well, mo ghràdh. We will be fine."

"Get back," the officer yelled.

Anna glanced up a second too late to see Ian's gun already raised a second time.

"Drop it." The police chief did not wait for Ian to adhere. He took aim and fired; the shot intended to hinder, merely grazed Ian.

He screamed and clutched his bleeding shoulder.

Despite his injury, the officer dragged Ian up off the floor, kicked his gun to the side of the room and slapped handcuffs on him. "Do not move," he demanded.

"I'm bleeding, I need a medic," Ian whined.

"It's a surface wound. I will have someone dress it once you are locked in a cell."

He returned seconds after locking Ian in the cruiser. "I will need information about what happened here."

Anna glanced up at him, shaken at his request. "He held a gun on both of us. All you need to know right now is that Joseph has been shot, and he legitimately needs a medic. Your report is the least of our concern."

"I will stitch it myself. 'Tis but a graze, the bullet went clean past the skin. Get me a towel to tie off the wound and I will drive back to my cabin to stitch it," he said to Anna.

Officer Bane crouched down in front of him as Anna jumped to do his bidding.

"Where are the bairns?" Joseph asked.

Anna stopped her search for clean towels, spun too quickly then had to hold herself against the counter until the room stopped spinning. "Oh, dear God, Clara, Thomas, do not let them see their da in the police car."

"We already saw what he has done," Clara spoke shyly as she came from behind the pantry door, holding the hand of their neighbour, Mrs. Nelson.

Mrs. Nelson gasped at the scene, let go of the children and covered her mouth with both hands.

"Are you Clara?" Chief Bane asked.

She nodded. Both children ran to Anna and clutched her legs. She threw several tea towels to the officer who crouched to help Joseph tie off the wound. "The child called the station, identified herself and said her Auntie Anna was being held at gunpoint. Thank goodness I was at my desk and just minutes away. You can credit her with saving your life, Mrs. Gordon."

Anna crouched down and pulled both children to her. "Oh, Clara, you are such a brave girl. How did you ever—"

"I helped," Thomas piped in.

"Of course, you did," Anna ruffled his hair and kissed them both.

"Mama taught me how to call the police station in case papa ever hurt her. You told me about Mrs. Nelson's phone when you explained how ours would work once it got installed."

The officer shook his head at the child's confession. "Mr. Campbell has some explaining to do and he will not be leaving a jail cell for a very long time!"

Anna stood, glared at the officer, cleared her throat, and nodded down to the children.

"Oh, goodness, I have said the wrong thing. I am so sorry, Ma'am, children. Joe, are you sure I cannot get you an ambulance?" Chief Bane asked redirecting his awkward exchange.

"I will be fine wi' Anna's help. We will manage." He inched himself back and leaned his head against the kitchen cupboard.

"Ian also said Marcy is out of the way; he may have done her some harm," Anna said.

Chief Bane shook his head. "Marcy is safe in a guarded home. The only one aware of her accommodation is her brother, who has visited her regularly."

"And you don't suppose Ian has been in contact with his brother-in-law? They have been known to scheme against Marcy in the past."

The officer's brow knit. "I hadn't realized they were so close. I will keep that in mind when I question Mr. Campbell." He lowered his gaze and smiled at the children. "Thank you, Miss Clara and Master Thomas, for your quick action, and Ma'am thank you for assisting the children. I will be back to speak with all of you." The officer tipped his hat to Mrs. Nelson, and she nodded slightly in return.

"We will get your Mama the help she needs so you can get back with her soon. In the meantime, you will be safe here with me." Anna smiled at Joseph over the children's head, and he winked back despite his pain. "You will be safe here with Joseph and me."

~

With Ian behind bars, they all relaxed. As a newly instilled teacher at the Kincardine Central School, Nellie was able to advocate on behalf of the children to have them registered with a next-of-kin signature. Following the first day of nervous tears, both Clara and Thomas came home bursting with stories of their accomplishments and acceptance. They were excited to make friends and visibly calmer and more animated, which enthusiasm may have been due in part to the regular presence of Joseph and the renewed happiness of their aunt.

News of Castle Gordon Fine Jewellery spread quickly through town. With the children enrolled in school and Christmas only a few weeks away, Anna spent many hours a day in her workshop filling special orders and crafting new designs. The Saturday before Christmas week, Clara asked to join her aunt in the workshop. "Having you here reminds me of the days I worked alongside my da at Hatton Garden."

The girl hugged her aunt, bringing tears to her eyes. "I miss them so much."

"Will you teach me?" Clara clasped her hands together and held them under her chin as she gazed hopefully at her aunt.

"I would love to. Pull up that stool."

Clara knelt on the stool and leaned closely over Anna's work bench. "What are you making?"

"I'm in the midst of a few projects I've promised townsfolk for Christmas presents, but this—" She held up a small sterling silver ring with a large oval blue stone in the centre and two smaller white stones on either side.

"That's beautiful."

"Our Joseph requisitioned this one." She grinned at the girl.

"Is that your engagement ring?" Clara's mouth dropped open.

Anna nodded. "It is indeed. He wanted a stone the same blue as my eyes. He said the colour reminds him of the ocean off the coast of the Isle of Skye."

"Our lake isn't that dark. Is that a sapphire like you told me before?"

"Oh, see, you're learning the trade already. And yes, sapphires are similar to this colour. But this dark blue stone is called a kyanite. The name kyanite is from the Greek word 'kyanos' which means blue. Although strangely there are no kyanites in Greece. This one came from Switzerland. And the stones on either side are diamonds."

Clara nodded her appreciation and crawled closer leaning her forearms on the workbench. Anna instinctively reached behind the child and pulled the stool closer.

"I am to have this to Joseph by next Friday. Nellie is coming to stay with you and Thomas. Joseph is taking me out to dinner, and I expect he will come up with some grand gesture to propose once again."

"How romantic," Clara whispered, never taking her eyes from the ring.

～

Friday came and following a lovely candlelight dinner together in town, Joseph took Anna's hand and walked with her outside the back of her house to the edge of the lake. Under the stars of the darkest night of the winter solstice in the same spot on the beach where he first proposed, Joseph once again dropped to one knee and placed the stunning blue kyanite ring on her left hand.

"My mum used to say a blessing on the winter solstice. I can't remember exactly, but something about finding peace in the promise of more light; that the cycle of nature brings faith to yer soul. She told us to rejoice in the darkness, in the silence find rest, for the lighter days that followed would be abundantly blessed."

"That's beautiful." She smiled lovingly and held his hand tightly.

"Well, it was when she recited it properly. Anna, ye bring faith to my soul and light to my heart at the darkest of times. We had a rough start, but I have grown to love ye like no other. It only seems proper that on this dark day, I ask ye to bring light to the rest of my life by becoming my wife. Will ye have me, mo ghràdh?"

She pulled his hands and brought him to stand up with her. "It is a perfect day to propose and a wonderful idea to put the darkness behind us and look forward to lighter days ahead together. I love you too, Joseph and I would be honoured to be your wife."

He reached both hands around her waist and pulled her to him, crushing his lips down on hers. She left the bedroom drapes open that night so they could see the stars as they made love slowly and passionately.

Having slept late, Anna rushed around the kitchen table clearing the breakfast plates. "I'm sorry children, I have so many orders to finish today with Christmas only a few days away." She turned to Joseph. "Shall I see if Nellie is available to come back and attend the children?"

"Nonsense. The weans and I are heading to town. We have some shopping to do ourselves." Joseph winked at Clara and Thomas, and they wiggled with excitement.

~

With only three days until Christmas, Anna wondered if she had bit off more than she could chew by accepting every order that came to her since opening just weeks before. Focused and trying not to rush, she gasped and turned abruptly when the bell above her workshop door startled her from her intricate work. Anna berated herself silently for forgetting to lock the door after Joseph left.

Despite his slight stature Everett filled the doorway, his angered expression immediately stirring Anna's apprehension. She cleared her throat and forced a smile. "Oh, Everett what a pleasant surprise. Is Marcy well?"

He took one step inside, stood silently and stared at her.

"I'm afraid I am dreadfully busy. What brings you here today?"

"That's been the question all along, hasn't it?"

"I don't understand." Anna's brow knit.

"You. I'm talking about you. What are you doing here?"

"I live here. I bought this house." Suddenly overcome with alarm, she reached slowly to her workbench as she stood and wrapped her hand over needle nose plyers, the only sharp object in sight.

"Not here." He waved his hands about the room and took another step toward her. "I mean, what are you doing in Kincardine? Why didn't you stay where you belonged in England or Scotland or wherever your kin are?"

Previously an entryway for boots and coats, Anna's workshop was small, with her workbench against one wall, and a long dresser behind her to hold her tools. The door between the house and the front room stayed open to provide her heat when she worked. Joseph was in the process of building a small reception counter to keep customers on one side and her work and the entrance to the house on the other, while she wrote down orders or showed her creations. She wished she had the benefit of that countertop now to distance herself from Everett. "My only kin are here, Graham's family, your sister's family is all I had left. Although that shall not be the case going forward."

"War widows are not welcome here."

She pulled herself tall and discreetly scooped the plyers into the pocket of her coveralls. "Judging by the notes Marcy sent me, I believe you and she seem to be of the same opinion although I'm lost to understand why."

"Marcy can't read nor write. I delivered the notes to the house."

Anna blinked back in surprise, instantly questioning if she had ever seen Marcy reading. "Why would you do such a thing?"

"We don't need more of your type."

"My type? Again, I don't understand." Anna took a side-step toward the door that connected her to the house.

"People ridicule misfits and foreigners like you behind their backs; no one can be trusted." His lip curled in a snarl.

"I'm not sure I believe that. Perhaps Joseph's friend Nancy made a comment or maybe her mother. But otherwise, the people of Kincardine and Tiverton have been most welcoming."

"You are a fool to believe their sincerity."

"People are relocating all over the world now that the war is over. Many were left with no one when loved ones were killed. That aside, I'm staying, and I am currently very busy at my new business with Christmas so near at hand. I would appreciate if you answered my question. Why are you here in my home?" She tipped her head and squinted at him.

"You have treated me with disdain since we met; your unwanted arrival brought misery to Ian's life and broke up a loving relationship. I'm here to avenge it." He took a step back and closed the door behind him.

Anna held up her hand. "Please, stop where you are. We can discuss this. Surely you can appreciate how I rescued Marcy. Their marriage was anything but loving. I helped her get away from that vulgar man, who I have no doubt would have killed her if left to his own devices. I am caring for their children. How can you accuse me of anything untoward? This is ridiculous."

Everett stepped toward her. "She didn't need rescuing. You have no idea what we have sacrificed for her, and now you have started gossip that will get Ian jailed for life. Marcella is awaiting transfer to the Ontario Hospital. She can't speak, nor eat, and their troubles are all because you came to town and ruined everything."

Anna retreated closer to the inside door. "We? You and Ian? What do you mean sacrificed? He lied his way into your father's graces, took her away from Domenic, the love of her life. He took money from your father and then he raped her, kept her locked from her children and poisoned her with his damn tea. Ian's aberrant behaviour ruined her life and his own, not anything I've done." Despite her racing heart, her voice remained calm as she pleaded.

Everett's head jolted back. "Is that what she told you?"

Anna mirrored his flinch. "I believe Marcy has told me the truth and I have been witness to Ian's behaviour and to their relationship, which started with marriage to a man she didn't love. No thanks to you, I should add."

"Foolish girl, she believed all these years that it was Ian who charmed Papa into the union. Who do you think told him that Marcy had been with Domenic, and that he should marry her to Ian?"

Anna gasped. "What? Why would you do such a thing to your sister? Your actions sentenced her to a life of misery at the hands of that violent man. She is much better off without him."

"She lied to you, or more likely you are making up lies. Ian is a generous and loving man." He jumped forward and gripped her arm roughly. "You are coming with me."

"No, I am not." Anna wrenched her arm free, drew the pliers from her pocket and aimed to thrust them into Everett's neck.

He dodged her attack, spun away, and pulled a revolver from his coat pocket. Anna screamed, shocked by his strength and his swift movements. She scrambled for the inside door. He overtook her, grabbed her around the neck and pointed the gun directly at her head.

"I tried to get you to leave town quietly, but you are too high and mighty for your own good. You have ruined everything that means anything to me and now you are going to suffer as I have," Everett said through clenched teeth.

Chapter Twenty-Five

Clara barged excitedly into Anna's workshop. "Auntie Anna, you won't believe what we got—"

"Ye didn't give away any surprises now did ye?" Joseph smiled at Clara when she returned to the kitchen moments later.

Clara pouted in reply and slumped in the chair at the kitchen table.

"What troubles ye?"

"She's not there. She said I could help her wrap up the jewellery for delivery when we got back, and she left without me."

"I'm sure she ran out for a quick errand, and she will include ye when she get's back. She cannae be far wi'out the use of the truck. Perhaps ye and Thomas could make a card or a nice drawing to give her wi' yer Christmas gift."

Clara thumped away unenthusiastically to find her brother, drawing a chuckle from Joseph.

Over an hour later, Joseph's uneasiness increased. He scanned Anna's workshop surprised to see her tools scattered across the work bench and her creations left in mid task. One step closer he found her engagement ring sitting in a small dish on the top corner of her bench. He picked up the ring and turned it gently in his fingers. "Where are ye, my love?" He placed the ring back in the dish and locked her shop door.

"Clara, Thomas," he called upstairs from the kitchen.

They appeared instantly.

"I will need ye to get yer coats and boots. I'm a wee concerned about yer auntie being gone so long. I've a mind to have a keek around town."

"May we come too?" Tears pooled in Clara's eyes, and she reached for her brother's hand.

"Dinnae be dowie my sweet. I will find her, and we will be back before ye ken."

～

After an hour of searching with no success, Joseph bought the children ice cream and returned to the house hoping Anna had returned. Her workshop remained empty and the house eerily quiet. Joseph's anxiety reached a new high. Using the newly installed telephone, he rang the neighbour.

"Mrs. Nelson, 'tis Joey Hendrie here."

"What a pleasant surprise Mr. Hendrie. How are you today?"

"I'm well and please call me Joe. I'm next door at Anna's wi' the Campbells' bairns."

"Lovely, how are they all adjusting. Poor dears."

"The weans are managing well. Tis Anna I'm worried about. I wonder if ye may have seen anyone at the house this afternoon. Anna vanished while the bairns and I were in town. I'm afraid she has come to some harm."

"Gosh with her wonderful jewellery business, she's had plenty of visitors to her shop. But, yes, I do recall one vehicle pulled in around one this afternoon. I was just taking my dinner and I heard the loud engine, so I glanced up. Just a lone man in the car. I thought how nice a gentleman picking up jewellery for a Christmas present."

"The car, Mrs. Nelson, do ye ken the kind of car or truck or who the gentleman may have been?"

"He wore a dark toque with his coat collar up. I didn't see a face. But the car was black and roundish, one of those beetle bug types."

"Everett, damn it."

"Pardon me?"

"Gosh, I beg yer pardon, Ma'am. I'm so worried for my Anna. Pardon my language, no offense meant."

"Oh, goodness none taken, my dear. Can I help? Shall I watch the children for you?"

"Aye, bless ye. That would be a huge help."

Chapter Twenty-Six

"You're going to call the police chief now and tell him you were covering for Marcy and that it was you who was on the pier that night fighting with Ian." Everett barked at Anna, just inches from her face, causing her to recoil from his rancid breath.

"I'll do no such thing. He would never believe me." Anna knew better than to admit the police already had a statement from Miriam.

He held the gun to her throat. "You will do as I say and if you are not convincing enough to get Ian released, I will kill you and Marcy and those despicable children along with you. No one knows where we are, and I will be long gone before anyone finds the lot of you."

Anna swallowed and forced back tears, fearing for herself and her unborn child, but even more for Clara and Thomas. She saw no logic to his plan, but having witnessed Everett's violence firsthand, she knew better than to take his threat lightly. He had stopped her escape at the house, forced her to his car at gunpoint, then punched the side of her head with the butt of his revolver when she attempted to escape the car as he put it in gear to back from her driveway. She barely recovered the black out enough to walk into his house on their arrival. While she was still dazed, he tied each of her wrists and ankles to the four legs of a wooden kitchen chair. Based on the view of a barn and several large pine trees, through a partially opened curtain, she guessed they were at the back of the house far out in the country. The small kitchen was dirty and cold and smelled of rotten food. "Fine. Untie my hands and I'll make the call."

"Tell him the joint bank account was acceptable to you and you're no longer pressing charges."

He untied only one hand, leaving the other hand and both feet secured to the chair. A loud knock interrupted him as he reached for the phone on the wall.

"Damn it." Everett grabbed another piece of rope from the kitchen table and tied it forcefully around her mouth before bolting to the front of the house. From the front room, he pulled the heavy curtain barely an inch and watched as the police chief and Joseph Hendrie, knocked again, exchanged words, and then finally retreated to the police car.

Soundlessly, Everett entered the kitchen from a door at the far end of the galley. Anna jolted at his reappearance and dismissed any hope of freeing herself.

"What do you think you're doing?" He untied the knot at the nape of her neck and ripped the raw cord across her mouth.

She reached her still free hand to press the bleeding cuts on her lips and cheeks.

"Looks like the police chief is out making house calls. You will have to wait until tomorrow to call in." He smirked then walked away to the window.

"If he is already knocking on your door, he will figure you out. You best let me get back to the children or you will end up in jail with Ian."

He tapped the side of his leg as he stared out the window. His silence gave her hope that he was pondering her suggestion.

"You know I am right. They will go to Marcy next, so if she knows the truth, you better let me go and get running now." Anna spoke to his back.

"Shut your mouth. The house will be dark soon, my car is hidden in the barn, and Marcy can't tell them anything. With the help of that menacing woman, I have kept her more sedated than Ian ever did. The idiot botched our whole plan."

Anna's intake of breath was loud in the quiet room, drawing Everett's attention from the window.

"Why so surprised? What did you take me for, a simpleton?"

"Look, Everett. I don't know what plan you and Ian had cooking, and I don't need to know. If you were in business together or even if you intended to cause Marcy harm, I don't know anything about it and I am quite happy to keep it that way. Let me go. I will walk back home, make up a story about visiting an acquaintance while making deliveries and you can be off, no one the wiser."

He stomped from the kitchen window, wrenched her free hand behind her and roughly tied it back to the chair. Facing her again in one step, he breathed heavily when he grabbed her throat and leaned within inches of her face. "You will stay here until I say you can go." He tossed her head back, left the room and slammed the door behind him.

"Damn it." Anna slumped painfully in the wooden chair.

Chapter Twenty-Seven

"We should have broken the door down." Joseph rubbed the back of his neck with one hand as he gazed out the window of the police car.

"He wasn't home, and we can't go barging into people's empty houses. He could well have picked up a necklace for his sister for Christmas and now he's out buying a ham. Everett Rossi is a reputable citizen. We have no reason to suspect him of any wrongdoing."

"Ye have no reason; but I have never trusted the shifty character. If he was the last to see Anna, I have some questions for him. I'm telling ye, Everett Rossi has something to do wi' her disappearance. Mrs. Nelson saw his car in the drive shortly after I left wi' the weans for town."

"What is it with this town, that people cannot keep track of their own kin?"

"Derek, I'm needing ye to take me seriously. She was desperate to finish her jewellery pieces before Yule. She never would have up and left her work, firstly wi'out locking the door to her jewels and secondly wi'out so much as a note to us."

"Okay, okay. Tell me again what the neighbour said."

"She told me a lone man pulled up in a Volkswagen Beetle around one o'clock. That's what Everett Rossi drives."

"As I said, perhaps he was picking up a Christmas gift." He glanced at Joseph and raised his eyebrows.

Joseph flipped his hand back at the chief. "I'm telling ye, the man is too cheap to buy jewellery and he has nae had a lassie in his life as long as I have ken him."

"Well, now, that doesn't mean—"

"We can at least check wi' him as to Anna's circumstances when he saw her. Where's Marcy Campbell? She should ken the whereabouts of her brother, or she can tell us if he came by wi' jewellery for her."

He pulled into the parking lot behind the police station, shut off the cruiser and turned to face Joseph. "I am only telling you because you are so worried about your Anna. Please keep it to your—"

"Damn it, I dinnae care about spreading rumors. I care about my fiancé."

He motioned downward with his hand. "Okay, settle down. Let me finish a sentence. We have a safe house, near here. A retired nurse has several rooms, and we pay her to shelter the occasional witness, or victim from time to time. She also takes in ah, tenants or patients shall I say who suffer mental maladies, or limitations. She keeps them calm."

"Stoatin, more damn cuppa."

"Some days I have no idea what you Scots are talking about." He held his hand up and shook his head.

"Tea, Derek. I'm talking about the damn tea. Ian Campbell fed his wife a drink of his own concocting to keep her calm. And now ye say this woman is doing the same thing. Anna said when Marcy refused the tea, she was perfectly coherent and capable of daily life."

Derek winced. "My understanding is she has stopped eating and become somewhat confused to put it mildly. She's awaiting transfer to one of the Ontario Hospitals in either

Woodstock or Orillia for more definitive psychotherapy. I did get her statement about Ian Campbell's misdeeds but when I tried to speak to her at the safe house to ask more questions, they told me about the decline in her condition."

"A psychiatric hospital? Damn it. I need to talk to her."

"I am not sure you can. Let me call over and see if we can visit her briefly."

~

"Gwendolyn O'Malley, this is Joseph Hendrie. Joseph, this is Nurse O'Malley, who as I told you, runs our safe house and has done for several years." Joseph estimated the woman stood almost six feet tall. Although her shoulders were wide, her frame was slim. Her skin was ashen, the paleness exacerbated by the standard white dress uniform Joseph had seen on many nurses during the war. The hem just below her knees revealed muscular legs with bulging veins beneath sheer white nylons.

"Pleasure to make yer acquaintance." Joseph extended his hand which the nurse glanced at briefly before spinning on her white healed shoes, her hands remaining firmly pressed into the pockets of her uniform.

"This way."

The police chief raised his eyebrows and shrugged in answer to Joseph's puzzled expression.

The nurse retreated toward the stairwell giving Joseph a moment to scan the front of the large house. The door to the dining room stood open. Although the table had been set with at least a dozen place settings, no one was in sight. The door to the left of the stairwell was closed, as was what he assumed to be the door to the kitchen at the back of the home. The hairs on the back of his neck rose as he reached the bottom step. He hesitated mid-step, with his hand firmly on the railing.

"Make haste gentlemen," Nurse O'Malley bellowed from the top step.

Derek pushed on Joseph's back. He shook off the ominous feeling and ascended the wide carpeted staircase. Joseph twisted in a circle on the top landing. One closed door was to his left. An open door to a bathroom was in front of him. The disinfectant smell of the room permeated his senses and caused him to blink back tears. A decorative balustrade spanned to his right, with four closed doors opposite extending the length of the hallway. "Where did she go?"

"Marcy's room is second on the left; I came by last week." Derek pointed down the wide hallway.

The police chief reached for the handle of the bedroom he indicated but shot back as Nurse O'Malley appeared from a smaller doorway at the end of the hall. "Not that one," she yelled.

"She's in the attic?" Joseph whispered. "What's going on in this place?"

Derek faced his friend and shrugged a second time. "Best follow her."

Joseph ducked the doorway then crept up several thin, steep steps, checking over his shoulder to be sure the police chief followed.

The nurse pulled the cord of a single bulb light hanging from the ceiling of the room. Joseph gasped at the sight before him, drawing the nurse's stern glare. The attic was sparse of furnishings or decoration; the walls and ceiling comprised of bare wooden boards. A tiny glass window was unadorned at the far end of the room. A small, braided rug lay beside the bed on an otherwise bare wooden plank floor. Marcy lay flat on her back on a single cot, her hands strapped to the sides of the bed. She had one small pillow beneath her head and a plain white sheet covering her to her chest.

"What have you done to her?" the police chief demanded. "Is she alive?"

Joseph leapt to her bedside and reached for the restraints.

"How dare either of you question my treatment of the infirm. I had no choice but to restrain Mrs. Campbell and keep her sedated. She has been a disruption to the other tenants with her crying and screaming and she has tried to escape on a number of occasions."

"No doubt she has. I was nae aware she had been imprisoned." The nurse ignored Joseph's angry glare and swatted at his hands as he unbuckled the tight ties holding Marcy down. "I ask ye to step back, Nurse O'Malley. Mrs. Campbell does nae appear too threatening. There is no need for this."

He perched on the side of the cot and reached for one of her now free hands. "Mrs. Campbell, tis Joseph Hendrie, a friend of yer sister-in-law, Anna. Do ye ken?" He rubbed her hand in his own and leaned closer. "Marcy can ye talk? We need to find yer brother, Everett."

"Everett, he'll kill..." Her head slowly rolled back and forth on the pillow.

"I'm here too, Mrs. Campbell," the police chief added. "I won't let anyone hurt you."

"Us, he will kill us, me and Anna." Barely above a whisper, Marcy's words were slurred.

"She's trying to tell us something." Joseph glanced over his shoulder to the police chief.

"She must be talking about Ian trying to kill her and Anna." Derek furrowed his brow and reached for his notepad.

Joseph squeezed her hand. "Yer safe from yer Ian. He wilnae hurt ye nor Anna. Can ye help us locate Everett?"

Her head rolled more violently on the pillow. Her eyes blinked slowly, once then twice like she forced them to stay open. "No, no, Everett will help, Ian kill me, kill Anna."

"Ye've sedated her so that she can't even keep her eyes open nor speak." Joseph pinched his lips and shook his head at the nurse.

Dismissing Joseph's concerns, the nurse addressed Derek directly. "You see what I meant Chief Bane, utter gibberish. She's trying to tell you Everett will help you. And Ian Campbell tried to kill her and this Anna person. Her devoted brother has attended her day and night since she's been with us."

"When was he last here? Everett that is."

"Why he was here just this morning and he agreed to the restraints." The nurse pulled herself up straight with her defensive answer.

Joseph and Derek shared an angered exchange.

"You and Mr. Rossi entrusted Mrs. Campbell's care to me and now you're questioning it?" She tipped her chin up at the police chief.

"Beg your pardon, but I wonder if you might leave us for just a few moments. It's a matter of police business I'm not at liberty to discuss." He smiled at her, placed his hand on her back and attempted to usher her toward the stairs.

The nurse huffed, shook her head quickly and stood unmoving with her hands on her hips.

"Miss O'Malley." The police chief removed his hand from her back and motioned toward the stairs.

"Fine, I will allow you five minutes. It is time for her medicine in any event."

Joseph turned a wide-eyed glare on his friend and waited until he heard the door latch at the bottom of the attic steps. "Medicine? How much more can they sedate her?"

"Something odd is going on here," Derek agreed.

"She is in no danger from her husband now he is behind bars. Ye had her admitted to protect her from him and now she needs protecting from the protector."

The police chief nodded. "And possibly from her own brother. I don't know what to do. This is a very strange turn of events." He raked his hand through his hair, walked the length of the room and crouched to gaze out the small window.

"I would like to take her back to the house. She's the only one who will be able to tell me where Everett is."

"Joseph, we can't… that is… I can only have her released to family."

"I'm soon to be married to her sister-in-law, and I'm currently guardian to her children."

"That's a stretch, Joe. Anna is the children's guardian and Marcy has an immediate family member in her brother. He has to make the decisions."

"Aye, and he is nowhere to be found and may be of a mind to kill her and my Anna."

"We do not know that." Derek tilted his head and glared at Joe.

Joseph turned his gaze to Marcy who commenced mumbling as if talking in her sleep. "Give me one day to sober her up. If she's still rambling by Yule, I will have her admitted to the O.H. myself."

"I think I will be the one committed if anyone finds out I helped spring a restrained patient from a safe house. I must be daft believing you, but I have always had suspicions about Nurse O'Malley and some of the treatments she inflicts. Something is definitely off here."

Shuffling down the wide staircase carrying a mumbling Marcy wrapped in only her nightgown and a thin sheet, Joseph took off running for the door as Nurse O'Malley called after the escapees.

～

"Make way children," Police Chief Bane said as he entered the front room of Anna's house.

"Auntie Anna." Clara jumped up to great Joseph despite the officer's direction.

Joseph carried Marcy who lay limply against him. "I have yer mum wi' me. But she's feeling poorly so we need to give her some space."

"Mama!" Thomas bolted to them and wrapped his arm around Joseph's leg, causing him to stumble forward into the room.

Mrs. Nelson grabbed the boy and pulled him back. "Let's give the men a chance to get your mum into the house shall we."

"Where's Anna?" Tears pooled in Clara's eyes.

Joseph lay Marcy down on the couch in the front room, covered her gently with a throw blanket, then turned to address the room. "I will nae mince words, Clara. Ye too, Mrs. Nelson, Thomas, come and sit wi' me." Clara pinned herself to the chair when Joseph sat opposite Marcy. Mrs. Nelson pulled Thomas onto her lap as she sat at the foot of the couch and glanced over to their sleeping patient.

Police Chief Bane stepped toward the chair. "I'm heading back Joe. I will ring you the minute I hear a word."

"As will I once she starts talking."

The men shook hands before Joseph turned again, all eyes on him in anticipation.

"Mrs. Nelson, I can't thank ye—"

"Please call me Audrey."

"Thank ye, Audrey. Ye've been a tremendous help."

"And I'm happy to stay on. Anna and the children have been such delightful neighbours. Please tell me what I can do. What's happening? And what's wrong with Mrs. Campbell?"

"Mrs. Campbell has been staying at a safe house. Initially, she went there until…" He stopped and glanced to each of the children.

"I witnessed the trouble with their father, no need to explain." Audrey tilted her head and smiled in understanding.

Joseph nodded. "Yes, right, ye where here that day. Well—"

"I know the police kept mama hidden from papa. We were here too when the police took him away to jail," Clara stated.

"That ye were." Joseph sat back in the oversized chair, opened his arms and both children clamored up with him, one on each knee. "I'm so sorry ye have to see all this. The reality is yer mum seems to be sedated. That is, she has been given some sleeping medicine."

Thomas' brow knit.

"Is she sick?" Clara asked.

"No, I think wi' our care, she will wake up and have some answers for us."

"Did Auntie Anna go away?" Thomas asked.

"I believe yer mum may be able to help us wi' that puzzle to."

"Why don't I start some supper?" Mrs. Nelson stood. "Clara, would you like to help me?"

She hesitated and looked up to Joseph. He nodded to her. "Go help, I will be right here."

Clara reluctantly left Joseph's lap and followed the woman into the kitchen.

"Thomas, let's ye and I go get a few things for yer mum."

By the time they returned with more blankets, a pillow and a warm washcloth, Marcy was already lolling her head and murmuring. Joseph perched on the edge of the couch and reached for her hand. "Thomas use the cloth to wipe her brow."

The child rubbed the cloth gently over her face, then glanced back to Joseph for direction.

He nodded and reached for the cloth to set it aside. "Ye did fine. Try talking to her."

"Mama," he whispered.

"We are safe here son. Speak up so she kens 'tis ye."

"Mama, it's me Thomas."

Joseph winked at the boy when he turned with a grin. "That's it." He nodded encouragement.

Marcy's eyes blinked open briefly, then several times, then closed again. She mumbled a few words, then her arms began to flail in front of her.

"Yer safe, Marcy. 'Tis me, Joseph Hendrie." He reached for her hands and pulled them gently to rest at her sides.

Her eyes opened now, and she stared at Joseph, her forehead creased in confusion.

"Clara, come see yer mum," he called to the kitchen.

She peered tentatively around the corner and Joseph waved her closer. "Come; dinnae be scared. Look her eyes are open."

Clara stepped to the couch and stared down at her mother. "Hello, Mama."

Marcy extended a hand slightly toward the girl, but Clara retreated out of reach.

Joseph stood and motioned for Clara to take his place on the couch. "Don't be scared," he repeated. "Sit here and talk to her wi' yer brother."

Clara glanced to Thomas who was beaming. "She woke up when I said my name." He wiggled proudly.

She smiled at her brother, then turned a frown back to Joseph. "I would prefer to help Mrs. Nelson. May I be excused?"

Joseph flinched but nodded; then watched her sullen return to the kitchen.

"Okay, Thomas, 'tis up to us. Let's see if we can get yer mum to have a chat wi' us."

By dinner time, Marcy had already become more lucid. Covered in a blanket, she sat, propped up by pillows, and held the plate of food Joseph offered.

Chapter Twenty-Eight

What seemed like hours later, Everett returned to the dark kitchen, punching a light switch with one hand and holding a plate laden with cheese, bread, and nuts in the other. Anna's first thought was who compiled the food and from where, given she sat in the kitchen the whole time he was gone.

She blinked at the light; her eyes having adjusted to the darkening room as the sun had set. "I need the facilities. If you don't untie me, you will have a mess of a puddle under the chair momentarily."

He dropped the plate loudly on the table, huffed and rolled his eyes before removing the ties from each arm. She immediately rubbed feeling back into her wrists, wincing at the cuts left on her skin from the harsh ropes. Before untying her ankles from the front legs of the chair, he pulled her arms forward, held them together at the wrists and bound them once again to each other. She stumbled forward when he undid her ankles and hauled her to her feet, her bound hands nearly missing the plate of food as she steadied herself.

"Dare I ask how you expect me to navigate the loo with my hands tied?"

His vicious squint sent a chill up her spine. He turned to walk from the room. Anna tentatively followed, her heart thumping almost as quickly as her mind churned with possibilities of escape. She trailed behind him through the back the door, down a beaten path to an outhouse. He unceremoniously held the door open, then slammed it on her entrance leaving her in complete darkness.

The stench had engulfed Anna as she approached the outbuilding, but now shut inside, nausea overwhelmed her ability to maneuver her task especially with tied wrists. Pitch darkness proved a blessing as she faced the bench and leaned over the hole. Stabilizing herself with her hands fisted together against the back wall, the force of dry heaves shook her body. "Open the God damn door," she screamed.

The squeak of hinges and influx of cold, fresh air snapped her to awareness and saved her from crumpling unconscious in the confines of the rancid outhouse. Dizzy from lack of food and movement over the last several hours, it took all her effort to pull herself upright and turn to the open door. She gulped fresh air as urine trickled down the inside of her pant leg, leaving a pool gathering in her shoe.

"Are you done?" His harsh voice startled her.

"If you must know, I've spent a penny in my drawers." She glanced down at herself unable to see the damage in the darkness of dusk. "Because your putrid outhouse made me convulse with vomiting and you won't untie my damn hands," she yelled in his face.

He gripped her arm and dragged her roughly from the outhouse. Her first step into sodden shoes brought on another wave of nausea she fought desperately to swallow down. He stopped them in the kitchen in front of the telephone on the wall. Surprised he knew the number by heart, she watched as he dialed the police station. He held her in place with one hand and held the receiver to her ear with the other.

"Chief of Police Bane please; it's Anna Gordon calling." She glared at Everett as she waited on the line.

He glanced down at her pants, then back to her face with a sneer. "You are disgusting."

Derek Bane was on the line before she had a chance to reply to Everett. "Mrs. Gordon, where are you? Joseph and I have been frantically trying to find you all day."

"It's lovely to speak to you as well Chief Bane."

"Pardon? Are you well, Anna?"

"No, I'm having difficulty getting all my orders filled before Christmas."

"Dear God, where are you? Give me a hint please as to your whereabouts. I can be there in minutes."

"You are too kind, thank you."

Everett squeezed her arm so tightly she gasped in pain. "Get to the point," he ground out through clenched teeth.

She cleared her throat to compose herself. "The reason for my call and I apologize for causing such inconvenience, but I would like to revise my statement in regard to the misdeeds of my brother-in-law, Ian Campbell."

"Can you answer this? Is someone forcing you to make the call?"

"Yes, yes, exactly right. I agree it is odd circumstances. And no, I'm too terribly held up right now to come to the station. I had hoped you could take notes over the telephone and save us both the inconvenience of another meeting."

Everett nodded to her. "That's more like it."

"Keep talking. I'm taking down everything you say. I understand, you are being forced to call, and someone is holding you."

Chief Bane's perception almost brought her to tears. She swallowed her emotion and cleared her throat once again before she spoke. "Correct. I'm sorry I must admit it, the whole situation with the bank appears to have been a misunderstanding. I actually found a note in with my belongings that I recently unpacked at my new home which stated the bulk of our account, mine and my late husband's that is, had been kept in our account in England. A silly mistake, entirely my fault. I hope you'll forgive me. It's family, you must understand. My family money never got transferred. The money transferred to Ian Campbell was directly from his brother, and a result of the Campbell family's savings. Turns out the account in question was all his own business dealings."

"Family. Okay, I understand, it must be Everett like Joseph said. Ian is in jail. Marcy is completely unwell. There is no other family. Joseph told me the neighbour saw Everett come to see you earlier. We knocked on his door, but no one was there. Are you with him? Is it Everett holding you against your will?"

"Yes, thank you so much Chief. I appreciate your understanding more than you know. I believe whatever accounting he provides to be the truth."

Everett squeezed her arm once again. "Tell him about the pier."

Discomfort overtaking her fear, she turned a glare on him before returning to the call. "One more thing Chief Bane."

"I'm listening, please keep talking. I'm putting it together. Rest assured; I will be there very soon with back up. Please stay strong."

"Thank you again, Sir. I appreciate your indulgence. I'm sorry to also have to admit that my information about the pier may have been somewhat misleading to your investigation. The truth is, Ian Campbell and I had a disagreement that night. I stormed from the house, and he followed to check on my welfare. We had a quarrel on the pier and, well, I lost my temper and threw a rock in his direction. I imagine that's what Mr. Eastman witnessed, the yelling and the splash. Entirely innocent family argument."

"I know you're aware it was Miriam on the pier. I told you myself."

"Yes, precisely. Once again, I thank you for your understanding."

"I'm going to hang up now. Keep talking on the phone if you can. We will be at Mr. Rossi's home in minutes and get you home safely."

"Thank you, thank you so much for allowing me to speak my mind."

Chief Bane ended the call, but Anna attempted to buy herself some time as he suggested. "I will make every effort to come in and make a signed statement over the coming days."

Everett squeezed her arm tightly. "That's enough."

"I'm sorry, I need to let you go for now then. Thank you again for taking my call."

He grabbed the receiver and slammed it down in the cradle. "You better not have tried any funny business."

She wrenched her arm free, spun to face him and held her tied hands up in front of her to hold him at bay. "Everett, I have no idea what you hope to accomplish here, but I am pleading with you once again and begging you to believe me. After that phone call, I am certain I can make enough of a stir with the police to cause reasonable doubt so that they will have difficulty convicting Ian. I won't mention anything that transpired here today. Just let me go home to the children and Joseph and make an excuse for my absence. If I'm gone much longer, you will soon be tied into a crime of abduction which may not end well. Be on your way from town and let the chips fall as they may for Ian."

"You have ruined everything, and you need to pay," he growled.

She retreated slowly until her back ran into the kitchen counter. "I don't know what you mean. Ian is a vulgar, violent man and your sister is better off without him. I helped her by—"

He slapped her face so hard, her head spun and hit the kitchen cupboard behind her. "Don't speak of him that way. You are a disgusting, ill-mannered wench."

Dazed, she slumped against the counter to support herself. He hauled her, barely aware to the barn in the back of the property. Hands still bound, he once again tied her legs together at her ankles, then tossed her back into a mouldy pile of hay in the far corner of the barn. He threw a canvas tarp over her and what she guessed was a bale of hay. His car started and the engine ran only long enough for him to back his car out to the driveway. The barn doors slammed, and the wooden arm dropped, bolting them from the outside. Cold seeped through her wet pants. Her hands and feet went numb as her tears fell unchecked. She closed her eyes and her mind faded to black.

~

Flashing lights flooded the windows at the front of his house immediately upon Everett's return through the kitchen. Stepping out to the front porch, he was met at gunpoint by Chief of Police Bane and Officer Oakley.

"Gentlemen, please lower your weapons. What is the meaning of this?" he asked innocently.

Chief Bane inched forward. "Arms up Rossi. We have reason to believe you are involved in the disappearance of Anna Gordon. We are here to search your home. Step aside."

Everett initially held his hands up at shoulder height then dropped them as the officers approached. He graciously swept his hand in front of himself. "By all means, please come in; I have nothing to hide. I have no idea what you are on about, but you're welcome to come through the house."

The three stopped just inside the front door. The officers glanced briefly into the open rooms on either side of the foyer, then turned their focus back to Everett. "Where were you earlier today?"

"I have been about some shopping, and I did a repair job for some folks down in Goderich. Their front door blew clear off the hinges in the last storm." He chuckled.

"Mr. Rossi, you were seen at Anna Gordon's shop earlier this afternoon. What took you there to call on her?" Chief Bane asked.

His brow knit briefly and then he smiled. "I stopped to update her on my sister's condition. When I saw Anna in town last week, she asked that I keep her apprised since she's taken on the children. I fear my sister is not well. I am not sure what will become of the children if their father is sent away as well."

"Why did you not call her on the telephone? Why would you go in person?"

Everett blinked quickly. "Why I don't suppose I thought to ring her. I wasn't aware she had a telephone. I thought a visit in person would be more the thing. If you must know, I have had somewhat of an interest in courting her since she arrived and I had hoped, well, that is, I thought I might convince her to take tea or dinner with me."

"Are you not aware she is engaged to be married to Joseph Hendrie?"

Everett's head jolted back in legitimate surprise. "I, ah, well, no, I was not. It didn't come up in our conversation today."

"But you spoke to her just last week as well? What day was that?" Chief Bane reached to his inside pocket for a notepad and pencil.

"Well, yes, or perhaps it was the week before. My goodness with everyone rushing to finish tasks before Christmas, perhaps I have mixed up my days."

"Did you see Mrs. Gordon before or after you were in Goderich?" he asked as he flipped the pad open to a clean page.

Everett wrung his hands together in front of him and glanced down to his feet.

"Mr. Rossi? Before or after? And who's house did you go to for the repairs? We will need to speak to them to corroborate your story."

He straightened abruptly and huffed. "I was in Goderich this morning and at the market this afternoon. I stopped to see Mrs. Gordon before I came home for my supper. This invasion is utterly ridiculous. If that Hendrie man cannot keep track of his woman, that is his own issue and nothing to do with me."

"We have reason to believe otherwise. We will need to have a look around." Chief Bane glared at Everett who shrugged and extended one hand ahead of them.

The chief and Officer Oakley exchanged puzzled glances before following him up the stairs of his home.

After a thorough search of his home, the officers once again stood in the front foyer facing Everett. Chief Bane squinted at their suspect, frustrated at their unsuccessful search, and irritated by his smug expression. "Oakley, go check the outbuildings." He commanded his deputy but kept his eyes on Everett who flinched almost imperceptibly but recovered quickly.

"Really, gentlemen, is all this necessary? I've told you my whereabouts, you have scoured every inch of my home, much to my dismay." He finished with a tight-lipped sneer at the officers.

"Oakley, go." The police chief turned when his junior officer remained in the doorway.

"Oh, right, sorry Sir. You meant now."

The chief rolled his eyes, then turned back to Everett who crossed his arms in front of him then uncrossed them and ran his hands down his pants. "Now what?" Everett asked.

Ignoring Everett's request for information, Chief Bane glared at him once again. "Are you certain there is nothing you want to tell me before Officer Oakley searches your barns?”

Everett met the request with silence.

“I should tell you; your sister has been released from Gwendolyn O’Malley’s safe house.”

Everett’s eyes grew large. “Wh.. what, why?” he stammered.

“Is something wrong? I thought you might be pleased.”

“Well, no, I, that is.” Everett raked his fingers through his hair, turned away from the police chief and blew out a long breath.

“What seems to be the problem, Mr. Rossi?”

The officer raised his brow when Everett turned back, his eyes brimming with tears. “This is a distressing situation, Sir. I should have been the one to decide as to her release.”

“She was placed in safe keeping until her husband could be detained and she went voluntarily—”

“But Ian may be released and then they would have to live separately. I can’t take her in. What will become of her? She is alone; she can’t manage alone. She is unstable.” Everett’s voice escalated.

The chief shook his head quickly at Everett’s rambling. “The most important issue has always been her safety. With Mr. Campbell no longer a threat, there was no reason to keep her in hiding.”

Everett scoffed. “But the pier incident was a misunderstanding and she—”

Anna’s exact words came to mind. “Why would you say that? You were not involved.”

“Ian told me so. He said he followed Anna to the pier that night when she was distraught. This is all her damn fault for lying to you and mixing her dead husband’s money in with my, that is with Ian Campbell’s.”

The chief’s suspicions mounted with every word of Everett’s plea. “When would you have had the opportunity to discuss the events of that evening with Mr. Campbell? He disappeared before any of the details of the pier incident came to light and he hid away for almost two weeks before he was arrested at Mrs. Gordon's home. By chance did Mr. Campbell stay here, with you?"

Officer Oakley's reappearance interrupted Everett's reply. They both spun to the young man who shook his head as he came in the front door. "Nothing, Sir. There seems to be some evidence of someone having slept in the far shed, a cot with bedding and a lantern, used plates and utensils, but there were no footprints in the snow, and I didn't find anyone."

"The wind would have blown any prints away, Oakley."

"Right, Sir. Of course, I should have thought of that."

Chief Bane closed his eyes and shook his head slightly before he raised his brow back to Everett. "Mr. Rossi, I'll ask again. Did Mr. Campbell hide in one of your outbuildings? There are criminal charges for harboring a fugitive."

Composed once again, Everett frowned and shook his head quickly. "Don't be ridiculous. I had a farm hand who stayed there during the summer months and took care of the property. He's long gone now."

"You kept a farm hand in your shed?" Officer Oakley's brow creased.

Everett flipped his hand at the two officers. "Why would I hide my sister's husband? My concern has always been for her well-being and now you have removed her from care and she's unstable and alone."

"I'm not convinced she needed care, and she is not alone. She has two children. That aside, your brother-in-law, Ian Campbell will remain incarcerated and will not likely be released for many years. He is facing attempted murder charges for an attack on a Port Albert woman as well as firing his gun at Anna Gordon and Joseph Hendrie immediately before his arrest. Whatever Ian told you about the pier that night was a lie. He will also answer to illegal distribution of alcohol, and charges relating to several accounts now being audited at the bank."

Everett's mouth dropped open. "But—"

"If you abducted Mrs. Gordon or drugged your sister in an effort to shed doubt on our investigation into Ian Campbell's charges, you have made a grave mistake." Chief Bane stared at Everett who clamped his mouth shut and glanced down to the floor.

"Mr. Rossi, do you have anything else to tell us? Have you done Mrs. Gordon or your sister any harm?"

He lifted his head slowly and stared, tight-lipped at the police chief for several seconds. "Get out of my house."

"You don't make the demands. I have a mind to take you into custody."

"On what grounds?" Everett squinted, challenging the officers.

Chief Bane knew Everett was right. He didn't have enough information to arrest him or even take him in for questioning. "I will be back to speak to you further once I have taken your sister's statement. There will be more questions and I expect your cooperation."

"Get out." Everett pointed to the front door.

The officers stood their ground and stared at Everett a moment longer before the police chief turned and motioned Officer Oakley out the door.

Chapter Twenty-Nine

"I'm telling you, Joe, we went over every inch of his house, bedroom closets, cold cellar, even the barn. There was one chair pulled out at his kitchen table in front of a single plate of food, no evidence of a second person having been in his house recently or ever for that matter. I'll admit his emotions were all over the map. He spoke as innocently as the spring rain while he followed us about the house switching lights on and off to assist us. He was clearly surprised when we told him Anna was your fiancé and then upset to tears when I said Marcy had been released. He didn't get defensive until I rhymed off the charges Ian was facing and then he just turned angry."

"But ye spoke to Anna. She confirmed 'twas him holding her against her will."

"Well, not exactly. We spoke in sort of a code. Clearly someone was there and forcing her to make the call. Someone who wanted her to shed doubt on her statements related to Ian Campbell's charges, specifically the incidents at the pier and her trust account, as if that would help."

"But ye asked her specifically if it were Everett and she said aye. It had to be Everett; ye must go back."

"He did make one comment that sounded suspiciously like something Anna said. And he mentioned something that he shouldn't have known about Ian. I am thinking Campbell may have stayed with him during the days he was on the fly and given him an abbreviated scenario of his crimes."

"I dinnae care about Everett or Ian's misdeeds, Derek."

"I know, I know you're in a fright and I agree, we're missing something. But he was mostly co-operative and I'm telling ye, we searched every corner of that house. If he has her, it must be somewhere other than his house and I need something more to go on to take him into custody. He got angry when I told him I would be back after I got a statement from his sister. What have you got out of Marcy; is she awake? Shall I come and question her?"

"She is awake, and she has eaten and spoken somewhat clearly to the children. I was about to have a sit down wi' her now the children have gone to bed."

"Alright, ring me back if she has anything helpful. I have a man, a private investigator of sorts stationed outside of Rossi's house. If Everett makes any move to bolt or if Anna is somehow in the area, my man will report to me immediately. He has a two-way radio and I'm here at my desk."

Joseph hung up the phone in the kitchen and returned to sit in the chair facing a wilted Marcy. "As I told ye before supper, the police believe yer brother has taken Anna. Her life could be in danger. Ye must talk to me."

"It doesn't feel right. I barely know you." Her eye lids blinked heavily, and her head lolled back on the couch.

He inched to the front of the chair and leaned his forearms on his legs. "Stay wi' me Marcy. I need yer help. Anna and I are engaged to be married. She is carrying my child and we have been caring for yer bairns in yer absence. That makes me family."

Her eyes widened at the new information. "I had no idea."

"Of course, ye didnea. Ye've been sedated for a fortnight. And I have a mind yer brother may have had something to do wi' that."

Tears pooled and dropped on her hands when she hung her head.

"Talk to me please, Marcy. I'm begging for yer help. No one will hurt ye here."

She lifted her head and stared somewhat dazed, at Joseph. Her shoulders were stooped, and her hands stayed tightly clasped together.

Despite his impatience, Joseph remained silent, his own hands clenched tightly in front of him.

"I told Anna a story about how Ian and I came to be married. I explained that I was in love with another man and that my papa refused the man's request for my hand. Instead, my papa succumbed to Ian's charms which were all lies and married us off quickly and sent us to Kincardine along with my brother, Everett."

Joseph shook his head slightly and squinted at Marcy. "Anna told me something about that. I'm sorry for what ye went through, but I dinnae follow. What has that to do wi' Anna or Everett right now?"

She took a deep breath and blew it out quickly, then stretched her shoulders back into the couch. "There was a man called Domenic, and I loved him and pined for him for years. That part was true. But the part about Ian charming my papa, well that has been a story Everett and I have upheld for years, but it's not true."

"Okay." Joseph squirmed with impatience.

"The truth is, Everett was in love with Ian, and they had, well, a relationship. I caught them in the barn doing what appeared to me to be unnatural behaviour. I was young, and didn't understand and I ran to my governess—"

"Governess?" His eyebrows raised.

Marcy flipped her hand dismissing his surprise. "She was a domestic from Britain. My papa hired her in the late twenties after my mama passed."

"Go on."

"Everett had been such a quiet boy growing up and when he met Ian shortly after he came to Toronto, well Everett came out of his shell. They were rarely apart. I had never seen Everett so happy. Ian came around the house all the time. He certainly made some crude advances to me, but he never showed an interest in courting me once I came to my debutante year." She hesitated and covered her eyes with her hand.

Joseph stretched forward to pull her hand away. "What has this to do wi' Anna?"

"He is a disgusting man."

"Everett?" Joseph's brow furrowed.

"No, Everett was homosexual and frankly lonely and harmless. But Ian, he was, I don't know, deviant and evil. He took pleasures with men and women and whoever he was with, he dominated them in a violent way. I can't even—"

"Marcy, Ian is in jail." He pulled her hands from her face once again. "Bring it back to the present day."

She shook her head for what seem like minutes before she finally spoke again. "My governess, that is, our nanny, she told my papa what I saw, and he approached Everett. Everett denied it of course and then he threatened to tell Papa I was with child by Domenic if I didn't say I made it up. Ian suddenly began courting me and well before I knew it, I was betrothed to a man I didn't love nor trust. I suppose it was Papa's way of making the homosexual problem go away."

Joseph tried to force a sympathetic smile, but his frustration mounted. He threw his hands up in front of him and shook his head.

She motioned downward with her hand. "Just wait, I'm getting there. I'm trying to say I agree with you, it's Everett, it's got to be Everett trying to avenge Ian. I've spent so many years covering for them, I have a hard time, admitting the truth."

"Please tell me; it could mean Anna's life."

Marcy nodded slowly. "He has never let go of his feelings for Ian, nor his hope of them being best friends and lovers as they once were, despite the way Ian has treated him. I'm certain Ian took advantage of Everett's feelings to steel money from him. The two of them have barely tolerated my presence for the last ten years. I am frankly just a means to their acceptance in society." She glanced at her hands in her lap. "I vaguely remember Everett threatening me before I was injected with something at the safe house." She squinted at the floor trying to force the memory.

Joseph pulled up straight. "When we saw ye at the house wi' Nurse O'Malley, ye mumbled something about he'll kill Anna and me. We kent ye were speaking of Ian."

"Yes, that's it. He whispered to me; his face was pressed right up against mine. Yes, I remember. He said if Anna and I didn't convince the police that Ian was innocent, then he would kill us both and the children too. That's it." Her eyes grew suddenly wide with recollection, and she nodded profusely. She crossed her arms and squeezed the material of her sleeves. "You must go yourself. You must go and find Anna. She has to be at his house. Dear God, I hope he hasn't done her any harm."

"I will have to call Mrs. Nelson; I cannae leave ye wi' the bairns. Ye have barely come awake, and we have no idea what's going on around here." He sat back in the chair and shoved his hair off his brow. "Chief Bane said he searched the house and the barn, and he has an investigator on the watch. Where else would Everett go if he was nae at home?"

"They are my children, they are asleep, and I am perfectly aware of my surroundings. I will guard them with my life, I promise you. Everett has nowhere else to go, but his property is large with several outbuildings. And, he has cold cellars where he hid homemade wine and alcohol. He must have her there somewhere."

～

Joseph switched off his headlights and rolled to a stop a fair distance from Everett's house. Clad in dark clothing, he crept quickly and quietly through the field toward the back of the house. He yelped, wrenched free and spun around fists drawn when a strong hand seized his upper arm in a tight grip.

He dropped his stance and flinched in surprise. "Jimmy MacDougall?"

"Joey Hendrie?" He shone a flashlight directly at Joseph who held a hand to shield his face from the light. "Chief Bane told me ye might come sniffing around."

"Yer the police chief's investigator?" Joseph eyed his acquaintance cynically. A stout man, he barely reached Joseph's shoulders. He often smelled of whisky, had food on his shirt and was rarely seen without a pipe in his mouth.

"I help keep watch from time to time. Since my Marjorie passed—"

"Neither here nor there, have ye seen any movement here at Rossi's?" Joseph pleaded.

He shook his head. "A lone light up the top window since the Chief Bane left me on watch." He tipped his head up to indicate the single bright window in the otherwise dark house. "Nae a curtain nor a shutter even moved."

"I will bring ye a bottle of braw Scots' whiskey if ye keek the other way just long enough for me to sneak around the back."

"Joey, we go back some, but I cannae accept a bribe. I'm on duty. Derek will nae hire me again if he finds out."

The two stopped and spun toward a thud. "What was that?" The investigator asked.

Joseph bolted to the barn, the investigator plodding along behind. He threw up the wooden door latch and jumped back as the door swung open and Anna tumbled unconscious at his feet. The investigator gasped and shone his flashlight down at her bound, lifeless body.

Joseph scowled. "Get out of my way MacDougall and get Derek back here to arrest Rossi before I murder him wi' my bare hands."

Joseph untied Anna's hands while the investigator pulled the rope from her feet, then dashed back to his car as fast as his short legs would carry him and radioed the police chief to the scene.

Anna moaned against Joseph's chest as he held her tightly in the back seat of the investigator's car. For the second time in a day, Joseph carried a lifeless body into Anna's house.

Marcy jumped up, then reached for the chair back to steady herself. "Dear God, what has happened?"

She watched in horror as Joseph lay Anna down where Marcy had been.

"Yer brother Everett has near murdered her. Ring Dr. Woods while I get her out of these wet clothes."

Anna mumbled incoherently as Joseph once again applied a warm cloth and tucked in blankets as he had done for Marcy just hours before.

By the time the doctor arrived Anna had already declared herself fit and attempted to stand to get herself some tea.

"I will get ye a cuppa. Let him at least listen to yer heart and take yer pressure," Joseph insisted. "And wrap the rope burns before they become infected."

Anna smiled but waved him away and he retreated reluctantly to the kitchen.

The doctor chuckled. "Take advantage of it, Mrs. Gordon. I'm more often trying to convince husbands to cook and wait on their wives while they're unwell."

"I'm sure I fainted out in the barn due to several hours' lack of food, and movement. Well, and the frigid temperatures and my wet trousers didn't help."

The doctor nodded along with her. "Either cold or lack of food can cause a temporary black out, especially in the early stages of pregnancy."

"I do tend to get dizzy mid day if I forget to eat."

The doctor held the stethoscope to Anna's chest; then sat back and patted her hand. "I'm sure you will recover from this incident quickly. However, as the baby grows, you must remember to eat several small meals a day to nourish both of you."

"Aye, several meals." Joseph nodded when he returned to the room with a steaming mug in one hand and a plate of biscuits in the other.

"Come and sit with me love and stop your worrying. The babe and I are fine." Anna patted the couch beside her. Joseph placed the mug and the plate on the table, sat and reached for her hand.

"Is there anything else we should—"

His question to the doctor was interrupted by a knock. Marcy stood and opened the door to Police Chief Bane.

"Well, this is a pleasant surprise to see both of you ladies, awake and coherent." Chief Bane smiled briefly and removed his hat as he stepped in the front door.

"No thanks to Everett Rossi. I hope ye've put his sorry ass in jail."

The chief cringed in reply.

"I'll take my leave," Dr. Woods said.

"Thank ye so much for coming out so quickly." Joseph stood and shook the doctor's hand.

"Anna, Marcy, both of you rest for a few days and don't hesitate to call my office if you need anything else." The doctor tipped his hat to the officer on his way out and pulled the door shut behind him.

"Come in, come in." Anna waved the police chief in.

He sat in the chair facing the couch where Joseph, Anna and Marcy now sat in a row. "Firstly, Mrs. Gordon, my sincere apologies for not finding you when we initially searched the house." He took a deep breath before he continued. "Officer Oakley scanned the barn and he insisted—"

She held up her hand. "I understand. Everett threw me in a back corner and covered me in a tarp and haybale. I'm sure Office Oakley has learned from his error. The important thing is I survived and managed to roll my way to the door. I will be fine. I presume you have Mr. Rossi under lock and key." She forced a smile.

"Just the same, this has been a chaotic investigation, the result of which we did not anticipate and I'm sorry you have all been drawn into it so tragically." He shook his head.

"Ye look solemn, Derek. What else have ye discovered?"

He cleared his throat and stretched his shoulders back. "I am sorry to have to tell you Mrs. Campbell, that you brother has taken his own life."

Joseph rubbed his hand across the back of his neck and blew out a heavy breath. Anna gasped and covered her mouth and Marcy merely smirked.

"Officer Oakley is still on the scene awaiting the coroner. Everett left a note to you Mrs. Campbell and one for your husband. I'm afraid I had to open them and take a few notes as part of the investigation into his death. It would appear he wanted you and Mrs. Gordon out of the way of Ian Campbell's investigation. By his minimal understanding of the evidence, without your statements, no one else would be left to testify against your husband."

"Ridiculous man." Joseph sneered.

"As I explained to Joseph earlier, after we searched the house, I told Everett that Ian was facing numerous charges outside of those which you two women could corroborate. More specifically, related to his attack on Miriam Cooper, to bootlegging liquor and to fraudulent behaviour at the bank. I believe he realized his chances of freeing his friend, were limited. I also mentioned if he had been harboring Ian, or harmed either you or Anna, he could face criminal charges himself. I'm sorry he felt the situation was so dire as to necessitate taking his own life. I had no idea they were so close." He tipped his head and gazed sympathetically at Marcy as he handed her a small envelope.

She sat stoically straight, and dry eyed with her lips pinched in a straight line as she ran the card between her fingers and flipped it several times.

"Shall I read it for you?" Anna recalled Everett's comment that Marcy couldn't read.

Marcy tossed the envelope on the table in front of them. "No one had any idea Everett and Ian were so close. They spent their whole adult lives scheming to keep it that way. My brother ruined my life by his own selfishness. I hold nothing against him or any man for their preference behind closed doors. I know Everett was tortured by his homosexuality, but he could have thrived with groups of like-minded men without strapping me to a life of violence for the last dozen years. In the end, they were both willing to drug me and have me committed to live with the insane or worse kill me and Anna and my children. Their secrets are out. Neither man can rule over my decisions any longer. Now perhaps I can find some peace and enjoy my children. I will not shed a tear for either of them and I have no interest in what he has written."

"I'm sorry for what you have suffered Mrs. Campbell, all of you actually. Unfortunately, I will need you to confirm his handwriting to rule out any foul play."

She glanced at the envelope on the table and back up to Chief Bane but didn't move.

Hoping to save Marcy some embarrassment by her illiteracy, Anna reached for the note, opened it, and nodded her head. "It is the same scrawling hand as the mysterious notes I received telling me to leave town. While I was restrained in Everett's kitchen, he admitted to sending the notes in the hope I would leave town. Now I know the reason for his attempt to dissuade me setting up house. He wanted Marcy to remain friendless, and in a drugged state so Ian could continue their charade of a marriage and he and Ian could be lovers. What I don't understand is why Ian tried to play matchmaker and put me together with Everett, or why Everett himself asked me out and tried to keep me away from Joseph."

Marcy glanced first at the note in Anna's hand. "She's correct. That's Everett's handwriting." She then turned to Anna. "They likely schemed to marry you off to Everett to hide his sexual preference and to keep control over you and your money. Everett didn't want you for himself. You are correct, he simply didn't want you to settle here with Joseph and have the opportunity to draw Ian and I apart, which is exactly what happened. They deserve everything they got."

"The contents of the letter addressed to Mr. Campbell, would appear to corroborate both of your assessments of the situation between Mr. Rossi and Mr. Campbell. I agree it was also their plan to keep you drugged and confused as much as possible Marcy, to avoid the likelihood of you finding a confidante. Mrs. Gordon managed to sabotage that plan, hence their attempts at making her life so miserable that she would flee the country. I believe Ian hid out at Everett's until they both determined to take matters into their own hands. Once Ian botched killing Anna, Everett picked up where he left off by visiting and drugging you and then abducting Anna."

"I have never seen the likes of such violence in an effort to maintain a loving connection."

The chief nodded. "Perhaps Everett fancied himself in love with Ian, but it's my opinion from studying behaviour of violent criminals, that Ian's offences lend more to dominance and control like a rapist or killer, than to crimes of passion. I'm not sure much of what Ian Campbell has done over the last decade had as much to do with Everett as it did to one-sided, violent criminal tendencies."

"I can attest to that." Marcy smirked again.

"Nurse O'Malley has also been taken for questioning for her part in Mr. Rossi's plan to have you committed," Chief Bane explained.

"I can't believe she agreed with him to have me committed at the age of thirty, with two children to care for." Marcy huffed. "In fairness to the frightening woman, I have had some recall, and I believe it was Everett who did most of the drug administering, at least enough to cause confusion so that the nurse merely treated the delusions unbeknownst of Everett's prior treatment. I swear I'll never let anyone make my tea for as long as I live."

Anna chuckled and reached to pat Marcy's hand.

"I appreciate your candor, Mrs. Campbell," Chief Bane said.

Marcy nodded curtly in reply.

"I appreciate all of your collective help in the investigation. I will let you get some sleep and heal for tonight, but when you're all feeling better, we will need formal statements. Mr. Rossi will also be resting at the funeral home. As next-of-kin, you will need to contact them with some direction."

"Hmmph." Marcy dropped her chin to her chest.

"I am sorry Mrs. Campbell. I recognize how difficult all this must be." Police Chief Bane stood. "Unfortunately, we still have a way to go before Mr. Campbell will be tried and sentenced. After recent events, he may be facing further charges, but in any event, he will remain incarcerated. You ladies will have some finances and property to sort out in the interim." The police chief put his hat back on and nodded to the three on the couch. "I'll leave you and your lawyers to sort that part of things, and I will be back to speak with you soon."

Joseph met the officer at the door and shook his hand. "Thank ye Derek for all ye've done. We appreciate yer service, and we wish ye and Officer Oakley and yer families a Merry Yule."

"To all of you as well," Derek said. The officer tipped his hat to the ladies and ducked through the door.

Joseph turned to Marcy. "Some rest may help. Clara and Thomas are at opposite ends of Clara's bed so there's a spare bed for ye."

Marcy stood and hugged Joseph briefly. "I can't thank you enough. If you hadn't escaped that horror house with me in your arms, I would have perished in the attic or God knows where."

"My condolences, Marcy." He patted her shoulder as she stepped back.

"What a waste of a life." She turned and headed up the stairs.

Anna watched Marcy's slow climb. "I wonder if she meant Everett's or her own."

"Aye, I wonder too." Joseph pulled Anna to him, and her emotions let go.

"I was scared. I thought I would never see you or the children again. Worse, I thought he would kill the children after getting me out of the way." She wiped a tear off her face with the back of her hand.

"I was scared too. If I lost ye after just finding ye..."

She glanced up to see tears in his eyes too.

He kissed her gently, then pulled her onto his lap. She nuzzled her face into his neck and breathed in his familiar scent. Moments passed while he held her tightly.

"I need a bath and some sleep." Anna broke their silence. "And then I have designs to finish, and Christmas presents to deliver."

"Ye'll be having some company for all of those things." He smiled down at her and kissed her again.

"Just as I hoped."

Chapter Thirty

"I ate so much turkey, I think I may burst. This eating for two leaves much less room for sweets." Anna patted her belly and smiled at Marcy.

The children worn out from the excitement of the last few days as well as early Christmas morning festivities, had barely made it through dinner before they were happily dozing in their shared bed. Recovered but still weak, Anna and Marcy sat with blankets over their knees, comfortably full and equally exhausted after a huge Christmas feast. One on the couch and one on the high back chair, the women faced the fireplace and gazed at the flames while they spoke candidly as they often had over the last few days.

"Everett said he told your father that you had lain with Domenic and that's why he forced you to marry Ian."

"The part about me loving Domenic is true, and about my papa refusing his request for my hand. Everett and Ian both said they had told Papa lies about Domenic; whichever one took credit for it, depended on who was telling the story. They talked about it so much, that I think they honestly had themselves convinced that's how the events happened. It didn't take me long to figure out, Papa had suspicions about Everett and Ian's relationship. Even if one of them did tell him I had lain with Domenic or that I was with child, I think Papa had already made up his mind to force the union. He tried to convince me that we would all be able to live comfortably in Kincardine with the money he gave Ian and certainly subsequently with his inheritance, but really, I think he only wanted to avoid scandal."

"He could have considered how his decision would affect his daughter's life."

She nodded. "Yes, I have thought of that often; but his and Everett's social standing were more important to Papa than my happiness. As I think I also told you, things would have been much different if Mama had been alive. Everett and Ian have spent their whole adult lives scheming. Mama never would have stood for that from her son."

"What do you mean scheming?"

"For more than a decade; since they met in Toronto in their twenties, they have fooled all of society with a false façade, extorted funds and apparently been involved in illegal trading." She paused briefly, then continued. "I'm sure they plotted to keep Everett out of the military. I mean Ian dodged the draft with the claim of economic hardship. He argued essentially that the bank couldn't live without him, and we would all starve if he left. He went on about it for so long, they probably threw him out of the office."

Anna chuckled. "I believe they allowed married men with children to stay home under that claim."

"I don't know, but he sure whined about it for weeks. And I'm guessing Ian paid someone to forge a medical note for Everett. They had heard stories of torture and arrest of other, you know…" Marcy gave her a knowing look.

"Yes, I know, men who preferred men."

Marcy nodded. "Some were even killed at the hands of the Nazis in the early 40s. They were, well, especially Everett was terrified someone would catch on to him. I heard them talking about it. The military worked with psychiatrists to develop guidelines for recruiters to identify and exclude those types from the services. Everett made sure he had a note before he got any opportunity to fail that test. There was nothing wrong with his heart. He simply didn't want people to find him out. I'm certain that's why he took his own life, not because of criminal implications, but more to avoid scandal. Just like our papa." She stared at the flames and shook her head.

"So, Ian is homosexual as well? That doesn't fit; he tried to rape me, and Chief Bane told me some of the things he did with Miriam."

"I have no doubt that Ian played the part so he could control all our family money. I'm sure taking advantage of Everett's devotion included sex and I'm sure my brother interpreted that as a loving relationship. But no Ian wasn't homosexual. He didn't have any concept of love or passion toward a man or woman. I concur with Chief Bane's assessment, of Ian's one-sided violent preferences. As I said previously, I have nothing against Everett desiring another man, I only wish they had not used me as their pawn."

"I'm sorry to say, whoever forced whoever's hand, ultimately, it was your papa who used you as a pawn and who also instilled the belief into Everett that avoiding scandal was worth dying for."

Marcy nodded. "I know you're right, but I would like to think if Papa knew Ian's true nature, he never would have married me off, nor allowed Everett to follow Ian to a new town."

"Well, somehow Ian managed to make love and produce beautiful children and so perhaps we should be thankful for that blessing and find a way to move on."

Tears pooled in Marcy's eyes. "I'm sorry to ramble on in such a negative way and on Christmas day. I really am ready to forget about all of it, but I am just so angry and so embarrassed."

"The details are not your doing so you have nothing to be embarrassed about. And, while I agree that Ian is an evil man, I feel badly that your brother lived such a tortured life and never found his own way. He didn't need to abduct me or torment you or take his own life; it didn't need to be that way."

Marcy turned to Anna. "I agree, but I'm a long way off your compassion. And yes, Ian and I produced two beautiful children, but I would never use the term lovemaking for our procreating. I only pray to God that neither of them inherited his hunger for brutality."

Anna smiled. "Such gentle souls; I can't imagine Clara or Thomas ever instilling cruelty."

They both turned back to the fire and sat silently for a moment.

"Ian is the one who needs psychotherapy, not me. Perhaps they can send him to Nurse O'Malley." Marcy chuckled.

Anna smiled sadly and nodded her agreement. "One thing for sure, I hope he spends enough time behind bars to never see his children again."

"Sadly, I think they will be the last of his concern."

"And that will be his loss. What will you do?" Anna tilted her head and smiled with genuine concern.

Again, Marcy turned from the fire. "I've spoken to a lawyer. I can obtain a divorce on the grounds of cruelty. He seems to think Ian will consent to selling the house. It will take some time to figure out your money that he tried to hide as well as what he stole from mine and Everett's inheritance. Surprisingly, he is entitled to a nest egg if he ever gets out of jail."

"You're welcome to stay; we could arrange another bed—"

Marcy waved her hand. "You have been beyond generous, but I won't impose much longer. As next of kin, I can sell Everett's house immediately and that will allow me to buy something between here and the school so the children can attend class regularly and visit you and Nellie. I can help them with their lessons—"

"But I thought you couldn't read?"

Marcy grinned mischievously. "Everett told you that did he? That's one secret I managed to keep to myself and trust me having them think I was illiterate came in handy on more than one occasion."

Anna chuckled and shook her head.

"We'll be fine, and I will be set financially and certainly I can work if need be. When I wasn't being drugged on a daily basis, I had quite a knack with needle and thread. Perhaps I could make some clothes for the children or work at alterations and repairs for some of the locals to keep myself busy." She was silent a moment before she wiped at the corner of her eye and turned to Anna. "You and Joseph have done so much for me and the children, I am not sure I will ever be able to repay your kindness."

"I am glad I arrived when I did."

Joseph came into the room, a tray laden with tea and shortbread.

"I feel horrible sitting here while you do all the washing up from that huge dinner. What did I do to deserve you?" Anna glanced up at him as he placed the tray on the table.

"The feeling is mutual." He bent to kiss her gently. "I have one request."

"Name it." Anna smiled.

"When can I make ye, my wife? I was thinking Hogmanay."

"That's next Monday night." She blinked in shock.

"Aye 'tis." He grinned. "Do ye have something else planned to bring in the new year?"

Anna clasped her hands together and turned to Marcy. "Perhaps you can assist us straight away. Are you able to make a wedding dress, and two attendants dresses in less than a week?"

"Two dresses?" Marcy's brow creased.

"For you and Clara of course. And we will need two smart bow ties to match for our men."

Tears flowed freely as Marcy stood from the couch and bent to hug her rescuer. "Of course, I would be delighted to come up with something. After all we put you through, I don't deserve your—"

"Enough of melancholy, it is time for celebration." Anna jumped up and threw her arms around Joseph's neck. "We are family, and I have found home and there is no place else I would rather be."

His hands roamed down her back, stopping at her hips as he pulled her against him and kissed her deeply. Marcy felt like a welcome family member for the first time in her life. She smiled at the two who made it all possible and snuck quietly off to the stairs.

About the Author

My career has spanned many years in a mix of criminal and civil law and hospital surgical administrative work. Along with my work and life experience, I hold a Bachelor of Arts Degree in English and a Creative Writing Certificate both from McMaster University, Hamilton, Ontario.

I am thrilled to have had the opportunity to take early retirement and pursue a career in writing, a pursuit I have entered with energy and enthusiasm. I am currently a registered member of Toronto Romance Writers, Crime Writers of Canada, and Sisters in Crime.

My husband and I share our home in Grimsby, Ontario, with our youngest daughter, her boyfriend, and our dog and cat. But I spend a great deal of time at our cottage in Kincardine, Ontario near my daughter, son-in-law and first grandson. On these shores of Lake Huron, with some of the best walking trails in the country, my imagination soars and my best stories come to life.

https://suejaskula.wordpress.com/
https://www.instagram.com/suejaskulaauthor/
https://www.facebook.com/sue.jaskula
http://twitter.com/jaskulasue
https://www.goodreads.com/author/show/21295570.Sue_Jaskula
https://www.bookbub.com/profile/sue-jaskula

Other Books by Sue Jaskula

All Fired Up

Unexpected Connection

Death at Dawn

9 781778 149009